SHIMMERS

D1714989

J. P. STRECKER

For my beloved wife, Stacey, and my talented son, Josh. Thank you for supporting me through all my endeavors.

To my mother and father, thank you for loving us all unconditionally.

I would like to thank my siblings, Matt, Mark, Angie, and Heather, and my childhood friends Bob and Duane for all the lasting memories.

I would like to thank Arthur Fogartie, my amazing developmental editor. I appreciate your exceptional intelligence, commitment, and professionalism.

Thank you to Alexis Arceo, my proofreading editor, for your keen eye and tremendous work ethic.

Last, I also want to recognize my extended family, dear friends, mentors, childhood teachers, and current and former students, who provided the wisdom, joy, and resolve compelling me to write this novel. You will never know the positive impact you made in my life. Each of you changed my life for the better. I wish I could thank you all individually.

PART I
INTO THE LIGHT

PROLOGUE
A CRESCENDO OF CALAMITY

MARCH 1973
MILAN, OHIO

D AVID SPRINGER STUDIED the readouts like a man on the cusp of greatness. He looked for any sign, any hint, any movement in the numbers that might provide an advantage – something he could exploit to reach his Promised Land.

Springer was young for a scientist at Edison Lab. A few months shy of his 35th birthday, he continued to battle the "way we've always done it" mentality so embedded in federal facilities.

Founded in 1965, the Federal Accelerator Laboratory in Milan, OH, lay 60 miles west of Cleveland. Someone eventually mentioned Milan as the birthplace of Thomas Edison. In a grand gesture, the facility received the new name: Edison Laboratories. It was home to the world's premier particle accelerator. The proposed purpose of the lab lay in ramping up atomic particles to the threshold of the speed of light, colliding them, and investigating the interconnected nature of matter, energy, space, and time.

Springer liked to explain his work to non-scientific folks by saying, "It's like an amped up Demolition Derby." His colleagues did not approve.

Springer could not have cared less.

Short and borderline frail with sandy, blonde hair – turning gray at the temples – and premature eye wrinkles brought on by too much espresso and too little sleep, Springer exuded enough confidence to make his associates despise him. But his overwhelming ability, his near-superhuman intelligence, almost made them forget how much they wished he would fall on his face.

"Are you ready, Dr. Springer?"

Springer looked up from his calculations to see Dr. Eric Palmer, all 6'5" of him, standing over his desk. "Are we in a hurry this morning, Eric?"

No one believed Springer was unaware of his annoying voice – nasal, pinched, and invariably snide. "Do you have a squash game scheduled, Eric?"

Palmer chuckled. He knew he could smash Springer like a gnat, but he admired David's ability, even if the young doctor's personality was as loveable as a blobfish with a runny nose.

Springer continued. "We still have to wait on Kline – he should be rolling in here about a quarter past late."

"I heard that, David, and I'll have you know, I was only five minutes past on time this morning."

Dr. Lionel Kline, the senior, but lowest ranking

member of the team, possessed an easy – some said laconic – manner and displayed a noticeable paunch under his lab coat. His even-keeled nature made him a favorite in the lab, but everyone at Edison knew he could, if riled, roar like a Bengal tiger with a hangnail. The full team had been together for almost five years with, what was officially broadcast as, minimal success. The most common chorus in the back halls usually ran along the lines of, "With an old bull from Cal Tech, a superstar from Rensselaer, and the kid genius from MIT, you would expect something more laudable than the concoction 'Killer Hot Chocolate.'"

The concoction was good – no it was stellar, the best anyone had ever had – but given the brain power involved, and the overwhelming costs, no one was particularly pleased.

"Good morning, Dr. Buzzkill," Springer said. He and Kline often clashed on protocols. David always took the aggressive line – Kline, older and more-often scarred, preferred a more judicious approach. Although he typically acquiesced to Palmer and Springer, Kline routinely expressed concerns regarding the project's direction and aims.

Today's test required approval from all three scientists, a fact Palmer underlined just before Springer gave the order to "Commence."

"David," Palmer said, "we have a little problem with…uh…authorization."

Springer's eyes never moved from straight ahead. "Take care of it, Eric," he said.

"That might not be easy," Palmer said. "Dr. Kline has not signed off yet."

Springer's head whipped around. "Dammit, we're three minutes behind." He glared at Kline. "What's the problem?"

Kline was uncharacteristically formal. "Dr. Springer," he said as he adjusted his bowtie, "I have concerns regarding potential for dimensional surface decay."

"You're talking about fractional – no, minute – amounts of matter migrating via possible dimensions." Springer's face grew rosy and his eyes narrowed. "Nothing too dangerous in my mind."

Palmer slid between the two men. "I think Dr. Kline would like us to install and verify a few additional safeguards – right, Lionel?" He looked at Kline, who remained impassive. Palmer continued. "He wants to ensure our experiments don't lead to a mishap – a little extra precaution."

Kline nodded. "I understand the theory like anyone else," he said. "I accept the theoretical nature of the experiment. But what if multiple dimensions, alternate realities, and parallel universes exist? In that case, we must be careful not to open an unintended portal. We need to exercise caution, and that requires more stringent safety standards."

Springer's lips formed a strained line. "We have just applied for a generous grant, predicated on our results. If we choose to play it safe, that funding will undoubtedly dry up. I am not suggesting recklessness, but we must push the envelope before our monetary sources decide to back an alternative project, one willing to assume more risk, like the one in Chicago."

Palmer looked at Kline and said, "He isn't wrong, Lionel. In the last five years, we've had some serious financial shifting. Remember, no cash – no collider."

Kline shook his head. This was his moment to exert some influence. "What are they expecting? Are we supposed to develop time travel in five months? These experiments require a long-game approach, gentlemen. If we predict incorrectly – if we rush – we could have a disaster on our hands. I know (he held up a palm toward Springer, who was rising from his seat) – I know – the chances are low. But we should err on the side of caution. I do not want to be that arrogant scientist in all those sci-fi movies who ignores the signs and ends up initiating a catastrophe."

A phone on the control panel next to Springer rang just as the young scientist looked ready to implode. He snatched up the receiver.

"Springer," he said. "I know. (He looked at Kline.) Yes, all systems for Test 333-A are ready. Yes, I know you are waiting for my godda…for my order. Maintain energy levels for firing and stand by. We are working out a few details on this end."

Springer turned on the charm. "Dr. Kline – Lionel – listen, we have everyone standing on tip-toe. They are ready to rock n' roll. We ran last month's test with 10% less power and a fractional differential in the quantity of matter. Everything went great, right?"

Kline nodded without enthusiasm.

I got him, Springer thought. "Okay," he said. "If you approve today, I promise I will sit down with you and Dr. Palmer and anyone else you want, and we will talk this through to your total satisfaction."

He paused – *One Mississippi – two Mississippi…*

"Lionel, I need your approval – now."

The senior scientist looked ready to agree – he even nodded – then, David saw something flash in Kline's eyes.

Uh oh.

"David," Kline said, "you are a wonderful scientist. I realize you want this project to succeed. Still, you understand the concept of a tipping point. What if even an incremental change in power or material proves sufficient to create a cascading effect and, ultimately, different and drastic results?"

Springer turned to Palmer. "Want to help me out here, Eric?"

Dr. Palmer looked at Kline. "Lionel, due respect, but I think you're being a bit neurotic here. We've seen nothing to indicate a problem. Consider our past readings."

Dr. Kline pursed his lips, blinked, then said, "Alright, run it. But before we do another test, you *promise* we will talk, right?"

"Absolutely."

Palmer nodded, "Yes."

"Okay then. Dr. Springer, I give my verbal approval for Test 333-A."

Palmer recorded the verbal authorization on a clipboard and handed it to his colleagues to sign. Before the ink dried, and while Kline said a quiet prayer, Springer snatched the receiver from its cradle.

"Control, this is Dr. Springer. Commence Test 333-A."

The devices surrounding the scientists began to hum - deeply, resonantly – almost frighteningly. In a few moments, the ions would build up speed. Protons would hurtle around the injector rings, then head towards the central core, a location dubbed Edison's Curve. In his mind's eye, Springer could see the particles as they accelerated through this masterful creation of human ingenuity.

If anyone's going to unlock the secrets of the Universe, it's going to be us – here.

While Springer and Palmer stared at the dials, Kline chewed the inside of his mouth until it was raw and bleeding. He knew the likelihood of a cataclysmic event was quite small, but something gnawed at the back of his mind. He worried about future generations – he worried about irreparable harm – he worried about…everything.

In the deep recesses of his heart, he felt a crescendo of calamity. Though clueless as to its nature, instinct told him that he and his colleagues, instead of pushing the limits of human ingenuity, were engaged in something far more dangerous – something unnatural.

A few minutes later, the collision test concluded.

"Success," Springer said.

The trio of scientists began to analyze the data.

Dr. Palmer said, "Gentleman, we have a small issue here. I see a fraction less mass in the chamber than we had at the start. The reading indicates a bit of matter has left our collection matrix."

Springer snorted. "Care to be a little more vague, doctor?"

It's "vaguer," you insufferable twit, Kline thought. *No wonder no one likes you.*

Palmer ignored the cynicism. "As we all know," he said, "matter cannot be lost. Any diminution of mass means the missing matter is either somehow unreadable within the chamber or has been moved to another dimension or universe."

Springer looked like a third grader who'd won a spelling contest in the school cafeteria. "Precisely," he said. "See, Kline, I told you there was nothing to worry about. Gentlemen, I think we have discovered the power threshold for matter transfer."

"Or the tipping point," Kline said.

He opened his mouth to speak again when he saw one of the control panel dials spike – a quick swing to the right peg, then back to normal.

"I think there's an anomaly building within the core," Kline said. "Take a look."

The other two men peered over Kline's shoulder.

"Any theories?"

"About what?" Springer asked. "Everything reads normal."

"Oh hell," Palmer said.

The others looked up from the array of dials and followed Palmer's pointing finger all the way to one of the screens. A dark, spherical mist about a foot in diameter floated in the chamber.

"What is that?" Palmer asked.

"No idea," Kline said. "It's only on that single monitor."

Springer reached up and tapped the screen as it flickered, but the image was undeniable.

Palmer leaned toward the screen. "What is that? I've never seen anything like it."

The sphere slowly began to collapse back upon itself. As the sphere shrunk to approximately nine inches in diameter, a gnarled claw appeared out of the rolling mist. It was neither fully human nor a distinguishable animal. It swiped in a grabbing motion, then disappeared into the cavity from which it came.

The Shimmer dissipated into nothingness.

Dr. Palmer asked, "What in God's name was that?"

Dr. Kline turned to his colleagues his face ashen. "I'm not sure God has anything to do with it."

CHAPTER 1
THE MISSING
MAY 1973

ABOUT 15 MILES west of Edison Labs, Jimmy and Joshua, identical three-year-old twin brothers, played in the grass. They rolled a ball back and forth. They'd seen Daddy playing on the Pong game in the bowling alley – it looked like fun. Their mother Maggie, six-months pregnant, made dinner.

"Paul," she said, her voice carrying the usual hint of maternal concern. "Paul, are you watching the girls?"

Paul waved from the crest of a small rise, then snapped off a salute. "The Father of the Year is on duty," he said. "Angie and Heather are at the pool – lifeguard and everything."

The family loved the Webegone Campground. It was their favorite getaway spot. They could all be in the same place at the same time – but doing different things, something the girls thought was "way cool."

Josh tugged on Maggie's cover-up. "Mommy, I'm hung-we for spettios."

"…and, and, hot dos," Jimmy said, looking at his brother for approval.

Josh crossed his arms. "Yes, yes, hog dogs."

"Well," Maggie said, smiling, "come sit down at the picnic table to eat before you starve. It's been all of an hour since you had your snack."

The boys scrambled over the table, sat down, and tucked paper napkins into their shirts.

"Take your time," Maggie said. "Remember, chew your food."

The two boys devoured their food like hungry beagle puppies around a single bowl of chow, tossed their napkins in a trash can, then went back to their game. Maggie slapped a half-dozen hamburger patties on the grill and called to her husband.

"Paul get the girls. Burgers in less than 10 minutes."

When she'd finished preparing dinner, Maggie placed warm hamburgers on a plate, wrapped them in foil, and set them on the table. Then she went around the camper to check on the boys.

They. Were. Gone.

A few moments before, Josh had heaved the ball. It soared past Jimmy's outstretched hand. Josh chased it down the hill, and Jimmy followed right behind his brother.

At the edge of the forest, Jimmy stopped when he saw a spherical mist just inside the tree line. Six feet by 12 feet, it reminded Jimmy of the parachute his preschool class used for games.

"Jimmy, look at the big booble. Monkey in the Middle!"

Jimmy wasn't sure. He reached down and picked up the green ball, but he never took his eyes off the silver sphere.

Josh motioned. "Come on – Monkey in the Middle."

Jimmy shook his head; Josh edged closer to the Shimmer. The silver dome slowly expanded until it was five feet in diameter. Jimmy could not see anything inside but the silver mist and a faint shadow.

Josh, ever curious, thrust an eager hand through the middle of the "Shimmer."

"Jimmy…cold. Come here."

"Don't touch," Jimmy said. He felt his throat tighten. *This is bad.*

"Feels like snow," Josh said. He took his arm out and rubbed it.

Jimmy, now within arm's length, stabbed at the Shimmer with an index finger. The orb rippled like the surface of water.

"Come," Josh said. He stuck his hand through the wall again and giggled. "Cold."

Their mother's voice rose from just beyond the hill. "Josh! Jimmy! Boys, come here right now – you are in big trouble!"

Josh looked at Jimmy, grinned, and said, "Monkey in the Middle!" He jumped into the Shimmer, which immediately began to shrink.

Jimmy shrieked for his mother. "Mommy! Jimmy – ball!"

The boy felt a moment of relief when he saw Mom, Dad, and his sisters running down the slope. Dad looked annoyed. Mom looked terrified.

Maggie scooped Jimmy up. "Oh my God, you scared me to death. Where is your brother?"

"Ball," Jimmy said. He pointed to the silver sphere, now about the size of a large pumpkin. The sphere now measured only 12 inches across.

"What ball?" Dad said.

Heather snickered. "Liar, liar, pants on fire."

Jimmy thrust his hands down in frustration. "Ball!"

Dad took off into the woods. "Josh! Joshua! Where are you, son?"

Maggie's head swiveled, her eyes darting as she lived every mother's worst nightmare. Her voice came from someplace deep inside a breaking heart. "Josh!"

The girls began yelling, too. They were all looking away when a small hand squeezed through the Shimmer. The fingers opened and closed, clutching, grabbing only air. Jimmy reached out but only managed to brush Josh's fingertips before the hand was yanked away, as if pulled abruptly from the other side.

Jimmy heard his brother's tiny voice. "Big monkey."

Tears seeped from Jimmy's eyes. All he could say the rest of the day was, "Josh in the ball – big monkey."

FOR THE NEXT two days, multiple search parties scoured the area. Jimmy was questioned numerous times by his parents, the police, and even a psychologist. The boy's story never deviated; all it did was confuse the adults – *ball, hand, big monkey*. After an exhaustive search of the five-acre woods, the police ruled Josh's disappearance an abduction.

The family never quit hoping – praying – for Josh's return. But every day painted another layer of grime on the window of hope, and joy slipped ever farther into the realm of the past.

Jimmy had not seen his mother smile for three months until he went to the hospital to meet his new twin brothers. Still, the smile seemed forced – and her eyes remained sad. Maggie clung to her newborns with ferocity and foreboding.

In July, the local newspaper, the Bellevue Gazette, ran a story titled, *The Missing*. Ten people had gone lost from the local area under highly suspicious circumstances. They had all disappeared between early March to late May.

Josh had been the last.

CHAPTER 2
A FRIEND FOR EVERYONE
AUGUST 1975

IT HAS LONG been thought that a few select children (and even fewer adults) can perceive remarkable things elusive to those who live in a world of stark reality. On occasion, the gift (or curse, depending on one's viewpoint) finds itself fueled by circumstance or situational need. At age five, Jimmy did not know the difference.

Jimmy played quietly by himself in the corner of the great room, Dad's fancy term for a television room. Never far away from the eye of his vigilant mother, who was busy folding laundry in the adjacent bedroom, Jimmy sat beside the couch, positioned off the edge of the braided Chindi rug. He zoomed his toy cars back and forth, relishing the sound they made as they skidded across polished pinewood.

As Jimmy talked to himself, his two-year-old brother, Matt, worked feverishly to liberate himself from his playpen. Matt was already notorious for his dare devil escapes.

Matt, long, wiry, and towheaded, looked nothing like his twin brother, Mark, who was stocky and dark featured. Their physical differences were as disparate as their personalities. Mark loved to languish wherever he was placed, while Matt moved like someone who could not quite reach an itchy spot.

Maggie walked over to acknowledge Jimmy's chatter and to make her routine check. "Jimmy, it is so nice of you to talk to your brothers. That will help them learn."

Jimmy, brow furrowed, was about to tell his mom he wasn't talking to them, but she returned to her routine before he could speak. Her quick stride reflected the words, "So little time, so much to do."

She loved Saturdays at home, despite the flurry of activity. Her family pumped her full of energy and kept her from dwelling on what she referred to as "The Incident." Still, the constant activity threatened to drain every ounce of *uumph* from her body.

Jimmy's father worked a lot on Saturday mornings. "It is a good way to earn some overtime," Mom would tell Jimmy when he asked where Daddy was on the weekends. Jimmy didn't know what "overtime" was, but he knew he hated it.

Fabric tore. Cheap metal groaned. Jimmy looked to see Matt with one foot on a Fisher Price garage and the other most of the way over the top bar of the aging Pack 'n Play. Matt looked at Jimmy and babbled something. Jimmy understood.

Don't screw this up for me, buddy. I'm almost outta here.

Jimmy didn't care. He turned back to his cars.

Matt straddled the top of his pen, balancing like a flounder on a broom handle.

Angie, age nine, rounded the corner, her auburn hair bouncing up and down as she walked.

"Mom, Matty's breaking out again – I'll grab him."

Angie assumed the role of second mom. She cleaned, changed diapers, prepped food, and – mostly – corralled Matt.

"Not so fast, String Bean," Angie said. She eased Matt back into the pen, removed the "escape assisting" garage from the playpen and called to her mother. "Mom, this Pack 'n Play is shot. It's got more holes than a piece of cheese."

"Well I should think so," Maggie said, coming through the door. "We got it, originally, for you."

Angie handed Matt his stuffed toy, a Basset Hound named Brownie. "That should keep you entertained," she said.

"Thank you, Angie" Maggie said. She turned to the recaptured Matt. "Mister, if you try to sneak out again, I'll put you in your room – all alone."

Jimmy smirked. *All alone,* he thought. He knew Matt and Mark hated being away from each other. He knew all too well – because of Josh.

Jimmy brushed a tear away without looking up and acted like he was interested in a firetruck. Every time he thought about his lost brother, he got the same scary feeling – an all-consuming void of loneliness.

Matt knew Mommy was serious because she had used her mad voice. Rather than attempt another escape, he picked up a blue car in his left hand. Scowling, he hurled the car up and out of the pen. It clattered across the floor.

Angie shook her head and said, "You are so bullheaded."

Mark, seeing his car outside of the pen, reached his hands out, opening and closing them in the classic *gimmie, gimmie, gimmie* move. Angie picked up the car and delivered it to the toddler who squealed in delight.

Heather, Jimmy's other sister, age seven, bounded into the room. She was yelling – she always yelled. "Hey Angie, do you want to play dress-up?"

Jimmy slid closer to the couch. During their last session, Angie and Heather forced Jimmy into a green, lacy gown, and snapped a Polaroid picture of him. The photo had appeared at every family event since. Jimmy blushed every time.

He sat as still as possible, lowering his head below the edge of the couch like a lurking submarine. Lucky for him, Angie quickly said, "Of course," and the two girls ran up the stairs to play. Jimmy peeked back over the top to ensure they were gone. Periscope up!

Jimmy went back to playing with his cars. He spoke towards an empty corner, said, "Eddie, pass me the police car."

Jimmy didn't think it was nice that no one else

played with Eddie; as a matter of fact, no one even talked to Eddie. Jimmy liked talking with Eddie – well talking *to* – Eddie rarely spoke.

The first time Jimmy met Eddie was just after Josh disappeared. Eddie came and went as he pleased – every few days – every few weeks. No pattern.

Jimmy didn't mind though; Matt and Mark had each other, Angie and Heather had each other, and his mom and dad had each other. Jimmy was happy to have anyone after Josh went missing.

Jimmy knew Eddie was a little different. First, Eddie never got taller – or fatter – or changed his hair. Then, there were his clothes. He was always the same outfit: a dark blue coat with matching pants - the soft, fuzzy stuff Mommy called "velvet" – and a funny looking shirt. The jacket and pants had gold threading along the pockets and seams. Eddie's socks and lace-up boots extended almost to his shins.

The clothes were "old timey," like on television shows about a long time ago, but they always looked new. Sort of weird.

Eddie was pale; he coughed a lot. He complained about an upset stomach and almost always asked Jimmy for a glass of water. Jimmy brought it every time. Funny, Eddie never drank a drop.

Still, Jimmy liked his friend, Eddie.

Eddie glowed. He always looked like he was standing in front of a white light.

It's just like the silver ball that took Josh, Jimmy thought, *only white.*

Sometimes, Jimmy just looked up and Eddie was there.

Jimmy pushed the police car too hard and it skidded into the corner.

"Eddie, roll me the police car," Jimmy said.

"Who are you talking to?" It was Angie, who had come back downstairs to grab her favorite dress.

She rolled her eyes. "Mom, Jimmy's talking to his invisible friend again."

She pointed to the corner.

"There's nobody there, you wacko. The corner's empty."

As soon as Angie turned her head, the car came rolling across the floor and into Jimmy's outstretched hand.

CHAPTER 3
CRIES IN THE NIGHT
OCTOBER 1975

J IMMY SHARED A bedroom with his younger brothers – the house was too small for him to have his own room. He didn't mind – the extra company made him feel safe. Matt and Mark always laughed at Jimmy's antics. Their favorite game was when Jimmy would say a word repeatedly, like "doggie, doggie, doggie," pause for a second, and then say, "bone." When he imitated a puppy chewing on a bone, the twins howled with laughter.

Sometimes, he'd mess with them a little. "Cat, cat, cat" – then he'd bark. The twins would scowl, then laugh and start to meow as loudly as they could.

The one thing Jimmy didn't like about sharing a room were the noises – like when the twins cried – always at night – always when they were asleep. It was barely audible sound, as if muffled by a pillow.

One night, Jimmy decided he'd had enough. He slumped downstairs.

Jimmy's parents were watching *Gunsmoke* – Mom

was on the couch; Dad sat in his recliner. Paul loved his chair – it was his throne. Whenever Dad caught anyone in "The Captain's Chair," Tickle Torture followed. While all the children claimed to hate the ritual, they loved their father's attention. Jimmy was in no mood tonight to be tickled mercilessly, so he ran to his mother.

"Mommy, Matt and Mark are crying again," Jimmy said. Jimmy's father exhaled with paternal disapproval. "Can I stay down here and fall asleep on the couch?"

"No, honey," Mom said, "You need to be brave and sleep upstairs." She got up and smiled, but her eyes betrayed deep fatigue – and something else a more experienced person would recognize - the unending anguish of a mother who'd lost a child.

She walked Jimmy up the steps to place him back into bed and check on his brothers. Her hand was soft, but her grip was firm, reassuring.

She pulled the covers up to Jimmy's neck and tucked him in "snug as a bug in a rug." When she kissed his forehead, he caught a whiff of perfume and hairspray – a mixture uniquely hers. He loved her smell.

Mom turned and listened – a mama bear checking on her cubs. Not a sound.

"They've stopped," she said.

Jimmy wanted to protest. He could hear something – he knew it was his brothers. But Mom didn't lie – she never lied. He watched her take two blankets down from a shelf in his closet and drape one each over his sleeping siblings.

"Goodnight, sweetie," she said. She closed the door with a soft click.

Maggie slipped down the hall to check on the girls. The room was warm – much warmer than Jimmy's.

"Hi, Mommy," Heather said. "Everything okay?"

"Yes. Have you heard the twins tonight? Have they been crying?"

The girls shook their heads.

"Okay then," Maggie said. "Time for bed, girls. Dolls up – lights out."

Heather stuck out her bottom lip. "Fifteen more minutes – please?"

Maggie shook her head in resignation. "Fifteen – that's it. Don't make me come back up here. Okay?"

The girls nodded with enthusiasm, "Yes, Mother," they said in unison.

Paul looked up as Maggie walked into the den and retook her seat.

"Everything okay up there?" he asked.

"Yes, I think," she said. "Something's wrong with the heat in the boys' room. It's freezing in there. The girls' room must be 10 degrees warmer."

"I'll get after it tomorrow," he said. "Now, why don't you be a good girl and come sit on Santa's lap?"

Maggie smiled, walked over to the recliner, and settled into Paul's lap. They sat quietly with her head on his chest for a few minutes. Then, Paul's fingers wiggled against her waist.

No one was immune from Tickle Torture.

CHAPTER 4
THE BASEMENT

SEPTEMBER 1976

"EDDIE, DO YOU want to play ball?" Jimmy asked.

Eddie shook his head.

Jimmy said, "Well then, you come up with a game."

Eddie pointed to the basement stairs.

Jimmy looked left, then right; he wasn't allowed to go into the basement without his parents. He had only been down there one time before, and that was when city storm sirens went off. The horns wailed and screeched, and Mom had rushed everyone into the basement.

"It will be okay, guys," she said. "Everything will be okay. We will not leave this basement until it is safe – do you understand?"

Something in her voice told Jimmy this was more than, "No more cookies." If he disobeyed, something bad would happen.

When Daddy got home from work, he used weird words: "Twister…F-3…devastation."

Jimmy remembered a picture on the front page of the newspaper. The top of the water tower lay across the middle of the baseball field where Jimmy and his friends played tee-ball. It looked like something from the sci-fi books Daddy kept in his room. When his father looked at the newspaper, he winked at Jimmy and said, "We come in peace."

They both laughed – but quietly – Mommy never hid it well when she was upset. She scurried around, a mother hen protecting her chicks.

Jimmy did not want to disappoint Eddie, but he was afraid of the basement.

Well, maybe I'll just go to the bottom of the steps, Jimmy thought.

After another check, Jimmy tiptoed down the basement stairs. The bare wood looked old, and the wood planks were grooved and cracked – not at all like the stairs up to his room. Jimmy could see gaps behind each step. He took his time, worried, at any moment, he might slip and fall through. He clung to the railing despite the abundance of cobwebs and dust.

At the bottom of the steps, Jimmy shivered a little. The air hung heavy with an odd scent. Jimmy knew it – mold. Mommy hated mold and attacked it in the bathrooms with rubber gloves, a scrub brush, and gruesome smelling, eye stinging disinfectant. Mold always smelled like dirt to Jimmy – the stuff his father tilled in the garden, always after a rainy spring day.

Dim light fought its way through two small, grime-encrusted windows along the back wall of the basement. Jimmy, looking to add a bit of luminescence to the room, walked a few steps to the string dangling from the ceiling and tugged it. The bulb, covered in thick dust, filled most of the room with light, but the corners remained bathed in darkness and mystery.

Jimmy surveyed the forbidden wonderland. An old bed frame lay against one wall, a rolled-up carpet against another. A metal sea monster sprawled across the far wall – "the boiler" was what Daddy called it. Pipes protruded at all angles. Jimmy saw tentacles and imagined their coming to life, grabbing him, pulling him into its core – the mouth of death!

Icy fingers of fear ran up Jimmy's spine and he turned to run upstairs when Eddie said, "Want to see my hideout?"

But there's no place to hide down here.

"Where?" Jimmy asked.

Eddie pointed to the boiler monster. "Behind there," he said.

Jimmy felt the blood pulsing in his ears. He shook his head.

Eddie said, "Fine, then I guess I won't come visit you anymore."

Jimmy felt his heart sink. He couldn't take the thought of losing someone else. He walked to the edge of the boiler with unsure steps, ready to bolt at the first sign of trouble. He focused on the tentacles.

If one of those things moves – run!

He stepped to the edge of the behemoth and saw a battered wooden door.

Eddie's voice came from behind him. "Let's go in."

Eddie brushed past and opened the door. Jimmy gazed at the dark maw – a grim looking hole in the wall. A pathway littered with rocks carved through walls of packed, black earth.

Jimmy took a step – then stopped.

"Chicken," Eddie said – and encouraged him forward. Jimmy saw a Shimmer – a white dome at the back of the tunnel. An ever-undulating circular form pulsed like a beating heart.

"Come on," Eddie said. "Let's go."

Jimmy took a deep breath – one step – then stopped.

"I don't think my parents want me down here," he said. He looked down the pathway – the white Shimmer beckoning him.

Eddie scowled, "You're my best friend, don't you want to see where I live?"

Jimmy's eyes narrowed. *Live? What do you mean live? Eddie lives in a hole in my basement? I thought this was a hideout.*

Eddie grabbed Jimmy by the arm and began to pull him toward the wall. "Come see, come see. You can live here, too."

"Stop it!" Jimmy's voice sounded like a protesting crow. "Stop it, now!"

Eddie squeezed Jimmy's arm.

"That hurts, Eddie," Jimmy said.

Eddie stepped back, dragging Jimmy with him. The second Eddie crossed over into the whiteness, the Shimmer began to contract like a deflating balloon. Jimmy looked behind him – the boiler seemed very far away like it had been moved somehow.

When Jimmy turned back, all he could see was Eddie's forearm protruded from the cloud – his fingers clutched at Jimmy's arm. Jimmy remembered Josh's hand reaching – pleading – disappearing in the silver Shimmer in the woods.

Jimmy dug in his heels and pulled back, but Eddie hung on. The white light blinded Jimmy. Panic-induced adrenaline surged through his body. He jerked, thrashing, but Eddie's hand would not release him.

The Shimmer drew closer as Eddie pulled and was within an inch of Jimmy's forehead when he broke free and crashed into a crumpled heap on the floor. The Shimmer evaporated as it collapsed in on itself – and Eddie disappeared.

Jimmy scrambled to his feet and raced past the boiler, through the basement, then to the top of the stairs. He barreled into his mother's arms and started to sob.

"Jimmy, Jimmy, what's wrong?" Maggie clutched at her son and stroked his hair. "What happened? You're absolutely covered in filth. Where have you been? How did you get so dirty?"

Jimmy, trembling, pointed to the basement door.

Her caress was soft, but her voice grew hard. "You know you are not to go down there alone."

"But Ed-ed-eddie," Jimmy said before his stammering gave way to another wave of crying.

"Who the heck is, Eddie?" Maggie asked.

After a moment, Jimmy calmed down and explained.

Though angered by his disobedience, Maggie wondered what had happened. There wasn't anything – more importantly, *anyone* – in the basement.

Best to put this fantasy to rest before it grows, she thought.

With Jimmy clutching her hand, she walked down the steps into the basement. The place didn't seem as dark to Jimmy when his mother was with him. The boiler looked less monstrous as well.

Jimmy pointed to the door behind the boiler – it was still cracked open.

"Tunnel," he said.

"Oh honey, that is the old coal room. Before they had gas heat, people used coal to heat their homes."

She walked to the open door, bent over, and picked up one of the rocks.

"See, this is a piece of coal. Didn't know any of this stuff was still around," she said.

She placed it in Jimmy's hand. "There you go, sweetie. You can add it to your treasures."

Jimmy studied the rock. "But it was shiny, Mommy. White – and there was a ball."

She'd heard this story before with slightly different details, but the memory still pierced her heart like a hot stoking iron. She collected herself and thought, *no use upsetting the boy.*

She took the piece of coal, raised it close to the lightbulb between her thumb and forefinger, and rotated it back and forth. "See how the light hits it, Jimmy? It's just a reflection – see?"

Jimmy nodded. But he knew it was not the same as what he'd seen when he was with Eddie.

Maggie tugged at her son. "Let's go get you cleaned up before your father sees you."

They went straight to the bathroom. Soot poofed everywhere as Jimmy stripped out of his clothes. While the tub filled, Maggie asked the questions any good mother would ask. "How old is Eddie?" "Where did you meet him?" "When?" "What does he look like?" "Where did he come from?"

She listened patiently to all the answers, then said, "Let's make this our special secret. We won't tell anyone else – not even Matt and Mark – okay?"

Jimmy nodded and climbed into the tub. Maggie began to wash his shoulders, then arms. She stopped when she saw the fingerprints – swirling impressions on his blackened arm. She reached to inspect them closer, but Jimmy, all boy, began to splash, and the soot – and fingerprints – floated away in the ever-blackening water.

Jimmy didn't talk about Eddie anymore – not even to his mother. He also quit complaining about the crying noises, even though they continued. He kept hearing "overactive imagination." He didn't know what it meant, but he could tell from the tone that it wasn't something his parents liked.

It was just like Josh. He'd told Mommy and Daddy about it – the silver ball – his beloved brother disappearing into it. No one believed him. Not even the nice doctor who talked to him.

"He's lost a twin," the doctor told Maggie. "He's trying to make sense of it. It is going to take him a long time to work through his fears."

So, Jimmy didn't talk about Eddie. But Eddie still appeared. He still tried to get Jimmy to go back into the basement, but the only feeling Jimmy had that was stronger than needing a friend – was fear.

After a while, Eddie quit asking Jimmy to go to the basement, and the two friends would sit and talk for hours. Jimmy really liked learning about Eddie's family – especially about Eddie's younger sister, Clara.

Jimmy and Eddie talked all the time for the next year, but Eddie, of course, was no substitute for Josh.

CHAPTER 5
CLARA

APRIL 21, 1977

M ARK, FOUR YEARS old, walked over to Jimmy's bed about an hour after bedtime.

"Who's crying?" Mark asked.

Jimmy could hear the soft sob. "I thought it was you."

Mark shook his head.

"Matt?"

More shaking.

Jimmy got up and walked over to Matt's bed, careful not to wake him up. They both listened intently, but the sound emanated from behind Jimmy, not where Matt was sleeping.

Jimmy whispered – he didn't need to awaken Matt. "Point to the sound, Mark."

Mark's finger stabbed toward the far wall of the bedroom. A slight Shimmer – white. Jimmy had never noticed before. It reflected off the wall behind Mark's headboard.

Jimmy didn't know what to do. *Should I tell Mommy and Daddy? No, they'll think I'm making stuff up again.*

He looked at his little brother. *But Mark hears it, too.*

Certain his parents would believe him this time, Jimmy took Mark's hand and headed for the stairs.

"Mom, Mom, Mommy! Mark can hear the crying, too," Jimmy said. He bounced on the balls of his feet.

Mark slid a little behind Jimmy.

Maggie cocked her head. "Marky, is this true? Do not tease Mommy – I'm not in the mood."

Mark nodded and pointed towards his room. Maggie grunted and headed for the staircase, muttering under her breath.

She spoke to Paul over her shoulder. "Be back in a second."

Paul never took his head out of his book. "Enjoy the monsters," he said.

When they entered the bedroom, Maggie rubbed her arms. "Why is it so cold in here again?"

Matt sat up in his bed. "Mommy, what's that noise?"

Either they are messing with me or I am going deaf, Maggie thought. "Well," she said, "Mommy doesn't hear anything. What does it sound like?"

Matt and Mark began to mimic the cries in perfect unison. Jimmy moved his finger up and down in the same pattern as if conducting a symphony.

Maggie held up a silencing finger. "All right, boys. One second."

What had begun as a tingle at the base of her spine was now a bone-rattling case of "the shivers." She stepped into the hall.

"Angie, Heather, would you come here, please?"

The girls knew that voice – it was not a request. They put their toothbrushes in the holder, spat into the sink. Angie rinsed – Heather wiped her tongue on a towel.

"Ewww, gross," Angie said.

"If you tell Mom, I'll lick *you*," Heather said.

Angie and Heather walked into the boys' room wearing matching flannel PJs: Angie in red; Heather in blue. Maggie's finger was back in the air. All six stood, barely breathing.

"Can anyone hear anything?" Maggie asked.

Three hands – the boys' – went into the air.

Angie was the first to speak. "I can't hear anything."

Heather was frowning. "I can hear something. It sounds like a sick cat."

Matt, ever the prankster, hacked and pretended to cough up a furball. Mark laughed, then pretended to throw up.

Everyone laughed – everyone except Jimmy. He wanted – needed – his mother to hear the crying. He'd endured it for years.

This is not a joke, Jimmy thought.

The tension gone; Heather turned for the door. "Outta here," she said. "Feels like an igloo."

"An igloo," Angie said. "You are so stupid."

Heather turned. "Am not," at the same time Maggie's bark cut through the air. "We do *not* call people stupid."

As the girls left, Maggie said, "I'm not sure what you boys heard, but I don't hear anything. Sorry."

She turned for the door but froze when Jimmy shouted – his voice a plea for help. "Eddie told me his little sister, Clara, cries a lot. He told me not to tell you, but he said she is sick."

Maggie stiffened. "Paul, you need to get up here, now!"

Matt said, "Who's Clara?"

Mark said, "Who's Eddie?"

Everyone turned to Jimmy.

CHAPTER 6
TIME TO MOVE
SPRING 1980

MATT, MARK, AND Jimmy made a pact never to mention the crying to anyone. Ever. The topic seemed to upset their parents. It wasn't a big deal to Jimmy anyway. Most nights, it didn't happen. Jimmy noticed the crying only happened when the room got cold – and when he could see the white light – the Shimmer.

Dad had a very simple explanation. "It's probably a cracked pipe," he said. "Makes a whistling noise – something only young ears can hear – you know, like a dog, and, of course, our boys."

A leak in the heating system might explain colder temperatures, but the frosty air was confined to the boys' room; the girls' room stayed toasty all winter.

The house was old, circa the 1870s, so it required regular maintenance and more than occasional renovation. In the spring of 1980, Jimmy's father hatched a plan to replace the plank siding on the exterior.

"This place is beginning to look like the Adams Family lives here," he said.

Angie lowered her voice and croaked her best Lurch impression. "You rang."

With Maggie's prodding and the promise of homemade pie and plenty of beer, Paul convinced a few of his bowling buddies to help.

"We're going to check the pipes from the basement as well," Paul said. "If we get lucky, we'll kill two birds with one stone – new siding and no more whistling."

Mark started to cry about "the dead birdy." Maggie hustled to the rescue with an explanation for Mark and a death stare for Paul. "No Mark, Daddy is not going to kill any birdies."

The project commenced in May. Jimmy sat for hours, fascinated as his father and "the crew" removed each board, inspected it, discarded it, or put it in a pile to be resurfaced and reused. The work involved a good deal of banter – and Pabst Blue Ribbon beer.

Jimmy proudly carried the title of "Designated Beer Restorer." Whenever any of the guys held a can aloft and yelled, "Hey, Jimmy," the boy darted to the cooler in the backyard and returned with a cold one. He tossed the fresh brew up and caught the empty on the way down. Then, Jimmy's favorite part – he ran to the sidewalk, where he crushed the used can underfoot.

Each evening ended with a cookout. The children attacked a pile of hotdogs and burgers (sometimes chicken when one of the mothers expressed concern about "all that red meat"); the men assaulted T-bones the size of trash can lids.

Every night, Paul offered Jimmy a steak. "You're part of the construction gang," Paul said.

Every night, Jimmy went with a burger. "Too much work – all that cutting."

Jimmy had never seen a "naked house" before. Every removed plank exposed a little more of the dwelling's skeleton. All Jimmy knew about building stemmed from the Lincoln Log huts he built with his brothers – and sometimes with Eddie. He remembered how he'd play Lincoln Logs with Josh. It would make him sad for a bit, but he was happy to play with his little brothers, too.

Once the buildings in their little towns were complete, they played "Godzilla," Jimmy's favorite monster show. Matt and Jimmy pretended to be monsters and wrestled around and through the Lincoln Log homes. Little maple logs and green roof planks scattered everywhere. Matt particularly liked the demolition process; Mark, not so much – but he always watched.

On the last day of pull-down, his father's friend, Chris, yanked off the final section of planks along the back of the house, near Jimmy's bedroom window.

"Hey Paul, check this out."

Chris handed Paul a wooden box covered with ornate carvings and wrapped with a corroding chain. A rusting padlock fastened the end of the chains together.

"Dusty as all hell but in good shape," Paul said.

He looked at the box, shook it, brushed off a bit of dust. He turned to Maggie and said, "Come on over here honey, check this out."

When Maggie came over, the guys had encircled the box, staring at it like a work of art.

Chris pointed at the lock. "Must be something valuable in there," he said.

"Hey, Stretch," Buzz always used Paul's high school nickname, "maybe you're rich."

Paul smiled without enthusiasm. "Probably full of worthless pictures. Otherwise, it wouldn't be here."

They all stood around anxiously awaiting the grand reveal. Chris tossed a PBR to Buzz and Jimmy – "That's for your dad, kid" – then took one for himself.

"Have to be prepared to celebrate," Chris said, while looking at Jimmy with a beer in his hand.

Maggie snatched the can from Jimmy, popped the top, and took a sip.

"Hey, that's mine," Paul said.

Maggie shook her head. "More opening – less talking."

Paul looked at Chris. "You find a key?"

"Nope."

Jimmy had a thought. *Maybe we can look for it – a treasure hunt.*

He opened his mouth to suggest just that, but Paul said, "Buzz, pass me those bolt cutters. Let's see what we have in here."

"Sure thing, Stretch."

With a quick click, the chain fell to the ground, along with the lock.

Jimmy picked them up and handed them to his mother for her inspection.

"Paul, this lock looks really old, like an antique."

Paul nodded. He never took his eyes off the box. Even though hard to detect in the sunlight, Jimmy could see a slight Shimmer drifting from the box. He said nothing.

Matt, Mark, Angie, and Heather, now joining the group, squeezed past the adults.

"Come here, kids," Paul said. "Let's see what surprises we have in here. Matt… Mark, you guys can do the honors."

With all the patience of a hyperactive Schnauzer, Matt grabbed the box. Mark reached for the lid, and the two boys opened it simultaneously.

Paul's look of expectation crashed onto the shoals of reality.

"I knew it," he said, his voice seeping with disappointment.

At the same time, Mark said, "Ah, cool."

Maggie patted him on the head as Paul removed the contents: a tin baby rattle, an old doll, and a stick and ball toy.

"I know what that is," Jimmy said. His voice took on a professorial tone. "You hold the stick at one end and try to swing that ball into the cup that's on the other end. I saw one on a field trip to that museum place."

I hope Dad lets me have it, he thought. *The girls won't want it, and Matt and Mark are too young.*

Paul looked ready to toss the box towards the trash heap. Maggie reached in.

"Wait," she said. "There's something else."

She reached into the box and extracted a letter, folded and sealed with wax. Jimmy could tell from the deterioration of the seal and the age of the toys, the box had been placed in the wall a long time ago, maybe as far back as when the house was built. The seal had a barely visible "K" stamped into the wax.

Maggie pulled the seal away with the care of someone who'd bandaged thousands of scraped knees. She unfolded the note. Jimmy noticed the beautiful cursive handwriting on the letter as she began to read it out loud.

Dearest Friends,

This box was interred in the heart of our home in memory of our two children, who passed away this fateful year in 1877. Cholera first took our beloved baby daughter on April 21, and a few months later, our precious son on June 20. We have placed a few of their favorite items within the wall for safekeeping until they are rediscovered and remembered one last time. May our sweet...

Maggie stopped, her hand on her mouth.

Angie tapped Maggie on the shoulder. "Who, Mommy, our sweet who?"

Maggie swallowed, cleared her throat, and continued.

…our sweet Edward and Clarice rest in peace.

With loving devotion,

Mr. and Mrs. C. Kosar

Maggie looked at Paul – the two of them stared at Jimmy. Maggie repeated the names.

"Edward and Clarice – Eddie and Clara."

Her face twisted in confusion. Jimmy looked at his father, who said, "You gotta admit, hell of a coincidence."

The adults seemed transfixed. With all the excitement over, Jimmy wanted to play a little.

"Can I have the ball and stick?" he asked.

Maggie never looked at him – she stared into space. But her hand offered the toy. "Here, honey."

"Thanks, Mom."

Before he was two steps away, she said, "Jimmy!"

"Yes, Mommy."

Jimmy could see tears in the corners of her eyes. "Be careful," she said. "Please."

The boys no longer heard any cries at night. Eddie didn't come anymore either.

It didn't matter. Less than a week after they looked in the box, a Century 21 "For Sale" sign decorated the front lawn.

CHAPTER 7
MOVING DAY

SUMMER 1980

WHEN ASKED THE reason for moving, Jimmy's parents told their friends that a family of seven was simply too large for the three-bedroom home. Jimmy knew better.

He mentioned his concern once. "Mommy, are we moving because of the box we found?"

She touched him on the head. "No, honey, we're moving because we need more space, and you should have your own room."

But Jimmy noticed her eyes lingered on his. Did he need more space? Maybe, even though he would have preferred to share a room with his brothers.

Was Mommy worried about him? Absolutely.

Still, there was truth to his parents' claim. Matt and Mark were turning seven soon, and Angie and Heather were 14 and 12, respectively. His parents felt it was time to give everyone a fresh start.

Jimmy was excited to have his own space. However, he desperately wished Josh was there share it with him.

The hole in Jimmy's heart was seven years old, but it was still a hole, nonetheless. Jimmy looked for Josh everywhere – on his walks through the neighborhood – at his ballgames – at twilight when the stars seemed to be making their minds up about appearing – at dawn when the sun stretched its bright arms from underneath the horizon.

He has to be somewhere.

Their new house had five bedrooms, all of which were on the second floor. Jimmy hadn't even visited their new home yet, but Angie took the time to describe it in exaggerated, and exhausting, detail. When she finally quit talking, Jimmy decided the new place was a blend of the Astrodome, home of the Oilers, and the palace at Versailles. (The French Revolution fascinated him – guards, guns, gold, and a guillotine – what more could a kid ask for?)

After the initial barrage, Angie got her second wind. "The basement is huge; it has a playroom as big as a football field, a laundry room with a bathroom in it, a workspace where Dad can build things. It even has a room where we keep all the logs for our Christmas fires."

Jimmy imagined sitting by the Christmas tree next to a roaring fire, opening his gifts with his entire family.

She continued, "On the first floor, there is a living room with the fireplace, big dining room, bathroom, enormous kitchen, and breakfast nook."

Jimmy had no idea what the heck a "nook" was, but he nodded and smiled. Angie started over, adding more detail to her initial "high-level view," as she called it.

Jimmy heard snippets: "Mom and Dad...master... Mark and Matt...not with you...I'm with Heather... very unique...probably the best in the house..."

Then, the line she'd said before but one he could hear over and over again without becoming bored: "You get your own room – all by yourself."

Jimmy grinned until his face hurt. He couldn't wait to see every bit of his new house, but his 10-year-old brain could only focus for so long on Angie's verbose descriptions. When she started telling him about her room *for the third time,* Jimmy lost all interest. Matt and Mark ran past. Jimmy decided it was an excellent time to join them.

"I need to watch those two," he said. "They might get hurt."

Angie's voice screeched in protest. "But I haven't told you about the attic yet," she said. "Besides, you usually don't care if those clowns are playing in the street at rush hour – naked."

An image of his brothers' tiny butts dodging cars made Jimmy laugh and he chased Matt and Mark down the steps into the back yard.

After supper, as Jimmy lay in bed, he thought about his favorite part of getting a new home. Jimmy was moving down the street from his best friend, Bob.

Bob and Jimmy had met on the opening day of kindergarten. They shared similar interests, evident when instructed to pick a book from the library to take home. Bob picked *The Legend of Bigfoot;* Jimmy selected *UFOs: Reality or Myth.* Both were fascinated with the unusual: ghosts, Bigfoot, "Nessie," aliens. If it was weird, Bob and Jimmy loved it.

So far, their adventures had been limited to books and movies, but they'd agreed to become real-life monster hunters when they grew older. Jimmy thought this might be a way to search for his missing brother.

FINALLY, THE DAY arrived, July 18, 1980. It was much warmer than a typical northern Ohio summer day.

In the small town of Bellevue, Ohio, 20 miles south of Lake Erie, the area was typically a bit more temperate due to the cool breeze off the lake. Not on this day, however. The temperature reached triple digits with no relief in sight. Jimmy's dad kept saying he was "sweating his boys off." Jimmy had no idea what that meant, but he knew his dad was hot. The wind blew out of the southwest throughout the day and pushed both showers and thunderstorms through the area.

That morning, Jimmy's Mom and Dad, Angie, and Heather took off to move their family's things. Matt, Mark, and Jimmy were left behind with Aunt Peggy. Fine by them - she was a great cook. Each of the boys had a few toys to keep them occupied. Also, knowing Matt and Mark loved flipping through the channels, their parents had left the television as well.

"I want to watch cartoons," Matt said.

Mark grabbed the channel knob and twisted. "I want to watch animals."

He was continually looking for reruns of *Mutual of Omaha's Wild Kingdom*. On the last day of school, the faculty at Shumaker Elementary School showed a Marlin Perkins marathon in the gym. Mark had been hooked on animals ever since. The more he could learn about lions, elephants, and bears, the better.

Jimmy refereed – they settled on *The Little Rascals*. Jimmy thought Matt looked a lot like Alfalfa and Mark a bit like Spanky.

They made a cute pair.

Jimmy hated being stuck with "the little ones" while everyone else went to the new house, but he knew his brothers would just get in the way.

The twins were a mischief machine. Paul had nailed their bedrooms windows shut earlier that spring because they threw everything they could lift out of their second-story window. Toys, clothes, sheets, towels, and pillows littered the front lawn.

A member of the local Fire Department had stopped by when someone noticed Matt and Mark struggling to squeeze a mattress out of the window and called it in. The "Twin Tornados" were a local legend.

AT THE END of a very long day, Mom came to pick up the twins. Jimmy and his father went to The Pinewood Derby at Cub Scouts.

Jimmy was proud of his derby car, the "Scarlett Sensation." Jimmy was sure his Ohio State-colored speedster could win. To a 10-year-old, that hunk of pinewood served as an *all that was right with the world moment*, especially since his father helped him build it. The clatter of plastic tires racing down the wooden track filled the evening. It was an exciting night for Jimmy, and his father did his best to remain enthusiastic, even though he was exhausted.

Jimmy finished in third place – respectable. He beat Tim, his nemesis, but lost in the semi-finals to Duane, one of his best friends. Losing lost its sting a little when Duane won the whole thing.

The den mothers distributed the prizes: little trophies for the Champ and Runner-Up, "You Built a Car" ribbons for everyone else. Jimmy didn't care – he got to keep Scarlett Sensation – the best prize of all and one he reckoned to display in a prominent place in his room.

They rode home with the radio blasting *Magic* (Jimmy thought Olivia Newton-John was smokin') and *Another Brick in the Wall*. With no AC, they had the windows down. They passed Clancy's – a local hangout – and the air grew suddenly colder. The wind picked up. By the time they drove in front of Redd Middle School, the giant American flag was snapping and popping. Trees bowed as if paying homage to

Jimmy's performance, and the smell of ozone filled the front seat.

"Storm's comin'," Dad said. "Crank up that window, son."

Just as Jimmy's window closed, light bathed the entire town as if some Olympian god had taken a flash photo. A thunderclap rattled the car windows.

"That was a close one," Jimmy said. He wasn't afraid of storms anymore. In third grade, he had come to understand how they were created. Jimmy knew there was a connection between the light and the sound but, like most things academic, he didn't remember all the details – all he knew was that there was nothing to be afraid of. His parents appreciated the lesson as it led to fewer sleepless nights with Jimmy cringing between them.

He was still working on the calculations (*Was it one mile for every second – or five?);* rain pelted the car. Sheets of water slammed into the windshield with the sound of a thousand tiny hammers. Jimmy saw ice pellets.

"Look, son," Paul said. "We've got hail!"

"You mean like snow?" Jimmy asked.

"No, more like pure ice," his father said. "If you get caught outside in this stuff, it hurts. It'll shred an umbrella in a heartbeat."

Jimmy wasn't so sure about how cool the storm was anymore. "Uh…we okay in the car?"

Paul peered through the windshield. "We're fine

son." He patted Jimmy's knee. "Just let me concentrate on the road."

Dad drove with caution. He pulled passed Whitely's Grocery Store. The hail stopped as suddenly as it had started, and the rain began to lighten.

Jimmy looked into the upstairs window of a beautiful colonial home. He noticed what looked like a gray Shimmer flickering in the window. He quickly averted his eyes. He knew that mentioning anything weird would only frustrate his father, so he did his best to avoid it.

Jimmy looked back at his father. "Uh, looks like a quick hitter, Dad," he said, using his father's typical term.

His father smiled. "Sure does, son, sure does. Maybe it will cool things down a bit. Well, we can hope."

A few minutes later, his dad pulled down the alleyway and into the garage. Jimmy hopped in his seat. "We have a garage. That's awesome. Now my bike won't get wet all the time."

Jimmy collected his belongings, including Scarlett Sensation. They walked out of the side door of the detached garage and up a concrete path to the house. The night air was still cool, but Jimmy could feel the sticky return of the summer heat. He looked up at the night sky. Small holes in the dark purple clouds revealed the moon's silver glow. Jimmy stopped and stared.

"Majestic, huh," Dad said.

"It's pretty special, Dad." Jimmy said as his dad began to grumble.

"Oh, come on, do we have to have every light in the house blazing?"

Jimmy looked up and counted all the windows where he could see light. Even the three tiny windows at the very top of the house emitted a deep yellow sheen.

"This house is huge, Dad," he said. "How many floors?"

His father smiled. "Well, if you count the basement and the attic, it has four."

His old house didn't have an attic, just a little "door" in the ceiling where his mom and dad would stuff the Christmas decorations. Jimmy was never allowed up there, so he was excited to explore. He glanced up again to the highest windows and thought he could see something or someone moving – he wasn't sure.

He was about to point it out to his dad when they saw another flash of lightning in the distance followed several seconds later by a muted rumble.

Jimmy looked up at his dad. "That was a good one. Sounded like Grandpa when he snores."

They both laughed and went inside.

"Didyouwin – didyouwin?" Matt and Mark pulled on Jimmy and clutched at Scarlett Sensation. Jimmy began to laugh and was about to sit on the floor and show his car off when he caught the unmistakable aroma of chocolate chip cookies.

He looked at his mother. "Third place," he said. "Do I still get cookies?"

Maggie laughed and hugged him. "Of course, you do – these are to celebrate the new house."

Less than a minute later, Jimmy was sipping cold milk and anticipating licking gooey, melted chocolate off his fingers. Angie and Heather thumped up the stairs from the basement.

"Come see, Jimmy. Come see."

A dilemma – cookies or adventure.

Mom was still hovering at the oven, so he stood up to follow his sisters.

"Don't eat 'em all," he said.

With his patented, wide smile, Matt stuck out his tongue and wiggled his fingers next to his ears.

"Matthew, behave," Mom said. Matt suddenly feigned interest in the tablecloth. Mom continued. "I will save you some, go check things out. Matt, be nice."

Matt cocked his head to the side and delivered his best angelic smile.

Angie, Heather, and Jimmy ran down into the basement; it was just as Angie had described it earlier: a sizeable open playroom for them, a laundry room next door, and the workroom. Jimmy looked up and saw an open square conduit sticking out from the ceiling and asked Heather, "What is that?"

Heather said, "Oh, it's the laundry chute. There's a little door in the wall on the second floor. You drop your dirty clothes in, and Mom washes them and puts them back in our dressers."

Wow, this house is magical, Jimmy thought.

Angie then opened the firewood storage room. Jimmy could see logs lining the backwall. Jimmy imagined sitting in front of the fireplace at Christmas again and started whistling. Christmas was his favorite time of year.

"*Jingle Bells*?" Heather asked. "A little early, don't you think?"

Jimmy stopped and smiled.

As the old-slatted wooden door squeaked shut and the bolt slid back into place. They then ran back up the stairs.

After a quick tour of the ground floor, a large square perfect for endless games of chase, the three headed for the upstairs steps. A voice came from the kitchen.

"Cookies in two minutes."

But they hurried upstairs anyway. This was the moment Jimmy had been anticipating, the moment he would finally see his room.

Angie yelled over her shoulder. "Save us some."

They heard their mother's reply. "I'll try, but the barbarians are at the gate."

Jimmy had a mental image of Matt and Mark smeared with chocolate and crumbs.

At the top of the steps, Jimmy peered down the hall, and he could see five closed doors. Jimmy thought of the game show, *Let's Make a Deal*, and giggled.

I'll take Door #1, Monty.

First room on the left belonged to the girls. As described, it was two rooms in one. There was one door to the hallway; on the far wall another door led into Heather's room – a space with wall-to-wall windows. Jimmy could see all three sides of dark backyard.

He imagined it being the deck of a Star Destroyer. *I wish this was my room.*

Door number two was the bathroom. After a quick look, (*You seen one bathroom, you've seen 'em all*) they headed into the twins' room

Matt and Mark's room was at the end of the hall. Matt and Mark came running up the stairs shouting in unison. "Get out, get out! No girl cooties allowed!"

Heather swatted Matt on the back of the head as they slammed the door in her face.

Door number four stood directly opposite the bathroom. When they opened the door, Jimmy immediately recognized his parents' big bed and their other furniture. He felt a little odd. Dad had already mentioned a new prohibition.

"You're a man now, Jimmy. No more sleeping with us when you're scared. You have to learn to be brave."

Well, I am 10, he thought. *10-and-a-half!*

"One room left," he said. He looked down and paused. There was a small door just above the baseboard.

"Laundry chute," Heather said. "Remember? Pretty cool, huh?"

Jimmy opened the little door and peered into the darkness. A pair of white eyes peered up at him. He banged his head when he jumped.

His sisters laughed. He rubbed his head.

Don't cry. Don't cry!

He heard his mother's voice. "Cookies are on the table," she said.

"It's only Mom," Heather said. "She pulled that on us earlier."

Jimmy nodded and continued down the hall.

Angie opened the last door. Heather flung her arms wide and said, "Ta da!"

His room was by far the largest in the entire house. It seemed a little odd – one person will all this room. But he didn't say anything about his reservations.

Jimmy waffled between, *Don't mess this up* and *I don't want to be all alone*. It was in moments like this that his thoughts lingered on Josh.

To distract himself, he imagined setting up his RC racetrack and train set, and still having plenty of room to jump and play.

"You're across the hall from us," Angie said with a reassuring smile. Jimmy felt a little better.

Angie and Heather could no longer resist the smell of the cookies and ran back downstairs to get their share. Jimmy stayed back to plan how to set up his room, but he could not stop thinking about being the only occupant of such an expansive space. He perched on the side of his bed and noticed something strange: the room was not completely rectangular. One wall stuck out, like a large box situated on the side of the room– it jutted out a good five feet.

On closer inspection, Jimmy noticed a door – a

closet, he figured. When he opened it, he saw an ascending staircase.

Two things hit him in the face – a blast of stuffy air – and a vile odor. He'd smelled it before – once.

While exploring outside Bob's grandmother's house, the two boys had come across a dead cat. Granny lived next to a set of railroad tracks. With active tracks all over town, only God knew the total of squished kitties in Bellevue. The carcass was mangled almost beyond recognition. Bob took the discovery pretty hard – he had a few pet cats.

Jimmy remembered putting his hand on Bob's shoulder. "Sorry, buddy," he said. "I know you like the kitties."

"It reminds me of my cat Tiffany, that's all," Bob replied, while wiping away a tear.

The smell made Jimmy sick to his stomach. On the way back to Granny's house, Jimmy saw buzzards circling above. They swooped ever lower in a circular pattern; their approached slow but unyielding. Jimmy watched until they landed. When the scavengers began tearing at the cat's flesh, he turned away and ran for the house.

He hadn't been able to get the smell out of his nose for days.

Jimmy's father walked into his bedroom and jolted Jimmy back to reality.

"Found the attic, I see," Dad said. "Don't worry. We won't use it much, so we won't be in your room very often."

"Dad, it stinks," Jimmy said.

Dad's nose wrinkled. "Ugh," he said. "Gross, huh. Probably a dead a bird or mouse. Maybe a squirrel. I'll check it out. Okay?"

"Okay."

"In the meantime, keep the door shut. Mom will spray a little Lysol – it'll get better."

Paul opened a window.

"Let's wash up and get at those cookies. Whatdaya say?"

Jimmy acted nonchalant. Then raced for the door.

"Last one down is a rotten egg," he said.

CHAPTER 8
SWEET DREAMS

SUMMER 1980

L ATER THAT NIGHT, Jimmy headed back upstairs to begin working on his bedroom. The heavier items were already in place – the bed, dresser, and toybox. Jimmy liked his room "just so," but for the most part, his parents did an excellent job of organizing his room. Plus, he didn't want to complain after his parents did all the work for him.

I'll change a few things – it'll be great!

The house was nearly 80 years old – that's what Dad said. With no overhead lights, Jimmy relied on a trio of lamps. He liked the warmth of the yellow light from the 40-watt bulbs. The soft shadows make him feel safe – at home. One of the lamps was missing a shade.

Must be in one of those boxes.

On the way across the room, Jimmy snatched Darth Vader from the toy box. He held the action figure next to the naked bulb and grinned at the nine-foot menacing silhouette cast on the far wall.

Jimmy did his best Lord Vader impersonation: "I find your lack of faith disturbing."

Jimmy had to admit, for a bad guy, Darth Vader was one cool character.

Jimmy found the shade in the corner of the room and put it in place. He returned the Dark Lord to his spot in the carrying case and began to imagine the great Star Wars scenes he could recreate in all this space.

He liked to fanaticize about living in the *Star Wars* universe and piloting the Millennium Falcon or X-Wing fighter in an epic battle to save the galaxy. Who knows, maybe he would even learn to use the Force. He held out his hand to "force move" his train set together.

Nothing happened.

I guess I will have to put it together myself, he thought, which he did.

He had just finished placing the "Scarlett Sensation" at the top-center of his toy chest when Mom came up the stairs.

"Jimmy," she said, "time for bed."

"Ugh," he said, "I haven't even finished putting my racetrack together or testing my train set."

"Well, tomorrow is Saturday, and you've got all morning before you go visit Bob," his mother replied.

He and Bob had been planning on spending the entire day together.

When he heard his Mom enter the girls' room, he ran to the bathroom to brush his teeth.

Dad walked past the door. "Goodnight, Boy."

Jimmy loved it when Dad called him, "Boy." His father always said it with a hint of pride. Jimmy yelled through a mouth full of toothpaste, "Goop Nigh," then drooled into the sink.

Jimmy liked to be under the covers, ready to go, so his mom could slide the blanket up under his sides. Of course, tonight, it was too warm, so Jimmy elected to push his covers down to the end of the bed and use only the sheet.

Maggie came through the door, kissed him on the head, tucked him in, and asked, "Do you want me to read you a story?"

Typically, this was a quick "Yes," but Jimmy could see his mother looked exhausted. He replied, "No, thank you, Mom. You still have to wrestle the Twin Tornadoes," and laughed.

She smiled with a sense of relief and appreciation and said, "Yes, the clowns await," then left the room after turning off his lamp.

She closed the door behind her, and the light of the hallway slivered into a faint line, then disappeared. Jimmy felt the darkness closing in around him – a cocoon of gloom. Jimmy hated the dark, but he fought the urge to turn on the lamp.

"I have to learn to be brave," he said, echoing his father's admonition.

Besides, he and Bob planned to be ghost hunters – they were going to capture Sasquatch. What kind of Bigfoot stalker was afraid of the dark? Still, no matter how hard he tried, his mind would drift towards isolation and fear.

Sleep came slowly – and did not last.

When Jimmy woke up, the only light came from the green glow of his clock. The corners of the unfamiliar room hid the unknown. Jimmy shuddered.

He shut his eyes for a moment but bolted upright in bed when he heard a faint scratching above his head. He remembered what his father had said – something about birds and mice. Jimmy considered getting up and telling his parents, but then he looked at the clock – 3:33 AM.

If I wake them up, they'll be upset. Stay brave.

Somehow it felt better to talk out loud. "Little animals in the attic – no big deal, no worries. I chase birds around in the yard; we have mice for classroom pets at school. I've even held them."

He remembered Mickey and Minnie, which put a smile on his face and relaxed him. Jimmy suspected they were both boys, though – no baby mice – and they both had a little pink bulge under their tails. Jimmy started to grin when something above him thumped – heavy – loud.

That was no mouse.

He flattened his hands on the bed, preparing to race for the hallway and looked over to the attic door. He could not see it very well from his vantage point, but it looked shut. He waited.

After about a dozen deep breaths, he lay back down

and went to every child's "go-to" move, covers up to his chin and lay as still as possible. The noise wasn't "blanket over the head" scary, but it was close. Jimmy did not dare move; a single creak might alert whatever was in the attic to his presence.

He looked at the clock – 3:55. He'd been frozen for a while. His back started to itch – a hair – sand – a bug – *a spider* – something irritated his skin.

Don't move!

Then – a miracle. His father, a regular smoker, commenced with one of his nightly house-shaking hacking fits. The smell of smoke made Jimmy queasy – and his mother furious.

"If you ever take up that filthy habit…" She never finished the tirade, but Jimmy knew he'd have a better chance of living after getting a tattoo than if he ever smoked.

Paul had very distinctive coughing jags: a loud bark followed by two lighter coughs, then the clearing of his throat. When the "phlegm hocking" started, Jimmy was prepared. He flipped on his side with only a slight squeak from the bed and began raking at the small of his back.

When nothing appeared from the attic, he relaxed, closed his eyes, and slept through the night.

CHAPTER 9
THE PERFECT DAY

SUMMER 1980

JIMMY WAS AWAKENED in the morning by shrieks of delight and boisterous laughing accompanied by the TV downstairs. His brothers were singing – or screaming, depending on your musical taste – along with a jingle. "I'm just a bill, I'm only a bill, and I'm sitting here on Capitol Hill."

As he was getting dressed, he noticed the RC track still in its box.

Putting this together is going to have to wait. I need to go see Bob.

Jimmy picked up the RC box and placed it in the closet on the other side of the room. As Jimmy turned around, he noticed something peculiar: the door to the attic was slightly ajar. He nervously walked over to the door, pushed it closed, then tugged on the door to check the latch; the lock held tight. He twisted the knob, and the door clicked open. Jimmy, still a bit nervous from the night before, peeked up into the attic and noticed the stairs. Seven steps ascended to a landing, then ascended again to the right. Jimmy listened for a second. When he didn't hear anything, he closed the door and hurried downstairs.

Five steps down – 90° left turn – seven more steps.

Jimmy made the connection. *Must be like the attic, only in reverse.*

A chill inched its way along his spine. Jimmy looked over his shoulder – all clear.

Matt and Mark sat in front of the television and shoveled cereal into their mouths like they were racing. Without looking, Jimmy knew the contents: Count Chocula for Matt – Boo Berry for Mark.

Mark looked up. "Come watch *Super Friends* with us. It just came on."

A few cartoons before heading to Bob's would be nice.

He headed to the kitchen.

Ah – jackpot! Mom was pulling out all the stops at the new house. Jimmy grabbed the box of Lucky Charms, then realized Matt was using his favorite bowl. It was an old, extra-large Cool Whip container. Grandpa had brought it last Thanksgiving – his contribution to the feast. While Jimmy shoveled the topping, Grandpa said, "You want some pie with that Cool Whip?"

It was the same joke he told every year, but it always made Jimmy laugh.

The tub's logo had disappeared about twenty wash cycles ago but since it held more cereal than anything else in the house – Mom wouldn't let him use a mixing bowl ("You're not Jethro Bodine," she said) – Jimmy loved the Cool Whip container.

Jimmy walked back into the den. "Matt, you took my bowl."

Matt looked up. A slimy river of chunky chocolatized milk dribbled from his mouth back into the bowl.

"Want it?" he asked – his cheeks bulged like a chipmunk's.

"You are so gross," Jimmy said.

"Takes one to know one," Matt said and resumed his vigorous consumption.

Jimmy shook his head and went to get a bowl of his own.

Angie and Heather sat in the breakfast nook. Jimmy slid onto the bench across from his sisters.

"Umm, you guys hear anything last night?" Jimmy asked.

"Besides Dad?" Angie said.

"Yes."

"Nothing," Heather said. "Well – that's not completely accurate. There was an owl out back. He hooted off and on for a while before I went to sleep."

"Nothing in the house – besides, you know, Dad?"

The girls shook their heads.

Angie took on the role of mother. "Mom and Dad left for work. Are you still going over to Bob's house today?"

"Heck, yes!" Jimmy replied.

"Alright then, get some breakfast, get changed, and I will take you over as soon as you are ready."

Jimmy scarfed down his cereal, ran up the stairs, threw on jeans and a Cleveland Browns tee-shirt, and was back downstairs in less than 10 minutes.

ANGIE WALKED JIMMY down to the street corner and pointed down to Bob's house.

"Okay," Angie said, "check back in around 1:00 PM."

Jimmy nodded.

"Good," she said, "I will have lunch waiting for you. Fried bologna okay?"

Jimmy gave her a thumbs-up. "It's all you know how to cook," he said. He was already running when he yelled over his shoulder. "With lots of mustard."

Angie had already called Debbie, Bob's oldest sister, to let her know Jimmy would be there this morning, so Bob opened the front door as soon as Jimmy hit the front lawn.

"I want to show you my new books," Bob said.

Jimmy whistled when he saw the titles: *Bigfoot Hunt – Men from Mars – Tracking Nessie – Scary Ghost Adventures*. Bob picked up *Bigfoot Hunt* and began to read.

"What's this word?" Jimmy asked, pointing to the large word on the page.

"Cryptozoology," Bob said.

"What the heck?"

"I think it is the study of the stuff we like. You know, Bigfoot, Nessie, and the Mokele-mbembe thing in Africa."

They both thought cryptozoology was a pretty impressive word and began saying it over and over. Jimmy listened intently, while Bob continued to read. When he finished, Jimmy said, "Let's go to the park. It's time for The Adventurers to try to find a Yeti again."

Just before he slammed the front door, Bob called back into the house. "Debbie, we're going to the park." The boys didn't stay long enough to hear her response.

GREENWOOD HEIGHTS PARK, named for the street on which it was situated, featured swing sets, climbing poles, ball fields, tennis courts, jogging trails, and little wobbly animals on huge springs, where kids rocked back and forth, while parents tried not to get sick. Bob and Jimmy loved to see if they could touch the ground with their backs. More than one scar attested to the boys' inability to hold on when the creatures rebounded.

The center of the park had four full-size baseball fields. The boys loved to get their friends together to play – but they preferred hitting a tennis ball. A little tougher to field, but they could launch homers like Dave Kingman.

As Bob and Jimmy walked past the concession stand, they spotted tiny white flowers dotting the outfields.

"My Granny says those are White Dutch Clover," Bob said. "Honeybees love them."

They could see bees swarming around the buds – skittering from one blossom to the next. In the morning quiet, they could hear the buzzing.

"Sounds like a bunch of people humming," Jimmy said.

They walked the track in silence for a moment before Bob said, "Did you hear about the guy from the other side of town that appeared out of nowhere?"

Jimmy shook his head, but his eyes opened with piqued interest.

Bob continued. "Yeah, yeah, my dad told me the story last night. Some guy was swimming in Lake Erie by Port Clinton – he said he was Roger Byrd."

"The dude who disappeared?"

"Yep," Bob said. "Went poof about seven years ago. Then he appears right out of thin air. He seemed really confused so the police came out to talk to him. They asked him the year. Guess what he said."

"How would I know?" Jimmy asked.

"He said it was the year 2043. Crazy right?"

Jimmy didn't answer. He saw Josh – smiling – playing – running – disappearing.

"So, what happened?" Jimmy asked.

"Get this. When the real Roger disappeared, he was 16. That would make him 23 now, right?"

"Yep."

"Well, this guy – the swimmer guy – was old – you know, wrinkly skin and saggy butt and everything. When the police asked him what happened, he told them he was going down the street and walked through a small vibration or something.

"Geez – that's creepy."

Bob's eyes gleamed. "Oh, it gets weirder. He claims he lived wherever he was for 70 years – says he settled into a routine there. Then earlier this month, he was swimming in the Lake. He paddled through this vibration thing again and came back here."

"Okay."

"No, no – wait. There's more. They took him to where he said he grew up on Harkness Street. His parents lived there."

"They must have been really happy."

"Well, yes and sort of."

"Huh?

"Get this," Bob said. His voice sank to a conspiratorial whisper. "They were thrilled because their little boy was back – I mean they asked him all sorts of things and finally figured out it wasn't some con job. The guy was their son."

"So," Jimmy said, "they all lived happily ever after, right?

"I guess." Jimmy leaned in – he could barely hear Bob. "Jimmy, the guy, the swimmer dude was *older than his parents!*"

"I call bullcrap!" Jimmy said.

"I thought the same thing. But it's true. They've got that guy down at the State Hospital. They are running all sorts of tests, and his parents visit him every day.

Jimmy began to run the numbers through his head. *If the same thing happened to Josh, he'd be...* He shook his head. *No, no, this is made up stuff – too weird.* He didn't want to imagine his brother getting old like that.

Jimmy looked at the woods, ready to change the subject, and said, "Crazy, now let's find that Squatch."

They reached the back corner of the park. The flat, open terrain gave way to a densely wooded forest. The ground sagged under their feet.

"Watch it," Bob said. "It's muddy."

"No kidding, genius," Jimmy said. He handed Bob a stick from the ground. "Use this," he said, "but be careful. There's an electric prod on the other end – just in case we need to defend ourselves."

"Did you perfect the tracking function?" Bob asked.

"No, still working on it – we'll have to find the beast on our own."

The boys knew not to tromp over tracks. They learned a lot from *Wild Kingdom*. Using Jimmy's invention, they probed the ground and moved leaves, sticks, and other debris out of their path. "What are we looking for?" Jimmy asked.

"Tracks, either predator or prey. If we can make our way up the food chain, we might find a Bigfoot. You don't think they get big by eating plants, do you?"

Jimmy smiled as he thought of the enormous Bigfoot creature sitting on a stump munching on wild raspberries.

Bob continued, "They need to eat meat like all predatory animals. They probably even crack open bone to get to the marrow."

"How do you know so much?" Jimmy asked.

Bob removed his backpack and took out a stack of *Safari Cards*. Each card had a picture of an animal on the front. The back contained a treasure trove of information.

"I've been studying these," he said. "You can borrow them if you want."

"Cool!" Jimmy slipped them into his back pocket.

The boys found a lot of prints – dog – rabbit – even a few from a deer. Bob took out an egg of Silly Putty and tried to make a casting.

"You think Bigfoot roasts his meat?" Jimmy asked.

"I'm thinking he eats it raw, with blood dripping," Bob said. He put his hands up to his face and mimicked the act of biting flesh off prey, then smiled.

Jimmy shook his head and laughed.

Bob peeled the putty out of the track. "Ugh," he

said. "It's just a muddy blob." He shook his head. "I thought this would work."

Jimmy patted his buddy on the shoulder. "Good try," he said. "I think we have to use some kind of paste – ah – plaster, I think."

"Well," Bob said. "At least we found the tracks."

Bob and Jimmy continued along the fence line until they came to the abandoned quarry. They both thought if there was a place for Bigfoot to live in Bellevue, this would be it. Since neither boy had ever left Ohio, they thought their assumption was perfectly reasonable, astute even. No one had mined sandstone in Bellevue for a long time, but the quarry was popular as a swimming hole. Jimmy heard about kids who were a little older than Angie coming here at night – but he couldn't imagine why. Nothing to do in the dark.

"This place is so cool," Jimmy said.

They spent the next hour exploring the area. Every so often, one of them would point something out that piqued their interest. Any large bird became a pterodactyl; any movement in the tree was the Mothman. If the water moved, they stood poised to repel an attack from Nessie.

The boys knew their sightings weren't real, but they were training. In the right place – at the right time – they would be prepared. They took a break and talked about the Bellevue High football team and skipped stones across the smooth surface of the pond – Jimmy won with a "fivester."

"What time it is?' Jimmy asked.

"Ten 'til," Bob said.

"Ten 'til what?"

"1:00."

"Holy crap," Jimmy said. "We gotta go. Angie told me to check in at 1:00."

He imagined his sister doing a full-on Mom impersonation, waiting on the porch, hands on hips, clucking about the fried bologna going cold and the Ballreich's chips getting stale.

They ran to Jimmy's house. Angie was not on the porch, and the lunch was fine. She'd anticipated Bob's attendance, so there was enough for everyone.

After showing Bob the house – everything except the attic – they assembled the RC track and spent the afternoon crashing Matchbox cars into pyramids of Styrofoam cups. They paid no attention to the time until Jimmy's mom called up the stairs.

"Boys, it's almost 9:00. Bob needs to get home!"

They scurried to clean up the room. Bob was closing the toy chest when Jimmy had a thought.

Next time The Adventurers get together, we need to investigate the attic.

THE STREETLIGHTS FLICKERED to life, while Jimmy walked Bob home.

"…there was a big thump – then I went to sleep," Jimmy said.

"I bet you were scared."

"Nope." Jimmy hoped he hadn't answered too fast.

Jimmy stayed at Bob's house a lot. Bob knew his friend was afraid of the dark.

"Yes, you were," Bob said. "Don't worry – even the best ghost hunters get scared. You can be afraid and still be brave."

Jimmy nodded. "Well, it was a little weird, that's for sure. You want to go up there with me? It's probably just a few small animals."

"Who are you trying to convince?" Bob asked. "Me – or yourself?"

But Bob thought it would be fun. The boys discussed constructing a trap to catch whatever was up there. Bob described a crude device, basically a box, stick, and pull string. Jimmy thought it sounded brilliant.

"We could bait the trap with fried bologna."

Jimmy started singing, "Cause Oscar Meyer has a way with b-o-l-o-g-n-a!"

When Jimmy returned home, he found his entire family in the living room eating pizza and getting ready to watch a movie. Matt and Mark finished theirs like two inmates in a French prison, then raced to the basement. Moments later, Jimmy heard the telltale "pinging" of pellets bouncing off the furnace ducts.

Another pea shooter war, he thought. *They're gonna make a mess, and Mom is going to freak.*

He laughed to himself – it was sort of funny when Mom lost her marbles with the Twin Tornados.

Maggie looked at Paul. "Do you think Jimmy is old enough to watch this movie?"

"He likes monsters and the like," Paul said. "You need to worry about the girls."

Jimmy sat between his sisters. The movie seemed boring at the beginning – a guy chasing a girl named Chrissie down a beach. Then, things got interesting. Chrissie went into the ocean to swim, while the boy struggled to get his shoes off.

When the shot switched to an underwater view – Jimmy knew something was up. Suddenly, Chrissie screamed – she heaved violently from side to side, propelled through the water by an invisible force – something under the moonlit waters. The girl, still shrieking, reached the safety of a buoy, only to be dragged under the surface. The camera showed the boy who'd been chasing her, asleep on the beach as the surf washed over his legs.

This is great, Jimmy thought.

"What's the name of this flick, Dad?" Jimmy asked – he felt grown up when he said "flick."

"*Jaws*, son," Dad said. "Came out about four years ago – already a classic."

For the next two hours and ten minutes, Jimmy was riveted to the screen. Whenever the music began to thump – duunnn dunnn… duuuunnnn duun… duuunnnnnnnn dun dun dun dun dun dun dun dun dun dun dunnnnnnnnnnn dunnnn - he had to claw his way out from under the blanket his sisters had yanked in front of their faces.

At the end of the movie, the girls were crying. Jimmy felt alive and energized.

"Dad, are there any Great Whites in Ohio?"

Paul shook his head. "They won't let anything that small in Lake Erie," he said.

Jimmy's eyes opened wide – then he saw his father's smile. "Da-ad," he said.

But when Jimmy went to bed, he checked the back of the Great White Safari card just to make sure.

CHAPTER 10
DOOOOO I RUN (RON)?
SUMMER 1980

THE BEDROOM ROUTINE was a bit more uneventful his second night. Mom and Dad were watching another movie – some old thing in black and white. Dad kept saying, "Here's looking at you, kid," and Mom kept acting like she was fainting.

The peashooter war in the basement was called off because about the time Sheriff Brody said, "I think we're gonna need a bigger boat," Mom came up from the basement carrying the two combatants – asleep on her shoulder. Angie and Heather were in their room screaming along with *Da Doo Ron Ron* and swooning over some goofy looking guy named Shawn.

At least it won't be creepy quiet while I'm trying to get to sleep.

With all his lamps on, Jimmy got his room ready, his way to ward off the unsettling feeling in the pit of his stomach – like snakes slithering through his lower intestines. Jimmy checked the attic door: shut and latched – check. He turned off two lamps, then looked to the third lamp on his bed's nightstand – check. At the last second, Jimmy decided to leave his bedroom door open a bit, so the hallway light would shine through the crack. He lay in bed, closed his eyes, and said the short prayer his grandmother had taught him.

Before he was halfway through "Now I lay me down to sleep," he was off to Dreamland.

A piercing noise made Jimmy bolt upright. He stared at the clock: 3:33 AM.

Same time as last night.

He looked across the room. His door was shut. The feeble green light of his alarm clock barely illuminated the room. He listened for a few moments and honed in on a faint scratching noise coming from above his bed. Something moved in the attic – he flinched, and a sensation came over him – like when your throat tickles, and you know strep is on the way.

It certainly wasn't the pitter-patter of little mouse feet – he was sure of that.

Jimmy saw a sliver of light invading his room from beneath the attic door.

I don't think that was on when I went to bed. Or maybe it could have been.

The light glowed yellow – weak – maybe one 40-watt bulb for the entire attic. When he shifted to get a better look, his bed squeaked. The noise above him stopped. Then he heard it again, moving across the attic towards the stairs.

Jimmy could not have gotten out of his bed if

he tried. His eyes were held captive by a specter – a definite shadow shifting and waving from underneath the attic door. It fluttered like sunbeams creeping along the bottom of a swimming pool.

All Jimmy could think of was the stupid song he'd heard before falling asleep – *Da Do Ron Ron,* which sounded more to him like, "Do you run – Run!"

No way I can outrun whatever that is, he thought.

This entity was something much larger than the mouse or bird he'd imagined the night before, but whatever it was, moved away from the steps and back across the attic floor. Jimmy heard a small squeak – like a struggle or tiny protest – or he thought he did.

Jimmy sat back against the headboard but did not close his eyes until the morning's rays began to lick at his windowsill. Only then, did he dare fall asleep.

CHAPTER 11
EXPLAINING THINGS
SUMMER 1980

JIMMY WOKE UP and decided it was time to tell his parents about his 3:33 AM wake ups. Sunday morning meant family breakfast. Jimmy did not want to talk about the attic in front of his siblings. The girls would mock him. The Tornado Twins would: a) be frightened and cry or b) race to his room to attack whatever creature was lurking in the eaves. Jimmy felt the only people equipped to help were Mom and Dad.

And maybe Bob.

After a morning filled with pancakes, sausage, bacon, eggs, and more cereal (Matt and Mark insisted), everyone raced off to whatever they wanted to do. Jimmy hovered. "Mom, Dad, can I ask you a question?"

His father said, "I'm sure you can – you also may if you wish."

Typical.

Mom said, "Yes, honey."

"I keep hearing things up in the attic," Jimmy said.

Mom's face "squenched" into something resembling a jack-o-lantern two weeks after Halloween – Dad made a noise with his lips – "Pppfffffsssst!"

Dad patted Jimmy on the shoulder. "Son, please don't make me look bad, buddy. I let you watch *Jaws*. Remember our talk about bravery?"

Mom's voice carried some edge. "Paul, don't be like that." Then, softer, "Let's go upstairs and talk about it."

Paul shrugged. "He's all yours, honey. Just don't make my first-born son a softie."

Maggie recoiled without a word. Josh had been the official first-born by five minutes.

Paul, realizing what he had done, stammered, "I…I am so sorry, love." He dropped his head. "Oh geez – I didn't mean…"

His fingers trailed gently across her back as he walked out onto the front porch. Jimmy saw his father sit in the big rocker and wipe away a tear.

Mom swiped at her cheek, then focused on Jimmy and said, "Come on, sweetie."

When Jimmy turned toward his room, Maggie went in the opposite direction. "I'll be right there, sweetie. I need to get something." A moment later, she entered his room. "Okay," she said, "tell me about the attic."

Déjà vu hit Jimmy. *Just like when I told her about the boiler in the old house. That went super – huh? Maybe this time will be different.*

They sat on the bed, and Jimmy explained

everything – the sounds, the shadow, the light, the door. Though she'd always considered Jimmy a sensitive child, she was certain he'd heard an animal.

Maggie walked to the attic door and opened it. "Let's go," she said.

The attic covered the entire length of the house. The expansive space was dusty, dark, and – except for a few scattered boxes – empty.

"You know this house is old, sweetie," she said.

Jimmy nodded.

"Well, I imagine there are some gaps around the roof. Something could get in here – nothing bad, just little things like squirrels and mice. I'll get your father to set some traps. It'll clear things up in no time."

Jimmy, seeing something in the corner asked, "What's that?"

In the corner, a dead mouse lolled on its side. It looked as if it had recently died. Jimmy had seen a dead mouse before when poor Minnie died due to old age; at least that is what the teacher told the class. This one appeared different. It appeared almost flat, like an anvil from one of those *Road Runner* cartoons had smashed it.

"See Jimmy, that is what was probably making the noise last night."

Jimmy didn't say a word, but rather took notice of the footprints beside the rodent. The prints looked remarkably like the deer tracks he'd seen with Bob.

How in the world did those tracks get up here?

85

Jimmy, after seeing the attic and talking to his mother; felt a bit better about the situation. He decided to accept the mouse idea – or maybe something a little bigger. He doubted a deer was up there, so those prints confused him. Bob would surely have an answer. Jimmy nodded to his mother, but she noticed doubt in his eyes.

They walked toward the steps. Maggie paused.

"Did that help, Jimmy?" she asked.

"Yes," he said. "Now that I've seen it, I feel better. I'll be fine."

Before going back down to Jimmy's room, she stopped and reached into her back pocket. "Tell you what – never hurts to be safe. Let's put out a couple of things to keep us all safe."

She held out a wooden crucifix attached to a thin leather strap.

"My Grandma Morrow gave this to me when I was about your age," she said.

Jimmy examined the intricately carved form of the crucified Christ, while his mom continued. "She was a very religious woman. She got this from the Holy Lands – it's made of olive wood."

She reached over and looped the strap over a nail embedded in a post to the right of the stairway.

She shut the door with a firm push and then, reached into her large robe pocket and extracted a leather-bound Bible. "This," she said, "was your great,

great Grandpa Cooper's. Put it by your bed and touch it every night before you go to sleep."

Jimmy turned the Bible in his hands. The cover was ornate with an oval groove encircling the front. Ridges ran along the spine, and worn, gold lettering read: *Holy Bible.*

"Do you always carry *the whole Bible* with you, Mom?"

"No, honey, but I thought you might need some reassurance. I slipped this into my robe on the way up."

"Would it be okay if I put it under my pillow?"

She nodded. "Sure."

Just before she reached the door, Jimmy said, "Can you lock the attic door?"

Maggie returned a minute later with an odd-looking key. "It's the only one we have, Jimmy. Your Dad and I will keep it. Don't even think about trying to get it because if you lose it, we'll have to call a locksmith, and Dad will make you pay for it from your savings."

She and Jimmy moved to the attic door. She placed the key into the hole and invited Jimmy to turn it. The resulting *thunk* was so loud, they both jumped a little – then laughed.

Maggie looked at her son. "Well, one thing we know for sure."

At the same time, they said, "It's locked!"

JIMMY HUNG OUT with Bob the rest of the summer. They frequently visited the park to look for Bigfoot and searched the night skies for UFOs. When they went fishing in one of the local reservoirs with Bob's father, they kept watch for "Reservoir Rampager," a myth they tried to invent – but none of their friends bought it.

Since the attic door was locked, they made no attempt to capture whatever dark menace was roaming there. Besides, after Jimmy had spoken with his Mom, nothing else happened – for a while.

CHAPTER 12
RESEARCH

FALL 1980

THE SUMMER TRANSITIONED into fall. One rainy Sunday afternoon Bob's father, "Big Bob" – Mr. Bellard to Jimmy – took several pounds of ground beef out of the refrigerator and began to cook.

Debbie and Robin, Bob's other sister, were helping to prepare the meal. Robin asked, "Dad, why are you cooking so much meat? We can't eat all this."

Big Bob shrugged. "It'll probably go bad in a day or two. If we cook it up now, it will keep a bit longer."

He continued flipping and sprinkling the burgers, while a lump of lima beans sizzled and smoked on the other burner.

Bob's eyes popped when he got to the table. "Wow, what a feast!"

Rail thin, Bob made the same exclamation whenever he had an entire box of animal crackers to himself. Jimmy always thought his friend would make a great zombie.

The room descended into silence broken only by

an occasional mouth-stuffed request for mayonnaise, beans, or more chips. The rain began so suddenly, everyone at the table looked out the window at the same time.

"Too bad, Bob," Big Bob said. "I was going to suggest you invite Jimmy over."

Before his father could add anything else, Bob was dialing.

"Jimmy – come over for dinner. I know it's raining, but *we have burgers.*"

Bob came back to the table with a look of satisfaction on his face and a jar of Plochman's Mustard in his hand.

"He'll be here in 10 minutes."

THE FOUR OF them huddled at the window. A few minutes later, Robin said, "Here he comes, peddling like a demon."

Big Bob whistled. "Look at that rooster tail."

Jimmy's bike cut through the standing water like a ski boat. When Jimmy came through the door, Big Bob hit him in the face with a towel.

"Don't take another step into my house until you dry off, Jimmy."

Jimmy dragged the towel over his head, slipped out of his soaked shoes, handed his rain jacket to Robin, and said, "Let me at 'em!"

Before everyone sat back down, Jimmy had already polished off the first burger. Within a matter of minutes, he'd reduced the Bellard's surplus hamburger population by a total of five. The boys excused themselves and walked up the stairs to play with Bob's *Star Wars* action set. The last thing Jimmy heard was Debbie saying, "What did I just witness?"

The boys tired of Chewbacca and Luke Skywalker after a while. Bob held up a book.

"Not this again," Jimmy said.

"You gotta try it," Bob said. "It's really good."

Jimmy turned the book over in a reluctant hand. "*Ghostly Adventures,*" he said, reading the title. "Well, the attic has been quiet. Why not?"

On the opening page, the boys saw the translucent figure of a woman holding a candelabra and descending a wide winding staircase. Each page offered another rendering of an apparition or haint.

Bob's eyes were wide. "It says here that when you are in the presence of the Spirit World, you can feel your hair standing on end or you feel changes in temperature."

Jimmy bit his lip. *That's what happened when I saw Eddie,* he thought.

Bob jabbed at the page. "This indicates these creatures – Ghosts, Bigfoot, UFOs, Nessie – they may not be of this world – and they bring a little of wherever they come from with them."

"What if they do?" Jimmy asked. "That might be a

way to understand how to get rid of them or better yet, capture one." He grimaced in thought. "Maybe that's why they are so hard to find."

Bob twitched in his chair as if ants were crawling up his bare legs. "Wow, what if we could talk to one of them? Think of everything we could learn."

"What's that?" Jimmy asked. He pointed to the book.

"Nothing," Bob said. "Last page stuff – a letter from the author. I always skip it."

He reached to close the book, but Jimmy grabbed his wrist.

"Not so fast, Flash Gordon," he said. And he began to read aloud.

Dear Reader,

While not scientifically proven, as we are only in the infancy of our understanding and research of apparitions and ghostly occurrences, we firmly believe we will eventually be able to communicate with those across the ethereal plain. We believe there are individuals who possess the power to open themselves up to these realities and step across the veil from our world into the next. Only then will we be able to communicate across this divide – to invite them here or visit them there, wherever "there" may be. Over time, we will seek out a way to identify locations where the barrier is weakest, so we may study these phenomena more readily.

Fellow investigators, if you dare, we wish you well on your future investigations.

In Mystery,

Dr. Philander X. Doster

Jimmy said, "Bob, I have to tell you something."

"Okay."

Jimmy took a breath. "It's about a boy named Eddie."

Jimmy outlined the story – he told Bob everything – the crying, the basement of his old house, the shimmering light, and the box in the wall. Bob was transfixed, "Too bad you don't live there anymore."

Jimmy said, "It may not matter, I found something really unusual up in my attic a while back. It may be important. My mom took me up there to show me there was nothing to be afraid of. We found a dead mouse."

Bob said, "I have seen plenty of those. You know, Tobey brings them as gifts."

"Yeah, yeah, but this one was completely squished and all around it were these strange tracks. They looked like deer tracks but wider."

"In your attic? That makes no sense. Let's go check them out."

"We can't, my mom locked the door."

"Dang it! Well, tell me more about Eddie."

After a little more explanation, Bob said, "Maybe

you are one of these people the book talks about, you know, the explorers – the ghost hunters."

Jimmy shook his head. "No, we're a team – we're in this together."

Bob nodded proudly, "You're right."

"We'll have to get back in the attic once I figure out how to get it unlocked."

Bob stuck out his hand. "Adventurers and friends," he said.

Jimmy pumped his friend's hand. "Friends and adventurers," he said.

CHAPTER 13
EDISON LABS
SPRING 1983

OCTORS SPRINGER, PALMER, and Kline continued forging the path for future subatomic collisions. They had recently taken on a new scientist, Dr. Roarke Benjumea, a top mathematician from the Fermilab in Chicago. The quartet was working with a new measuring technique designed to replicate the events of 1973.

"Gentleman," Springer said, "as you know, we have been working for 10 long years, trying to generate the anomaly again. In many ways, it has slowed our progress substantially. We have taken necessary precautions; yet, we still cannot replicate. If we are unable to recreate the anomaly in the next few tests, we should shift gears and focus solely on attempting to replicate the birth of the Universe, as per our mission objectives."

Anyone who knew Lionel Kline well could tangibly see the frustration building. An explosion was not far away.

"David," he said breaking his usual lab protocol,

"We undoubtedly punched a hole through our Universe, and something came through to visit, even if only for a moment. But we do not know why. It seems unreasonable – imprudent – to escalate the program until we have some answers."

Springer's eyes narrowed, "*Dr.* Kline, it would be most heartwarming to have your full participation and commitment to this endeavor."

Without realizing it, the two men had moved to within a foot of one another. Eric Palmer slid his imposing frame between them.

"I see both sides," he said. Kline and Springer stepped back a little. *I can't keep separating the children,* Palmer thought. He continued. "Let's talk this through again and agree on a course of action."

Kline scratched his chin. "Let's determine a quantity of replication tests. After the series, even if we have been unsuccessful, I will feel we have exercised all good judgment and I will concur with exploring another route."

Springer went to his standby – sarcasm. "Well, that's so very—"

Dr. Benjumea, who rarely contributed, spoke from across the lab. "Maybe it is less about the precision of the experiment and more about the probability of replication." His eyes never left his desk.

The trio looked over. Palmer seized on the opportunity for *detente.* "Please elaborate," he said.

Benjumea looked up. "Well," he said.

He's a smug little sucker, Palmer thought, though he remained hopeful of a solution.

"As I see it, having reviewed the '73 tape thoroughly, the anomaly only sustained itself briefly – here for a matter of 4.36 seconds, then gone. What if it is like a weather pattern? Almost identical conditions can eventuate into dramatically different results."

"Sounds like my golf swing," Palmer said. He got a chuckle from Kline, a smirk from Springer, and a blank stare from Benjumea.

And people think I'm a dork, Palmer thought.

Benjumea shrugged off the comment he had not understood. "Think along the lines of Chaos Theory."

"The Butterfly Effect," Springer said. He never wanted anyone to even consider he did not understand everything, even though the complexities of effective social interaction lay far beyond his ability. "Lorenz used it in the context of atmospheric predictability."

Kline took up the "let's show off how much we know" challenge, although everyone in the room possessed a firm grasp of the concept. "His paper dealt with seagulls, did it not?"

Why not jump in? Palmer thought. *No reason to give them a reason to think I'm uninformed.* "Yes," he said. "Phil Meriless changed the name to *The Butterfly Effect* in 1969."

Benjumea shook his head. "Okay, now that we're all finished showing off, let's work the problem."

"Dr. Kline, I have read everything you wrote about

the '73 incident. I unequivocally believe you opened a portal to somewhere, although I can't imagine where. Is it not possible, however, that contributory conditions lay outside this lab? Wherever that thing came from, its dimension must also be factored into the equation. Does the relative distance of the dimension play into the possibility of crossover? What are its properties? Can we determine anything about this new – ah, let's call it - realm?"

"Are you trying to convince us to continue the experiments or to abandon them?" Dr. Springer asked.

"Mathematical probability would suggest the likelihood of replication is quite small, unless you can detect the other dimension's existence and location." Benjumea realized he was enjoying a rare moment in the spotlight. "At the same time, if you replicate the crossover with higher energy transfer, whatever tried to come through might very well be able to visit if we can keep the portal open."

"Sounds a little ominous," Palmer said. He hoped his skepticism had not shown. Kline bit on the end of a pencil. "Is there a possibility we might collapse the entire system?"

"Certainly," Benjumea said with more conviction than he felt. "Look – we're scientists. We usually deal with measurable facts. In this case, they appear either to have failed us – or to have abandoned us."

Springer offered a rare smile. "Or they have confused us so thoroughly, we have no idea what we are doing."

The group shared an awkward moment.

"At any rate, "Benjumea said, "when facts don't align, sometimes we move into the area of speculation. I think that's where we are. My conjecture is just that – conjecture. The anomaly might reappear tomorrow."

"Or never again," Springer said.

Benjumea clapped his palms together. "Precisely," he said. "Dr. Kline, what is your fear?"

Having gnawed off the eraser, Kline began sucking on his bottom lip. "We could cause damage," he said. "Our actions might bring about a cataclysmic event destined to swallow this lab and every occupant whole."

Benjumea said, "I wonder (he looked around the room) …has anyone studied increases in unusual events within our area since the start of the experimentation – perhaps in places other than Edison Labs?"

Everyone shook their heads.

Palmer raised his hand. "I could take that on, Dr. Benjumea. What am I looking for?"

"Million-dollar question. What is it you thought you saw in 1973?" Benjumea asked.

The silence grew. None of the men of science wanted to give voice to the "myth" they witnessed. After almost a minute of roaring silence broken only by the ever-growing ticking of the wall clock, Kline spoke what was in each man's mind.

"A monster."

Unfazed, Benjumea took the lead. "Dr. Palmer, why don't we begin to investigate types of incidents such as hauntings, requested exorcisms, missing persons, and paranormal sightings. We can include reports of UFOs, Bigfoot, and other strange and bizarre occurrences for the fun of it."

Springer slumped into a swivel chair, his head in his hand. "I cannot believe we are considering wasting resources chasing Ripley's *Believe It or Not.*"

The lead scientist understood he'd lost the lead on the project when Benjumea ignored his moans and said, "Dr. Kline if we conduct this research, will you be more willing to move forward with experimentation?"

Kline issued a curt nod. "Well, at least it is something. So, yes."

Palmer bobbed his head.

Benjumea grinned. "Well," he said, "seems we have cobbled out our own little Camp David Accord here. Let's get to work. The resource allocation is certainly worthwhile. We'll debrief in a month."

The report sat in the middle of the table. At over 400 pages, it was as massive as it was comprehensive. Each member of the quartet had attacked his assignment with full scientific fervor.

Benjumea turned on the overhead projector. "Here is a summary of some of the more pertinent – and odd

– facts from Ohio, Indiana, Michigan, Pennsylvania, West Virginia, and Kentucky research from 1974 to 1982."

Springer made no attempt to hide his disdain. "You mean a summary of fanciful tales," he said.

"Whether we believe the events or not, David," Benjumea said, "we have *data* on the reports. No one has made an empirical assessment of the validity of the sightings – we simply compiled the information readily available."

The men stared at the image on the wall.

Event Increase, 1974-1982 (OH, IN, MI, PA, WV, KY)

Ghost/Sprit Sightings x = (32%)

Exorcism Requests x = (42%)

Missing Persons x = (47%)

UFOs x = (39%)

Bigfoot x = (80%)

Other x = (33%)

Event Increase, 1974-1982 (All Other States)

Ghost/Sprit Sightings x = -3%

Exorcism Requests x = (12%)

Missing Persons x = (3%)

UFOs x = -12%

Bigfoot x = (2%)

Other x = -12%

*Note – Illinois and Tennessee are the only other states showing statistically significant increase in all cases. Both states also have particle accelerators.

After a brief and contentious discussion, the group decided to resume testing while continuing to collect data on the sightings. They would vary frequency and energy to determine if a correlation existed. To placate an increasingly frustrated Springer, they agreed to increase the power and frequency of the tests first – and pull back later. Test 667 B, the most powerful test ever performed, was scheduled in two days.

CHAPTER 14
PREDICTING BOYFRIENDS
SUMMER 1983

DESPITE JIMMY AND Bob's enthusiasm, the next few years were mostly uneventful for the Adventurers and Friends. They would still conduct the occasional Bigfoot search, perform ghost research, and watch all sorts of scary movies, but Bellevue was just not the hotbed of activity for monster hunting – at least not until the end of their sixth-grade year.

Their summer commenced with a trip to the Public Library.

Bob stuck his head out of the car window. "Jimmy!"

Jimmy sprinted out of his house, then made an abrupt U-turn and caught the screen door just before it slammed. No use getting yelled at right as his vacation was beginning.

"Hi, Mr. Bellard," Jimmy said. He looked at Bob. "Let's roll."

Jimmy waved to Matt and Mark, who were taking turns falling off a skateboard on the sidewalk.

"I'll bet you a dollar one of them breaks an arm before the end of the week," Bob said.

"No bet," Jimmy said.

"You want part of that action, Dad?" Bob asked.

Mr. Bellard laughed. "Absolutely not. That pair is a disaster looking for a place to happen."

Typically, Jimmy wouldn't be caught dead in the library over the summer, but Bob had asked, and an afternoon with his best friend was better than sitting at home and waiting for a trip to the Emergency Room. It was Mr. Bellard's trip originally – he'd probably grab a few Ellery Queen mysteries, and they'd be out of there in less than 30 minutes.

Jimmy and Bob went straight to the Sports Section. Jimmy pulled out a book about his beloved Cleveland Browns. He saw all the greats, his favorite being Dave Logan. He reread the tragic story of Ernie Davis and wondered, again, how great the backfield would have been if he'd lived.

"Jim Brown and Ernie Davis," he said.

"I know, I know," Bob said. "They never would have lost a game."

Bob shelved the book, and they went to explore. In the basement of the library, an antique glass cabinet stood between two large card catalogs. Bob pulled on the door of the cabinet. It was locked.

Mrs. Lutz, the Librarian, who always reminded Jimmy of the Wicked Witch of the West from *The*

Wizard of Oz, walked by. "Can I help you boys?" she asked.

Bob withdrew his hand like the knob was a snake. "Not really," he said. "We're just waiting for my dad to finish looking around.

Mrs. Lutz turned, and Bob asked, "What's in the cabinet?"

When the woman pivoted, Jimmy expected her to say something about "you and your little dog too," but she was very nice. "All we have down here are historical materials about Ohio."

Bob thought for a second and then asked, "You don't have anything about haunted houses in Ohio, do you?"

The Librarian mulled it over and then produced a key ring, unlocked the cabinet, and pulled out a yellow book titled *Ohio's Ghostly Greats.* "Don't forget to check it out before you take it home," she said.

Jimmy and Bob raced for the Circulation Desk and found Mr. Bellard.

"Found two I hadn't read before," he said.

Bob signed the check-out card, and the attendant applied the dated stamp.

"Due in two weeks," she said. "The fine is two cents a day if you are late."

The boys didn't hear her. They were already halfway out the door.

Driving home, they looked at the Table of Contents. Bob pointed to the third chapter: *Ouija Board – Conversations with the Dead.*

"That needs to be the first story we read as soon as we get back," Bob said.

They ran up to Bob's room, their official ghost hunting headquarters, and opened the book. Careful not to tear a page, they thumbed to the story. Bob read in a breathless voice about a couple in Columbus, Ohio. They'd used the mysterious device to communicate with their child who'd died at the age of 10. As Bob read the final words of the passage, "Remember, never use a Ouija Board alone," Bob closed the book. "We gotta get one of those Ow-oo-jah things."

Jimmy laughed. "I think it's pronounced *Wee-gee,*" he said. "My sisters talk about it sometimes when they come home from sleepovers. And the game Light as a Feather and Stiff as a Board but think that game is just an excuse to touch each other's butts." They both laughed.

Bob asked his dad if Jimmy could spend the night. Of course, Jimmy was allowed. Mr. Bellard almost always said, "Yes."

That evening, the boys asked Robin and Debbie if they wanted to hear some scary stories from Ohio. The girls enjoyed a good fright, even though they had moved up from "campfire tales" to Stephen King and Dean Koontz. The kids took turns reading from the book.

Bob closed the session with the Ouija board story.

"I think we have one in the basement," Robin said.

"No way," Jimmy said.

Debbie said, "Well, you two should go down there and find it." She leaned over and whispered in Robin's ear, "Those guys won't get halfway down before they chicken out."

Jimmy looked at Bob. They nodded and headed for the kitchen, where the basement steps were located. On the way down the steps, Bob said, "Careful – we have a lot of spiders down here."

Jimmy wasn't afraid of spiders, but he could feel the hair on his neck bristling. *It's like someone's watching me,* he thought.

Two yellow eyes blinked up from the shadowy basement.

Jimmy was about to turn and run when Bob flipped the light switch. "Hi, Tobey," he said. "You looking for a mouse?"

A jet-black cat cast a condescending look at the boys, then began grooming his hind legs.

Bob spoke over his shoulder. "When he finds one, he likes to take it upstairs and give it to my sisters. Scares the crap out of them. They scream bloody murder and jump up on the couch. It's hysterical."

Jimmy let out a nervous laugh. *Hope he didn't see how scared I was.*

They surveyed the landscape at the bottom of the steps – boxes everywhere.

"This is going to take forever," Bob said.

Piles of books lined the walls. *If they built some shelves, they could have their own library,* Jimmy thought.

Then he saw it – a dim gray Shimmer emanating from one of the boxes in the back of the room. It wasn't as strong as the glow in his old basement – the one near Eddie – but it was there.

Jimmy walked over to the box. "Let's check this one," he said.

The box was secured by interlacing the flaps together – no tape. Bob popped his fingers into the small opening on the top of the box and pulled straight up. Jimmy could see a bunch of games he recognized – Monopoly, Sorry, and Trouble. Jimmy and Bob began pulling out the games one at a time. When he picked up the Risk game, Jimmy saw a cream-brown box.

"Viola," he said.

"Nice find," Bob said. "We could have been down here all night."

"Lucky guess," Jimmy said. He didn't think he should mention the Shimmer.

With Bob in the lead, they headed back to the stairs. As they were about ready to climb the steps, Bob flipped off the light. The second the darkness returned, Jimmy felt the "prickling" again. He took a moment to look back across the basement. His mind conjured up a thousand creatures moving towards him. He put his hand on Bob's back as they took steps two at a time and reached the kitchen a bit out of breath. Bob turned and looked at Jimmy. "Man, walking back up gave me the willies, like something was behind us."

Jimmy didn't say a word but nodded his head in agreement.

They placed the game on the kitchen table and stared at the cover. Bob read it aloud, "Ouija – Mystical Oracle by Parker Brothers."

"Parker Brothers?" Jimmy said.

Bob said, "Let's give it a chance. Maybe it only works for special people," and winked at Jimmy.

"Alright," Jimmy said. "So, we can test it properly, go get your sisters again. They can give us some questions to ask; this way we won't know the answers."

"You just think my sisters are cute," Bob said.

"Ewww, gross," Jimmy said. But Bob was right.

The girls giggled all the way down the stairs.

"I can't believe you toolboxes found it," Debbie said.

"X-ray vision," Jimmy said.

"Shut up," Robin said.

The board fit snugly in the box. Underneath the board was a blood-red case. Placed in a small hole within the case was this cream-colored, heart shaped device. It had a clear plastic circular section embedded in it. Jimmy surmised the "window" was to show the letter on the board when asking questions, like the top of the box displayed.

Debbie sat down at the table, and Bob and Jimmy placed their hands on the device situated above the board. Bob said, "I will be the leader since I just read the rules. Remember, we both need to keep our hands on the board."

Robin appeared with a lit candle. She placed it on the table and turned off the kitchen light.

"For atmosphere," she said.

"Debbie, we need you to ask a question we do not know the answer to, so we can check to see if this thing works," Jimmy said.

Debbie smiled. "Bob, ask if Eric Rank likes me?"

Bob repeated the question to the board. The planchette, the heart-shaped piece, remained in place for a second or two, then slowly started to move in an arching pattern around the board. Jimmy looked at Bob, and Bob looked at Jimmy, both surprised by the movement.

Jimmy saw – well, he wasn't sure – a mist – something like the Shimmer – collecting over the board – gray, like cigarette smoke. Jimmy looked over to the candle and then back to the board. He was about to say something when the planchette moved with purpose to "*Yes.*"

Jimmy looked up at the smile on Debbie's face and the gleam in her eye. He forgot about the Shimmer and said, "Unfair question, Debbie. Every boy likes you."

Robin gagged and Bob frowned. "Yeah, we need a specific question. Something we can test," he said.

Robin said, "Okay, okay, I like a boy who plays baseball. What team does he play on?"

Bob and Jimmy each thought it was a better

question, so Bob repeated it aloud to the Board. The planchette, once again, began to move. The device stopped on the *M*, followed quickly by a *C*, then after a long pause, left the *C* and returned to the *C* again.

The boys shook their heads. "Something screwed up," Jimmy said.

But Robin was bouncing in her seat. "Oh my God! It is going to get it right – It's McClain's."

The kids leaned in – hooked on the board's veracity.

Robin continued. "What's his number," hoping the Board would get it wrong.

Slowly, the Ouija board began to work its magic. A "2" followed by a "5." The planchette rested, waiting for its next command.

Robin's face went ghostly white. She stood up, banging the table with her knees. "Put it away! Put it away!" she said and then ran upstairs.

Jimmy and Bob looked at one another. "Confirmation," they said.

Jimmy was about to take his hands off the board when Bob said, "Jimmy, not yet! We have to say goodbye. Bad things happen when you don't say goodbye."

Bob and Jimmy said, "Goodbye," and moved the planchette to the word "Goodbye," then took their hands off the board. Debbie, also a bit nervous said, "Goodbye." Jimmy noticed as soon as they all said goodbye, the mist retreated into the board.

Debbie went to check on her sister, and the boys packed the game in the box.

They left the board downstairs with a couple of Bob's books on top of it, just to be safe. They were a bit creeped out. At the same time, they speculated the girls might have been faking their fear only to egg them on. Regardless, they felt the board provided some entertainment. They headed upstairs to call it a night.

Jimmy, lying in bed, stared at the ceiling and noticed a spider descending on a silver thread.

"Hey Bob, you remember my attic?"

"Yep," Bob responded.

While Jimmy waited for Bob to connect the dots, he watched as the spider slipped ever closer. A slight breeze from the open window made the spider sway like a pendulum, its legs spayed out for balance.

When Bob didn't speak, Jimmy continued. "Do you want to take the board over to my house and see what's there?"

"Sure, you hearing things again?" Bob asked. Jimmy could tell his friend was almost asleep.

The little creature was close enough now for Jimmy to count all eight legs.

"There's a noise occasionally, but nothing loud. Maybe the board might wake it up or something."

When the arachnid was a mere six inches from his face, Jimmy blew upward. The spider froze.

Bob, roused from his snooze, sat up, looked at Jimmy, and said, "Well, let's reopen this cold case."

Bob saw the spider hovering above Jimmy. "Another one? Those things are everywhere."

He closed his hand over the little creature, walked to the window, and placed the spider on the sill.

Jimmy was happy Bob hadn't killed his little visitor. "Hey, you got rid of my friend," he said.

Bob looked over his shoulder. "Maybe I don't want you to have another friend."

The boys laughed. Bob turned off the light.

CHAPTER 15
OUIJA
SUMMER 1983

T HE NEXT MORNING Bob and Jimmy got up and headed downstairs. Debbie and Robin were on the couch, still fretting over the events of last night.

Jimmy heard a tremor in Debbie's voice. "The boys probably overheard you talking about Terry earlier, and God knows they watch enough baseball to know who everyone is and what numbers they wear."

Robin sat balled up in the corner of the couch. "Maybe, but get that board out of the house, or I am going to burn it in the fire pit out back."

Bob and Jimmy both looked at each other. Jimmy said, "Get it – now!"

Jimmy slipped on his Converse high tops and waited outside. A minute later, Bob appeared, ghost book under one arm, the game under the other. As they crossed the street to pass from Union street to Greenwood Heights, Bob noticed Angie and Heather sitting on the porch. Jimmy knew Bob had a crush on them, as Jimmy had a crush on Debbie and Robin. Angie and Heather knew it as well.

"Hi, Angie, Hi Heather," Bob said in his best deep voice.

They both replied, "Hiiiiii Bob," batting their eyes. They looked at each other and giggled.

Bob froze momentarily. Jimmy shook his head. *They are so stupid.*

He grabbed Bob by the arm and dragged him into the house. Bob waved one last time and said, "See you later!"

They sat down at the breakfast nook. Jimmy said, "We need to think about what we want to ask the board."

Bob nodded. "Yeah, like who are we talking to for starters."

"Good point," Jimmy said. "We don't even know who's answering our questions."

"According to this," Bob said, holding up the *Ohio Ghostly Greats* book, "it could be someone different each time we use the board."

"Yeah, we don't want to invite in the Demon from Detroit," Jimmy said.

"Well," Bob said, "we're about to concoct our own story – The Banshee from Bellevue."

"Okay, I'll be right back," Jimmy said, as he stood up and ran into the next room.

He grabbed a yellow pad of paper and a blue Bic pen out of the dining room's curio cabinet. Mom kept all her office supplies in there, including a stash of caramels. Jimmy plucked four sweets out and returned to the table. He handed everything – except two of the caramels – to Bob. Bob took the supplies, placed the pen cap to the side, and wrote "Ouija Questions" on the pad's top line.

"Okay," Bob said, "question number one."

Jimmy, popped a caramel in his mouth, "How about, what is your name?"

They alternated.

"Where are you from?"

"How did you get here?"

Jimmy scooped into his ear with the pen cap. He extracted a ball of thick, yellow wax.

"Wow, that was a good one," Bob said.

"And you sound a lot louder," Jimmy said – and snorted.

"Pretty gross though, Michigan colors, blue and yellow," Bob said.

Jimmy flicked the wax onto the floor. "All fixed."

They finished the caramels, then consumed an entire box of Pop-Tarts. "We can ask the questions tonight," Bob said. "You think I can sleep over?"

"I'll ask Mom," Jimmy said. They smiled; they already knew the answer.

At 8:30 PM, the boys were on their way back to the Coopers' with Bob's stuff.

"Hey! You guys want to play Ghost in the Graveyard?"

Christi, the unofficial "vacation activities coordinator," and classmate to Debbie and Angie, was standing on the other side of the street.

"Sure, Christi," Bob said. She could have asked, "Do you guys want to run barefoot across broken glass?" and Bob would have agreed. Bob thought Jimmy's sisters were cute, but Bob thought Christi was gorgeous.

"Great," Christi replied. "Robin, Debbie, and I are playing Clue." She pointed to Jimmy. "Your brothers are with Danny out back. We'll come out as soon as we finish the game."

"Colonel Mustard in the Conservatory with the candlestick," Jimmy said. "Always a good guess."

Christi laughed. "Just don't let the Tornado Twins corrupt my little brother before I get out there."

Bob and Jimmy passed Christi's house and saw the younger guys playing whiffle ball in the backyard. Danny pointed to the fence with his bat, calling his shot like a miniature Babe Ruth. Matt fired a pitch, and Danny planted it over the fence.

"Homerun!"

He rounded the bases, tipped his cap to the imaginary crowd on the way home, then – in accordance with backyard rules – raced to the outfield and climbed the fence to retrieve the ball.

Mark laughed. "He hit the crap out of that one," he said.

Matt fumed. "Well, Mom will wash your mouth out with soap when I tell her you said crap."

The sky began its evening transition – blue to white – to pink – to orange – to purple – then the deep black velvet of an Ohio night. Maggie and Paul were sitting on the porch when the boys got home.

Jimmy said, "Can we go to Christi's to play Ghost in the Graveyard?"

"No going out of bounds," Maggie said. "Jimmy's Garage to Albina Drive and over to the Methodist Church. That's it – not one step over the line."

"Yes, Momma."

The boys started to run when Paul's voice locked them in place. "Stay out of Mrs. Skyler's flower garden."

Ever since "the flower picking incident" of the previous spring, "Old Lady Skyler's" property had been deemed off limits by all the parents. No one wanted a repeat of the spinster's tirade about "unruly, undisciplined, flower-pilfering hooligans." After Jimmy's dad had listened to her 10-minute tirade, he tapped Jimmy lightly on the head, adopted his sternest paternal tone, and said, "Father unequivocally condemns killing Edna's marigolds. Don't do it again!"

Mrs. Skyler *hrumphed* – she had hoped for the death penalty.

The streetlights flicked on. Bob and Jimmy made their way back to Christi's house.

When Matt and Danny were "it," Bob suggested he and Jimmy hide between McConkey Square Garden, the term used for the neighbor's basketball court, and the shed next to the St. Paul's Methodist Church. The boys took up the lookout positions – their heads on a swivel. Jimmy looked to the night sky in the east and saw a silver Shimmer. It was much bigger than any he had seen.

"Do you see anything in the sky above the church?" he asked.

Bob shrugged. "Just a whole bunch of dark."

"I think I see something above the church."

"Like what?"

All of a sudden, he heard laughter from around the corner.

"Nothing – never mind."

"Okay, keep your eyes peeled for Matt and Danny. They are small but fast."

They'd been playing for about an hour when they heard Bob's dad. "Bellards… hooooome!" He always stretched out "home," ending on as high a note as he could reach. Every kid immediately mimicked the call. Debbie and Robin rolled their eyes.

"Coming, Dad," Debbie yelled.

Rules were rules. The game ended when the first parent called – no questions asked.

Bob, Jimmy, Matt, and Mark all bolted for Jimmy's

house. Matt and Mark went straight to the basement to begin an evening of track and field championship on the Atari; Bob and Jimmy tromped upstairs. While Bob unpacked the board, Jimmy pulled out the banana split candle he had won at Natalie Claborn's birthday party. Jimmy would not admit the crush he had on her – and Bob was a good enough friend never to mention it.

Jimmy was coming out of his parents' room with a lighter when he heard his mother's voice.

"What do you think you are doing, Mister?"

"Ummm, I was planning to light my candle. Would it be okay?"

"That would be fine, honey," Mom said, "as long as I can stay in the room with you boys."

Jimmy's jaw clenched. "Mom, it's not my fault the girls almost burned down our last house because they put that stupid sheet over some stupid, old lamp."

Mom's face was stone. "Maybe not," she said, "but we're not taking a chance on another fire. That's the deal – you want a candle or privacy? Choose one."

Jimmy mumbled his response. "Privacy."

"That's what I thought," Mom said. "Use a flashlight."

Jimmy's mood lightened. "Great idea. Thanks, Mom."

Jimmy and Bob sat on the floor with the Ouija board between them. Two red flashlights, standing on their ends, shone up towards the ceiling.

Jimmy looked up and snickered.

"What?" Bob asked.

Jimmy pointed to the ceiling. "Looks like a giant set of boobs."

Bob looked up, then started jumping and grabbing at the light.

Dad's voice from downstairs stopped the action. "Are you boys jumping on the bed?"

"No, sir."

"Well, pipe down. I can't hear a word Hannibal Smith is saying."

Bob looked at Jimmy with a panicked expression. "A-Team or questions?"

Jimmy paused, his index finger to the side of his head. "Business before pleasure," he said. "If we're going to be great ghost hunters, we have to be serious about it."

"Okay."

Bob took out the list of questions, then motioned Jimmy to place his fingers on the board. "You ready?"

"I think so."

Bob, a bit on the theatrical side, started with his best Vincent Price impression. "Oh, spirits of the Cooper house, please join us."

Jimmy looked up. "Stop hamming it up."

Bob scowled, then continued with his mystic tone. "Oh spirits, if you are with us, please give us a sign."

Jimmy recognized the phrasing from the *Ohio Ghostly Greats* book. They waited.

Nothing.

Bob reverted to his natural voice. "Come on, great spirits, are you there?"

They heard a creak, and their attention snapped to the attic door.

"Whatcha doin?"

They spun to find Matt standing in the bedroom doorway.

Jimmy screamed, "Holy crap, Matt! You scared us to death."

Mom's voice echoed from the Great Beyond. "Language!"

"Sorry, Mom, won't happen again," Jimmy said. He whispered. "She hears like a bat."

"Can Mark and I play?" Matt asked.

Jimmy shook his head. "Sorry, it is only two players."

Matt said, "We get to watch, or I'm telling Mom you called her a bat."

He ran to the hallway and yelled into the laundry chute. "Mark!"

Matt had not been back in the room but a few seconds when they heard – they *all* heard – what sounded like a bowling ball bouncing down the attic steps. They jumped when something crashed into the attic door.

Mark walked in. "What was that?"

Bob took a breath. "Let's check it out."

They walked in a cluster – shoulders almost touching – towards the door. When they got close, the younger boys shrank back a little. Jimmy could feel Matt's breath on the back of his neck.

Bob jiggled the handle.

"Locked," he said – he sounded relieved. "Jeez, the handle is cold." Jimmy took his word for it. Bob placed his ear to the door. "Nothing," he said.

When he stepped back, he looked down. "What's this?"

He pulled on whatever was sticking out from under the door.

"That's the crucifix Mom hung in the attic," Jimmy said. "I wonder how it fell down. It was on a nail."

Bob placed the cross in Jimmy's palm. As Jimmy held it, he saw a dark mist seeping into the room – a rolling vapor, probing here – then there – looking for something.

No one said anything.

They can't see it, Jimmy thought.

Bob leaned down and peeked under the door. Even with the mist all over his face, he didn't notice it. But when he looked up, he said. "Wow, there is some significantly cold air coming from under this door."

Matt and Mark put their hands at the bottom of the door. They stood and rubbed their hands together.

"Cold," Matt said.

Mark nodded.

The mist swirled around Bob, Matt, and Mark – ivy-like fog wrapping around their ankles, knees, thighs.

"You see anything?" Jimmy asked.

"No," Bob said. "It's just really freezin' in here all of a sudden."

The cascading film moved past the boys' waists and up toward their chests. Jimmy slammed the crucifix flat into the door frame. The mist retreated under the door like a frightened cat.

A groan like the moaning of a dozen rusty hinges filtered across the room. The boys stood like statues – afraid to move – too startled to scream. When the sound trailed into nothingness, Mark looked at his older brother.

"Is that what you told Mom about?" he asked.

Jimmy, afraid whatever had created the sound would return, nodded.

Bob's voice was a croak. "Look at the board," he said.

The board had not moved, but the looking glass hovered very clearly over the word "Goodbye."

"Did you move that?" Bob asked. "Anyone kick it or anything?"

"We were right next to you the whole time," Matt said. Mark nodded in confirmation.

Bob and Jimmy spoke in unison. "Let's put it away."

After they packed the game, they put it in the closet. Jimmy put the Bible on top of it, just in case.

They all decided it would be a good night to camp out in the basement.

CHAPTER 16
SHARED GIFTS

SUMMER 1983

J IMMY AWOKE TO a thin shaft of sunlight shining
through the basement window directly into his eyes.
Like fine cobwebs, his memories were a bit tangled.
He wondered what was real and what was a dream.

Given he was in the basement with Matt, Mark,
and Bob sleeping next to him, he knew his recollec-
tions were accurate. He thought about the mist.

I saw it – but they felt it. He shuddered.

He turned on the TV. The basement shook with
the Atari Track and Field theme. Matt rubbed his eyes.
"Hey, turn it down! Holy cow!"

Jimmy replied, "You two left the volume all the
way up."

Mark yawned. "My fault; I beat Matt yesterday and
turned it all the way up to rub it in. Remember, Matt,
remember when I destroyed you yesterday?"

Mark didn't beat Matt very often.

Angie thumped down the stairs. "There you are," she said. "Breakfast in five."

Jimmy decided to ask. "Angie, did you hear anything weird last night?"

"Just you guys running downstairs like you were about to wet yourselves."

Always eager to impress the "older women," Bob jumped in. "Oh my gosh, we have to tell you what happened last night."

The boys relayed the events. Angie listened intently, but Jimmy could tell she was growing more uncomfortable by the minute.

When they finished, Angie's face was drawn and her voice a little strained. "Let me tell you guys about this scary dream I had."

Bob, Matt, and Mark unzipped their sleeping bags and sat up.

"I was in my bed, awake, but I couldn't move or speak. It was like I was paralyzed or something. Everything got cold in my room, and I swear I could see my breath."

Bob looked over to Jimmy and mouthed, "Cold."

Angie continued. "Something was pushing me into my mattress – all of me, like I was being crushed. I kept sinking into the bed. I couldn't breathe. Heather was there – in the dream. She asked me why the room was so cold."

"Then, what happened?" Jimmy asked.

"I woke up, panting like a dog – short of breath,

you know, like I'd been running. Crazy, huh? Gives me goosebumps to talk about it."

Bob asked, "Did you hear any noises or voices during your dream?"

"I thought I heard something, kind of like the sound before you ran downstairs, but this was later."

Jimmy tried to keep his voice calm. "Did you tell Mom and Dad?"

Angie said, "No, why would they care? Besides, I'm too old for that. But I know you guys like scary stories."

The boys were wide-eyed and quiet.

"Okay," Angie said. "It's creepy down here, and you guys smell bad. I'm gonna eat."

AFTER THEY ATE, Jimmy asked Bob, "Anything in your ghost book that might explain what this is?"

Bob said, "Let's go to my house and look."

Mark asked, "Can we come?"

"Wait here," Jimmy said. "We'll bring it back in a few and read it together."

They were back in less than 10 minutes.

Bob began to list the topics from the Table of Contents: "Haunted Castles, Haunted Mansions, Ghosts, Mediums…" Then he said, "Poltergeists."

"What's that?" Jimmy asked.

Bob was already headed to the Glossary.

"Poltergeist," he said. "A noisy spirit. It can make sounds and, if strong enough, move things physically. This type of creature also includes demon infestations."

Jimmy's head bobbed. "Sounds about right."

Bob's voice took on an air of foreboding. "It says here that they can grab, scratch, and bite and are considered dangerous. They can be held at bay with religious artifacts, fragrances, and spells. However, they are challenging to remove from a location."

Jimmy remembered the crucifix. "I wonder if the cross has been holding it in check. I need to get Mom to put it back at the top of the stairs."

"Don't do that," Matt said, "She will freak, and Dad will think we are all crazy."

"Or babies," Mark said. "Besides, one of you guys can do it."

Jimmy slapped his fist into an open palm. "We could, but the door's locked." He looked at his brothers and Bob. "But I will tell you this – I'm not sleeping in my room until the cross is back up."

An evil grin spread across Matt's face. "Mark and I know where the key is."

Of course, you do, Jimmy thought. *The CIA couldn't hide stuff from you two.*

"Where is it?" Jimmy asked.

"Won't tell unless we can help," Matt said.

Mark nodded. "Yeah, we want to help."

Jimmy looked at Bob, who shrugged. "We don't have a lot of choices here."

"Okay," Jimmy said, "but we're in charge. Where is it?"

Matt's face took on a conspiratorial gleam. "I was looking through Dad's top drawer. He always keeps a few Butterfingers in there. I saw this weird looking key with a long handle, a crazy design on one end, and then on the other, it only had two pointy things." Mark put his fingers down to show what the end looked like.

"That's the one," Jimmy said. "How are we going to do this?"

They looked up as Mom came through the door with a plate of crackers smeared with Jiff Extra Crunchy Peanut Butter and a handful of Sunny D packs. "Are you boys planning another adventure?"

Jimmy smiled. "That's what we do."

"Nice of you to include your brothers," she responded and began to distribute the treats.

Trying to sound as innocent as possible, Jimmy asked, "Where's Dad?"

"Taking a nap. He didn't sleep very well last night. Believe it or not, he had a bad dream. See, boys, you are not the only one who gets them."

Jimmy realized he would not be getting into the attic any time soon. But something else struck him:

Dad had a bad dream – just like Angie.

Mom walked back into the kitchen. Jimmy turned to the others, "We need to get the cross back up into the attic before whatever is causing the dreams gets worse."

There was a murmur of acceptance.

Dad finally got up – Mom's turn for a nap. She always tried to make up for the sleep she lost to Dad's buzz-saw snoring. After solemn vows that no one would work independently, Bob went home, the twins left for a birthday party, and Jimmy walked down the street to see Grandma Leona. She liked his weekly visits. It had been a lonely time since Wilfred, her husband of 66 years, died.

JIMMY WALKED INTO his grandmother's house, climbed the two stairs into the kitchen, stopped at the refrigerator for his traditional glass of purple Kool-Aid, and grabbed a handful of gumdrops from her pantry.

"Hi, Grandma. How are you doing today?"

"Jimmy, I can always tell you're here when the gumdrop dish rattles. Matt and Mark go straight for the chocolate tin." Grandma turned her thin face to the side, inviting her grandson's kiss.

"You look good, Grandma," he said.

"For a 105, you mean," she said. It was a running joke.

"Not a day over 96," he said.

Grandma Leona doted on her grandson – even more so since Josh's disappearance. Though she did not hover like her daughter-in-law, she called the Cooper home every day to check on Jimmy. Tall, slender, and smart as a whip, she kept her body sound – three-mile walk every day – and her mind sharp. She read every best-selling biography. She knew more about historical figures than a great many university professors and stayed current on politics, world events, and – to Jimmy's delight – sports.

"Browns going to be any good this year, Grandma?"

"Rutigliano's defense will be solid. Pruitt, Logan, and Newsome give Sipe some options. Still wish he hadn't thrown that pick on the last play against Oakland back in 81, Red Right 88 – ugh, but you know what?"

Jimmy knew exactly what she was going to say and mouthed the words along with her, "I think this is going to be our year."

After some more small talk – she always embarrassed Jimmy by asking if he "liked any special girl yet" – Jimmy said, "Grandma, weird things have been happening lately. Can I ask you a serious question?"

"Of course."

"Have you ever seen a ghost?"

Grandma didn't answer right away, unusual for her.

She sat in her chair, staring straight ahead.

After about a full minute, she responded, "Jimmy, you're old enough now. I think I can share this without scaring you. Since I was young, I would sometimes see different types of lights. For a long time, I thought there was something wrong with my eyes because no one else could see them." She paused for a moment.

"Do you remember the house I lived in when you were younger?"

"Yes, the one with the huge backyard. There was a spooky old graveyard way in the back. I never liked going there."

She smiled. "Yes, that's the one. I used to see things in that graveyard all the time. I was never afraid of them because there wasn't anything aggressive. Whatever was there floated without purpose and then disappeared. Besides, I never saw anything up close. Whenever I walked into the cemetery, the apparitions disappeared, but I could almost always see them from a distance."

Jimmy stared at his grandmother, his mouth agape.

Her gaze focused on something outside the window. "Since I moved into this house, I hadn't see anything in a long time. Then…" her voice trailed.

"Then what, Grandma?"

"Then your dear grandfather died."

"I miss Grandpa Will."

"Yes. Sometimes – if I'm being perfectly honest – I can feel him walking around in here."

Jimmy's eyes darted back and forth. He wasn't afraid. He loved Grandpa Will – but he wanted to see if he could detect something.

His grandmother smiled again. "I don't feel anything now, honey. I know when he's around. His light is warm and full of color."

"Like a Shimmer thing?"

"Hmm," she said. "Never thought of it that way

– very good. Yes, I guess you could say it's like that when I sense his presence."

She reached for his hand. Her skin felt brittle – like old paper – but her grip was strong. "Can you see Shimmers, Jimmy?"

Jimmy became very interested in his shoes. He didn't know what to say – he didn't want to lie to his grandmother. Mostly, he didn't want her to tell his parents, but he took a chance.

"Yes."

"Well, bless the Good Lord, Jimmy. I always knew you were special."

"Are there different types of Shimmers, Grandma?" he asked.

"I think so, Jimmy," her voice was measured and quiet. "I can remember four or five different ones – more of a feeling than anything else. There may have been more." She tapped her temple with her forefinger. "Not quite as sharp as I used to be, you know."

"You're still pretty sharp for 109," he said.

"I thought you said 96. I'll be back in a second, sweetie."

She retrieved a tin of homemade cookies from the pantry. Armed with three snickerdoodles, Jimmy said, "Tell me everything."

"Your grandfather's Shimmer is always colorful, like a rainbow," she said. "I know I've seen silver ones but not very often. They are usually pretty big. Saw one in a forest in Canada once – oh, and when I went to see some family in Iowa."

Jimmy thought about Josh – but decided not to mention it.

Grandma was lost in the trance of memory. "I will admit the time I was in Iowa, everyone was going on and on about something unusual in the sky. Even though no one else mentioned the Shimmer, I could see a silver aura in the air. It was round but moved like the Aurora Borealis. It looked a little like a non-slip metal plate, you know, with a crisscrossing pattern."

She paused, while Jimmy inhaled a cookie. "The graveyard mist was always either white or gray, and I could see figures – sort of. The gray ones always came a bit closer to the house, like they were looking for someone or something. The white figures were more aloof – appeared to be congregating."

"A party?" Jimmy asked.

"Maybe," she said. "Neither of those bothered me much."

She leaned in closer – her voice dropped to a whisper. "There was one more," she said. "Only saw it once when I was little. My parents and I stayed at the Tudor Arms in Cleveland. When we walked to our room, I saw a dark black cloud from under one of the doors. It felt alive. It was struggling to get out of the room we passed. Not sure why it couldn't get out, but I'm glad I didn't get any closer."

Grandma got up and refilled his Kool-Aid.

Jimmy chewed on his last cookie for a moment. "You ever try to go into one of the Shimmers?"

"Well dear, I could almost hear Wilfred – your Grandpa – telling me I could come if I wanted, but at the same time warning me not to."

"Why?" Jimmy asked.

"I really couldn't hear him, but I could feel his voice," Grandma said. "I know it doesn't make any sense but there was a – well – a vibration and it communicated with me. It told me some Shimmers have dangerous things on the other side – some horrible things. I worried I could get stuck there and never return. I thought maybe the colorful one would be safe, but I was never brave or foolish enough to try. Besides, when the Blessed Virgin is ready for me, she'll let me know."

Grandma Leona made the sign of the cross and kissed the crucifix she always wore on a chain around her neck. Jimmy had never seen her without the cross.

"Tell you what, Jimmy," she said. "Next time your Grandpa Will shows up, I'll ask him a lot more questions, okay?"

Jimmy almost jumped out of his seat. "That sounds like a great plan."

"But you have to promise me something, son." Grandma Leona's eyes locked on his – an iron grip, disguised in pale blue irises. "Promise me you will never go into one of those Shimmer things unless you have no choice."

JIMMY RAN INTO his house and only remembered to catch the screen at the last second.

That was close. I can't afford to make Mom mad.

At dinner, Mark asked, "Hey, isn't Bob doing a two-fer tonight? What time is he coming over?"

Jimmy smiled at Mark's use of Bob's catchphrase for a two-night sleepover. "I guess when he's done eating."

"Oh," Maggie said, "Big Bob called. Bob can't sleep over tonight."

Jimmy dropped his fork. "But we had plans!"

Matt and Mark stared at their brother. Matt said, "Yeah, Mom – plans."

Maggie's "Mom-dar" began to whirl. "What's the elephant in the room here, guys? You boys up to something?"

Jimmy shifted the conversation. "It's nothing, Mom. We were just planning on a big Risk game tonight – you know, it's more fun with four people."

Maggie spooned more beans onto her plate. "Well, not tonight, sweetie. Maybe later this week. Oh – no more sleeping in the basement. You goofballs have beds, you know."

They ate in silence until Mark spoke. "So, where's the elephant?"

Jimmy's mom blew water out of her nose from laughing and had to be excused for a moment.

Jimmy looked outside. The evening looked dreary, mimicking his mood. He noticed raindrops beginning to splatter on the sidewalk and street. Within minutes, everything outside was enveloped in a steady downpour.

This was no "quick hitter." Jimmy knew the weather would last all night – and maybe into the next day.

CHAPTER 17
A NIGHT ALONE
SUMMER 1983

JIMMY COULD HEAR the steady drumbeat of the raindrops as he walked into his bedroom and collapsed on his bed with a massive thump. He closed his eyes.

Focus, he thought. *Listen…smell…be alert.*

He opened his eyes. The lights from the trio of lamps cascaded across the ceiling, creating a kaleidoscopic Venn diagram. If he hadn't been so frightened, he might have appreciated the overlapping patterns more.

The musty smell of rain filled his nostrils. *Oh crap, I left a window open.*

He closed his eyes and locked in on a steady drip… drip…drip – a soft heartbeat of splashes by the attic door.

He pushed off the bed.

A small puddle gathered just below the windowsill. Jimmy's footfalls broke the surface tension of the water, and a small stream trickled across his room.

Jimmy raised the blinds and closed the window. He retrieved a towel from his bedpost, pivoted, and tossed the towel toward the water. Unenthused about his janitorial task, he moved the terrycloth across the water with his foot. He noticed the wooden crucifix lying next to the attic door – in a small puddle.

Crap!

He scooped up the cross. Varnish bubbled at the end of the transverse beam. Jimmy picked at it with his thumbnail. *Mom's gonna kill me*, he thought. *No way she doesn't notice this.*

A quick perusal of his closet revealed a piece of fine grit sandpaper, a reminder of Pinewood Derbies past. Jimmy smoothed the crucifix's damaged edge.

Better, he thought. *But it might be a good thing if Mom doesn't look at this for the next... 50 years or so.*

He put the cross down, picked up the soggy towel, walked down the hall, and listened as the towel thumped its ways down the laundry chute.

He turned around and bumped into his mother.

"Hi, sweetie," she said. "Want to help me rebuild Mount Cooper?"

"Sure, Mom," he said. He loved the name Mom gave to the pile of laundry that accumulated at the bottom of the chute. With seven in the house, the washer and dryer ran almost constantly.

Jimmy pushed dirty jeans, tee-shirts, and towels through the opening of the 18" x 18" "tunnel of dirt."

"All done," he said loudly enough for his mother to hear from her room.

"*All?*"

"Everything I'm gonna touch," he said. He drew the line at his sister's "unmentionables."

Maggie came out of her room shaking her head, "Honestly, Jimmy, they're just material like everything else."

Jimmy turned, squinted, and did his best Dirty Harry impersonation. "A man's got to know his limitations."

He was getting into bed when the twins entered. "Sorry about the key," Matt said.

"Well," Jimmy said, "if you want to be on the team, you have to do your part."

Matt struck a defiant pose. "I'll get it done."

Matt switched off the light as he left, and Jimmy pulled the covers up over his shoulders. The cobwebs in his head quickly morphed into dark curtains, and he was soon dead to the world.

IF SOMEONE HAD touched him on the shoulder Jimmy would not have been any more awake. He knew what time it was before he looked at the green numerals, 3:33, glowing from his clock. The door was still open – like Mom promised. He looked around, determined everything was A-OK, then flipped over to his left side.

His head thunked lightly against the headboard. Before Jimmy's ear touched the pillow, he heard a corresponding noise above him. Something was moving – dragging – *slithering?* – across the attic floor towards the steps. The noise seeped through pores in the wood, invading his room without resistance. Jimmy looked at the hallway door and thought about making a run for it but decided to wait.

Jimmy pulled the covers up over his head.

The noise reached the landing. There wasn't much space between Jimmy's room and whatever moved toward him – maybe 10 feet. Jimmy, once again, considered running, and he shifted in his bed to put his leg on the floor, letting out a "ping" from one of the bed springs. The pace of the steps quickened; Jimmy pulled his leg back under the blanket.

Silence settled over the room – for a moment. Then Jimmy heard the most frightening sound he could imagine – the unmistakable click of the lock and the creak of the attic door.

Oh my God, it's opening.

Increased pressure in the room passed over Jimmy like the front of a thunderstorm. An invisible wall of wind cascaded out into the hallway. The atmospheric drop brought with it another sound – the unmistakable click of *his bedroom door.* Now closed.

Steps approached his bed –

squishy like someone trying to tiptoe through mud.

Sploosh…Sploosh…Sploosh… the steps drew closer.

Where's the Bible? Where is it?

The steps continued, *Sploosh, Sploosh,,* growing ever closer to him. Without looking, he stabbed his hand out from under the covers and reached for his bedside table. He hit the Bible with his fingertips and cringed as he heard the holy book slide across the table and onto the floor at the precise moment the splattering footsteps turned into dry clatters.

Those are not footsteps – those are animal hooves, Jimmy thought.

Hail Mary, full of grace, the Lord is with thee…

As the words flooded through Jimmy's mind, the temperature plummeted. He looked to his left – his right – certain he would see the mist – the Shimmer. He saw nothing – but he felt the bone-chilling cold.

He felt pressure pushing on him, compressing his sternum, making it hard to breathe. Even in the darkness, he could discern the presence of a figure – no, an arm. He swatted at it – and felt like he'd tried to slap concrete.

The cross, the cross, he thought to himself. *What did I do with the cross?*

Jimmy could barely breathe, and the pressure on his chest mounted. His hand, now outside the sheets, slid down towards his chest.

I cannot breathe.

He felt – yes, he was sure – fingers – and at their ends, claws – thick, massive, blunt. He squirmed and kicked, trying to remove the force compressing his body.

He felt something hit his ankle in between his feet as he struggled.

That's right, he thought to himself, *that's where I left the cross. I left it at the end of my bed.* He maneuvered his feet into position as lightning bolts began to appear in his clouded vision.

With the quick thrust of his legs, he could feel the cross go airborne. The cross landed on his chest. Jimmy reached out with his right hand and grabbed the cross and pressed it to the thing's hand. The pressure in his chest immediately subsided. Air rushed into Jimmy's lungs and he screamed with every ounce of energy he could muster.

"Help!"

He ran towards his door, heaving.

The entire hall filled with a thick, dark black mist. Jimmy imagined the funnel of a tornado. He stood, mesmerized watching the rotation of the black cavity. Loud banging shook him from his trance.

Angie and Heather's room.

Fists pounded the door from the inside. "Let us out! Open up!"

The door cracked open about an inch, then slammed shut. The mist curled around the doorknob, shimmering tentacles of nothingness holding his sisters prisoners in their room.

Jimmy spun and saw Matt running towards him.

Halfway down the hall, Matt fell and disappeared into the hovering carpet of gloom. He tried to stand – but moved backwards – pulled by the swirling arms of mist – heading ever closer to…

…the laundry chute!

Maggie charged out of her room with fire in her eyes. Seeing Matt sliding towards the yawning hole in the wall, she lunged and grabbed her son by the arm.

Angie and Heather were still screaming, still beating on the door. Incoherent screams came from Mark's room. Mom clutched at Matt – grasping at an arm, a leg, hair, anything to save her child.

Dad, his hair askew and blinking his eyes, stared at the chaos in the hall in disbelief and bellowed. "What in the hell is going on?"

"I can't pull him back up, Paul," Maggie's voice choked with desperation. She began issuing orders. "Go downstairs, and do not let him fall."

"Jimmy, check on Mark."

"Angie and Heather, for God's sakes, shut the hell up!"

Jimmy ran by his mother to the end of the hall and watched the black cloud, menacing, approach like the jaws of the shark in the movie. The maw moving toward Matt even as his ankles, then knees, sank into the wall. Jimmy ran through it hoping it was not solid.

Maggie would not let go. If Matt went, she was going with him.

When Jimmy reached Mark, a viscous cloud of

darkness swirled over him. Jimmy tried to wave it away but when he swatted, the Shimmer pushed back. He could see wavy golden filaments flowing from Mark's body.

Oh God – life force. It's killing Mark.

Mark squeaked, "I can't breathe, Jimmy."

Jimmy saw terror in his little brother's eyes.

Jimmy said, "Hold on, Marky."

Jimmy sprinted to his room. He came back into the hall at full speed, crucifix in hand.

God, I hope this works.

He held the cross up to Angie and Heather's door. The mist was immediately recoiled and retreated like a skittish dog. The girls came bursting out of the room breathless and shaken.

No time for sympathy, "Angie and Heather, get over here and help me – now." Maggie screamed with tears of anger and fear pouring down her cheeks.

The girls pulled on Matt's arms. The boy slipped lower into the chute.

The opening had oiled its way to within a foot of Matt's head. He was squealing in pain and terror, pulled down by a force he could not resist – about to be consumed by a threat only Jimmy could see.

Mark was coughing, close to passing out. Jimmy raced to him and pressed the cross into Mark's chest. The Shimmer exploded in a thousand black BBs and threw Jimmy against the wall, as Mark sucked air into his thirsty lungs.

The sole blackness left in the hall focused on Matt. Jimmy saw the Shimmer grow darker, an angry thunderhead ready to burst in a furious and destructive storm.

Jimmy, his head throbbing, staggered to his feet and down the hall. Everyone was crying – everyone was screaming. It sounded like every tornado siren in the world was focused on the laundry chute. All Jimmy could see of Matt was his brother's forearms and hands.

If he falls, he'll be gone, Jimmy thought, *just like Josh.*

Jimmy said out loud, "not again."

Jimmy dove in between Angie and Heather and threw the crucifix into the hole in the wall. A sound like a hog being roasted alive filled the house, and the chute vomited Matt onto the carpet outside the master bedroom. Maggie clutched her son.

Jimmy heard footsteps on the stairs and his father's voice. "You got him? Do you have Matt?"

Paul threw his arms around his entire family in one big mass. Jimmy, situated between Matt and Heather, looked at his father's hand – and his knuckles wrapped around the crucifix.

JIMMY OPENED HIS eyes the next morning to find his entire family sleeping in the living room – his sisters and mother on the couch, Dad in his chair, and Matt and Mark next to him in sleeping bags. Jimmy was just about to explain things to her when Heather looked at him and shook her head. "I don't want to know, nope, I don't want to know," and pulled the blanket back over her head.

Jimmy wandered into the downstairs restroom with his cross in his hand. He turned on the hot water to wash his face. When the steam rose, memory's hammer struck him between the eyes.

Nobody saw it but me.

He flushed the toilet and washed his face and hands. With his chin still in a towel, he looked up and gasped at the nightmarish message he saw scrolled on the steam covered mirror.

"Goodbye."

CHAPTER 18
CLEANSING WHILE CAMPING

SUMMER 1983

"What's the lake house like, Dad?"

Matt had not stopped talking since they'd gotten in the car.

"It's just a cottage," Dad said. "A little place on Lake Erie – at Bay Point – a place we can go for getaways and such."

The girls seemed less enthused. "Do we have to fish all the time?" Angie asked.

Jimmy saw Heather act like she was putting her fingers down her throat.

Girls.

"No," Dad said. He turned to Mom. "Honey, you want to take this?"

Maggie's words were positive, but Jimmy noticed her subdued tone.

"You can play in the lake – we've rented a small boat – sort of like a test drive. You know, to see if we like it. You might want to try some waterskiing. Down the way from the cottage, there's a safari park, a beach, and the Cedar Point Amusement Park. But I want you all to check in regularly. It is important I know where you are at all times."

She's remembering the last time we went on a trip, Jimmy thought.

Matt decided – well, to be Matt. "There will be lots of boys." He dragged out the last word. It sounded like *bow-ease.* "Maybe they'll be desperate enough to talk to uggos like you."

"Matthew!" Maggie's voice had shaken the "subdued" part. "You will not insult your sisters. We take care of each other in this family." She'd swung around in the seat and was leaning into Matt's face. "Do I make myself clear?"

"Y-y-yes, Mother," Matt said. He didn't speak for the remainder of the trip.

Maggie had allowed Bob to come along since Jimmy didn't have a built-in buddy like his brothers and sisters. After Matt and Mark went to sleep – a little bit of a battle won only by Mom's iron will and her memory of Matt's mean comments – Bob and Jimmy sat on the dock and listened to the waves lapping the shoreline.

"Can't believe we get to stay up so late," Jimmy said.

"Just remember – if we so much as touch the water after dark, your Mom will make us come in."

Jimmy laughed. "And we'll probably have to go to bed before the twins."

The boys slumped in lounge chairs and relaxed into the dock as it bobbed in the light chop. Jimmy might have fallen asleep – he wasn't sure. The rhythmic slap of water on sand certainly was soothing. But he bolted awake when Bob asked, "You miss your brother, don't you, buddy?"

Jimmy was glad it was dark. He could feel the sting of tears in his eyes.

"Yeah," he said. "We were pretty tight."

"Disappeared into – what did you call it?"

"A Shimmer. Kind of like a silver ball of goo – only more like a mist."

"You think that's what came out of the attic?"

Jimmy checked before he wiped his eyes. "Not sure – the silver Shimmer that took Josh was like a creature, but this was something that came out of my attic and tried to kill Matt. It was a different color – black. Maybe there is a Shimmer ball in the attic?"

Jimmy knew Bob was a true believer. Still, Bob always asked the hard questions.

"You sure it wasn't a dream?"

Jimmy sat up and shifted his legs toward Bob. "Well," he said. "I thought about that, but remember, Mom and Dad are still freaked – they didn't see the mist – they didn't see the… ah… other thing-"

Bob interrupted. "Neither did you – remember? You 'felt' it, but you told me you had your head covered."

A lot of guys would have gotten mad, but Jimmy

knew Bob was a good investigator – he was going to probe for answers.

"True, but I touched its arm, club, or whatever. And I could feel its presence. I mean, the room temperature must have dropped 20 degrees and let's not forget about the mist in the hallway."

"Okay," Bob said. "What's the other thing – the other evidence? It wasn't a dream?"

"You see the scratches on Matt's leg?"

"I saw a bandage. Are they bad?"

Jimmy chuckled. "He was scraped up pretty solid. Mom acted like he needed surgery. She wanted to take him to the ER – Dad talked her out of it. They cleaned the leg – washed the cuts with alcohol—"

Another interruption. "I bet Matt loved that."

Jimmy's laughter echoed across the water. "He screamed like someone was killing him. Said he would rather have fallen down the chute. For once in his life, he wasn't Mr. Tough Guy."

"Classic." Bob wasn't going to let it go. "Was it the same thing as the one that got Josh?"

"I don't know, it was different – but the evidence suggests we're dealing with something similar. And I know one more thing."

"What's that?"

"The Ouija board didn't help a bit – in fact, I think it made things worse."

Bob crossed his arms and looked pensive.

"Jimmy," he said.

"Yep?"

"We gotta get that cross back in the attic and check for a Shimmer."

FATHER ROBERT PARKED at the back of the Cooper's house beside the garage. He turned to the younger man beside him.

"Father Jacob, would you be so kind as to get the Bibles and holy water? I will lead the cleansing – you will pray at the appropriate time."

They approached the house with limited enthusiasm.

"It doesn't look haunted," Father Jacob said.

"Have you seen many?" Father Robert asked.

"No, Father."

"Me either, but Leona Cooper is a pillar of our parish. She said her daughter-in-law and son were quite insistent there was a problem. We are duty-bound to respond."

Jacob located the key under the second planter. "Maybe this will get the Coopers to church a little more often," he said.

"I certainly hope so," Robert said.

The priests began in the basement, where they sprinkled holy water. Robert issued a blessing – Jacob said a prayer. They repeated the process on the first floor, room by room. They were headed upstairs when the front door opened. Leona Cooper jumped when she saw them.

"Oh, you startled me," she said. "I thought I might get here first."

"Leona, so good to see you," Father Robert said.

Father Jacob, the junior priest, bobbed his head in greeting but stayed silent.

"We were about to go upstairs to complete the blessing," Robert said. "Would you like to accompany us?"

The trio walked up the stairs. The priests blessed each room. The last one was Jimmy's.

Father Jacob, now more relaxed, pointed to the Bible on the bedside table. "A very good sign," he said.

Leona smiled. "That's been in our family for generations."

"And in the heart of the Church for millennia," Father Robert said.

The priests set about their ritual. Leona, who had not been upstairs in some time, inspected the room. She noticed a dark mist rising from the far side of the bed. She circled around the foot of the bed for a closer look.

She saw a brown corner of a box – probably a game. The mist was thick around the box's base. She started to reach for it, but Robert came around the bed with his aspergillum. He shook it several times as he recited the ritual.

When a droplet of holy water hit the box, the mist retreated under the bed – a reflex so fast, Leona would have missed it had she not been staring. A chill touched her spine.

It's the same as what I saw in Cleveland all those years ago.

"Well," Jacob said, "this is interesting."

He bent over next to the attic door and picked up Jimmy's crucifix.

"Not the prime place to keep it, but a nice thing to find in a young man's bedroom."

He handed it to Robert, who placed it on the nightstand next to the Bible.

"The house is cleansed and blessed, Father, according to the ordinances and strictures of the Holy Church," Jacob said.

Leona watched the mist slither from the bed to the attic door, where it disappeared.

"What about the attic?" she asked.

Robert pursed his lips. "We don't usually cover attics," he said.

She'd noticed how the mist detoured to avoid contact with the priest.

"Oh, come on," she said. "Humor an old woman."

The second they crested the attic steps, Leona saw the Shimmer, thick as a San Francisco fog. Careful to stand behind the men of the cloth, she said, "I'm so very grateful."

The priests applied the holy water, read the ritual,

and closed with a prayer. Just before they headed down, Leona took the aspergillum and fired a direct hit onto a pocket of mist she saw in the corner of the attic. It skirted into the darkness.

I swear I heard it whimper, she thought.

She said, "I'll see you gentlemen at mass – and I'll bring my checkbook."

CHAPTER 19
SKELETON KEY

SUMMER 1983

W HEN THE COOPERS got home several days later, Maggie called the church office. Father Robert assured her everything had gone well.

"Your house is blessed and safe," he said.

Maggie felt better, but dreaded the upcoming battle of getting everyone to mass for the next month.

A small price to pay for peace of mind, she thought.

"I'm going to find where they have your donations to the Goodwill," Paul said. "Maybe I can get some of my stuff back."

"Paul, those ties were out of style when you bought them," was her only response.

Maggie didn't want to dwell on what had happened. She simply told the children that the house had been blessed, and everything would be fine. The kids all shrugged and said, "fine." Since they'd been together for over a week, Bob went home with a promise to return soon to execute Operation Skeleton Key after

Maggie and Paul had locked the attic door upon their return.

Jimmy moved his nightstand, complete with Bible and crucifix, in front of the attic door. He found several plastic crosses in a drawer in the kitchen. He taped one – out of sight – atop every doorframe in the house. His last act of "self-preservation" was taking the Ouija board to the basement, where he deposited it at the bottom of a box of toys and games.

Still, when night came, Jimmy did not sleep much.

THREE DAYS LATER, Bob knocked on the back door. After a few Pop Tarts, Mark and Matt joined them.

"Mom and Dad are gone, right?" Jimmy asked.

"Yep, they left about a half-hour ago," Mark said.

Bob asked, "How have things been?"

"Fine, no problems," Matt said." Maybe those preacher dudes did it."

"They're called priests, Matt, and you know it." Jimmy was unusually firm. "Now's not the time to take the chance on making anything else in the Cosmic Universe mad."

"Yeah, whatever," Matt said.

"Okay, let's go get the key and put the cross back up in the attic," Jimmy said.

"Alright," Mark said. "Angie is on the phone talking

to her boyfriend, and Heather went – somewhere – who cares?"

Jimmy thought it was a bit early for Heather to leave, but he realized she was also the one who was most disturbed by "The Night." The boys ran upstairs. Matt kept lookout on the landing; the others went key hunting. Mark rummaged in his father's dresser for a while – not as carefully as Jimmy would have liked.

"He's going to know you were in there."

"Nope," Mark said. "I'm in here all the time swiping candy. I could replace all his socks with Mom's pantyhose, and he wouldn't notice."

"Good point."

"Now, Mom…" Mark's voice trailed off with a shudder.

Maggie Cooper was notorious for her meticulous nature.

At the same time, Jimmy and Mark said, "A place for everything and everything in its place."

"Yeah," Jimmy said. "She'd notice if a mosquito moved her hairbrush during a landing." He punched his brother on the shoulder. "Come on, dude. Where's the key?"

"Not here," Mark said. "It was right under the Butterfingers – well, there are Baby Ruth's now, but they were—"

"Shut up," Jimmy said. "We get it. Let's go. We gotta try something else."

OLD MR. HERBERT's Antique Shop stood between the Ben Franklin's Store and Clothes Hanger.

The bell tinkled when they entered.

"Look at all this old stuff," Mark said.

"It's an *antique store,* genius," Jimmy said. Sometimes, his brothers were so very embarrassing.

A voice full of gravel came from behind the counter. "How can I help you boys?"

Jimmy stared. Old Mr. Herbert's was run – apparently – by an old guy.

"Are you Mr. Herbert, sir?" Jimmy asked.

"One and the same," Mr. Herbert said. "You guys need something? 'Cause this probably isn't the kind of place you just want to wander around in."

His smile was warm, but not particularly genuine. Jimmy noticed. And the old man's eyes expected trouble.

"I think we're in the right place, sir," Jimmy said.

The eyes widened – the smile look less plastered on.

"Well, you certainly have nice manners, young man. What do you need?"

"A skeleton key."

"Is that right?"

Mr. Herbert walked to a drawer, opened it, rummaged around, and came out holding a large ring of antique keys. "Something like this?" he asked.

Mark whispered to Jimmy, "Yahtzee!"

Jimmy's initial excitement faded when he saw the plethora of keys – different sizes and shapes.

"How do I know which one I need?" he asked.

"Well, that all depends," Mr. Herbert said. "You know anything about the lock?"

"It's old," Bob said.

Herbert let out a hearty laugh. "Then, I ought to be able to open it with this." He extended a long, gnarled index finger. "And here I didn't think my arthritis was ever going to be useful."

Thoroughly entertained by his own joke, Mr. Herbert kept chuckling, while the boys looked at the keys.

"Um," Jimmy said, "if we were to get say…three, do you think we'd have a better chance of opening the door?"

"Good thinking, young man," Herbert said. "They all have different size bits – that's this part here. Wait a minute, let me explain."

Herbert took the boys through an elongated journey – the history of key making, different materials, and the parts of the key: bow, shank, collar, throat, pin, kitty wards, and bits. "Soref invented the padlock in 1924. Of course, there were a lot of developments—"

Jimmy had waited as long as he could and jumped in when Herbert took time to swallow.

"That's fascinating, Mr. Herbert. So, how many of these skeleton keys do you think we need?"

"You can have them all for a hundred bucks," the old man said.

Bob opened his mouth. "Do we look, ow—"

With his heel still implanted on Bob's foot, Jimmy said, "That's a lot more money than we have, Mr. Herbert. How much are the keys individually?"

"Two bucks," Herbert said, "but since you didn't let your friend there say anything smart-mouthed, I'll give you three for the price of two."

Jimmy pulled out a wad of one-dollar bills, counted out four, and handed them across the counter.

"Sorry, they're a bit wrinkled."

"Spend the same as crisp ones," Herbert said, as he put the bills into his cash drawer. "You boys have a nice day. You know, the history of combination locks is fascinating."

He looked up, but the boys were already pedaling away on their bikes.

THE BOYS SLUNG their legs over the center bars and stood on the pedal of their bikes as they coasted into the front yard. They jumped off, rolled across the grass, and stood up in time to watch their Huffy Dragsters roll into the hedges.

"Mom hates it when we do that," Mark said.

"I know," Jimmy said. "But it's pretty rad, right?"

"Did you guys find any keys?" Matt asked from the porch.

"We got three. We let Mark pick because he got the best look – we'll see."

They hooted and hollered all the way up the stairs – after all, Mom was gone; and they didn't care if they irritated the girls – they lived to irritate the girls. But the second they crossed into Jimmy's room; each boy sank into his own quiet space.

"Okay," Jimmy said. "I'll take the keys. Bob, you hold the cross. Mark, you hold the Bible. Matt, watch the door."

"Oh no," Matt said. "This time, Mark stands lookout."

The twins swapped spots. Matt pulled some wire from his pocket. "Got this from Dad's shop. That cross won't come down again."

"Good thinking," Jimmy said.

Jimmy put the first key up to the keyhole. "Too big," he said.

All three boys glared at Mark.

The second key slid into the lock easily but turned… and turned…and turned.

"Not getting any traction," Jimmy said.

"I think you mean *purchase*," Bob said.

"Duh," Jimmy said. Then added, "Shut up."

The third key did look a lot like the one his mother had used.

"Last hope," Jimmy said.

He inserted the key and felt the resistance. "This might work," he said. He snapped his wrist to the right.

Nothing moved.

"Let me try," Bob said. He got the same results.

"We're hosed," Jimmy said. "Three keys and no luck."

Matt grinned. "Only we have *four* keys," he said. He pulled a key from his back pocket.

"Where in the world did you find it?" Bob asked.

Matt rest his fists on his hips – the perfect Superman pose. "Henceforth, you shall refer to me as Detective Matthew P. Cooper."

"Matt, where did you find it?" Jimmy repeated.

Matt crossed his arms, lifted his eyebrows, and waited for due recognition.

"Dear Lord," Jimmy said and continued, "Oh Lord Supreme, Exalted Detective Matthew Paul Cooper, where did art thou find the royal key of attic?"

"I like it," Matt replied. "I found it under Dad's ashtray by his chair. You know, where he stashes his cigars."

Jimmy smiled. *Mom hates those cigars.*

"Nice job, Matt," Jimmy said. "Give it here before I thump you."

Jimmy had the key; Matt had the cross; Bob had the Bible. Mark had abandoned his post and was standing on his toes to watch the action.

Jimmy asked, "Matt, put your hands down by the bottom of the door. Do you feel anything cold?"

Matt replied, "Nothing, all clear. But if it comes out, one of you is going in the laundry chute – not me."

Jimmy slid the key into the keyhole, turned the tumbler, and grinned at the resulting *click.*

Jimmy's voice barely registered. "Okay, guys. Here we go."

Bob and Matt held up their talismans. Mark now had the wire. On Jimmy's signal, they moved forward just as he opened the door. When Matt hesitated, Jimmy grabbed the cross, held it in front at arm's length, and put his right foot on the bottom step.

Sunlight crept through the small attic windows and cast eerie shadows on the wall. Jimmy didn't see any Shimmer but found it hard to breathe because of all the dust.

Bob's hoarse croak came over Jimmy's shoulder. "You think that cross'll work?"

"Don't know," Jimmy said. "But it seemed to the other night."

When they got to the top, Jimmy scanned the attic. Darkness covered the entire area – a dark layer of gloom. The only light came from a far corner…

…a small, but unmistakable, black Shimmer glowed from behind a box.

Jimmy's heart pounded against his ribs – *The Opening.* He reached toward the nail where the cross had hung – and froze. Something slithered through the Shimmer. A snake repositioning. Then, so slowly the movement was almost imperceptible, it began to ooze its way closer.

Bob knew something was wrong. "What is it, Jimmy?"

"You can't see that, can you?" Jimmy asked.

"No, but if you tell me to run, you won't have to repeat it," Bob said.

Jimmy pointed to the wire. Mark, frightened by the look on his big brother's face, handed it over without a word. Jimmy held the cross against the post with his left hand. He and Bob passed the wire around the post as fast as they could.

"Geez, it got cold," Bob said.

Jimmy looked down at the mist curling around Bob's calf.

"Hit your leg with the Bible – now!"

Bob did not hesitate. When he swatted, the mist skittered away with something akin to a growl. It was not a cry of pain – but one of anger. "Hold that Bible out in front of you – give me a little time," Jimmy said.

The wire was cutting his hands, but he kept spinning it around the post. He never took his eyes off the Shimmer. The mist had gathered in the center of the attic and was rising in a pillar – taking shape – gaining mass. Jimmy could sense the roiling energy building in the column of fog.

"Done?" Bob said. "Let's get the hell out of here."

Bob missed the top step and fell into Matt's retreating back. The two boys pitched headlong into Mark at the landing. Jimmy heard a few mild curses, but no one cried out in pain.

He turned to see the Shimmer rushing at him with the force of a runaway train. It splattered against an invisible wall and shed to the sides, like a wave hitting a seawall.

The cross is generating a force field, Jimmy thought. *Thank you, Jesus and all the Saints.*

Jimmy wanted to run, but his legs would not move.

"I think it worked," he said.

"Get out of there," Bob said.

"In a second."

The "pieces" of the mist reassembled. Although without a distinct form, the creature –now the vapor – had shape. It looked like a distorted skull with deep-set eyes, flaring nostrils, and a bottomless gape where the mouth should have been.

The creature's gaze was locked on the post – no, the cross. A swirling appendage swept from the mass and slapped against the post.

"What was that?" Bob's voice quivered.

Jimmy didn't answer.

The creature was shaking its "arm" like a dog would shake a wounded paw.

"Did it work?" It was Matt – he sounded very small.

"I-I-I think it's trapped," Jimmy said. He opened

his mouth to speak again but froze when the creature's head turned toward him.

The voice came from nowhere – and everywhere – all at once. A deep, threatening hiss – Darth Vader – only scarier. "You…can…see…me." Everyone heard it, but only Jimmy could see it.

Jimmy took a step back. The vacant crater in the creature's face slowly took shape – lips – and teeth – row after row – sharp – fang-like – endless.

"Yessss…you…can." A pause – then – "Interesting."

Jimmy took a half-step back. His heel slipped off the top step, and he fell. Bob had come halfway back up the stairs. He caught his friend and, along with Matt and Mark, he guided Jimmy down to the landing and out of the attic.

Jimmy saw the terror in their faces when they all heard a demonic explosion of laughter from the attic. He slammed the door and locked it.

"Tell no one," he said.

CHAPTER 20
MANIACAL MADNESS
SUMMER 1983

JIMMY TOOK THE next hour explaining what he saw – he drew sketches to reinforce his points. Their initial reaction of fear eventually turned into fascination.

"I can't believe we trapped the thing," Mark said. "What is it? A ghost?"

Jimmy shook his head. "I don't think so. I think it is something else, more dangerous."

Matt said, "Jimmy, you should go ask it."

Jimmy's wide eyes reflected terror. "Are you kidding? You wouldn't say that if you'd seen it."

Bob stroked his non-existent beard. "Well, we should try to find a way to communicate without looking it in the face, or whatever the heck it has. Besides, we don't know if talking to it might screw up Jimmy in some way."

The boys stared at each other with what they assumed were their best pensive looks. Mark soon tired of trying to look thoughtful. "We've got walkie talkies."

"Great idea, genius," Matt said. "You going to stand up there and push the button for it?"

"I'm trying to help, smartass," Mark responded.

"Hey, I'm the only one allowed to cuss in this house," Matt said.

Mark smiled and thumped his brother on the arm, "You and Dad."

Bob's voice was quiet. "We could try the Ouija board."

"I was thinking the same thing," Jimmy said, "It's a great idea. We'll need to keep a journal. We need to know exactly what we're dealing with."

"Heck, yes," Bob said. We can publish it someday and make a fortune."

Jimmy stood – he was headed to the basement. "Fat lot of good money will do us if we're all dead," he said.

<hr />

"Mom's been down here," Jimmy said.

"How can you tell?" Bob asked.

"Telltale signs," Jimmy said. "One – the boxes have been moved and stacked neatly. Two – where's all the dust?"

"Good point," Bob said. "Can't believe I missed that one."

By the time they returned to Jimmy's room, Matt

and Mark were gone. Jimmy heard an argument from across the hall.

When Jimmy opened his brothers' door, Matt was on top of Mark.

"No wonder you always win," Matt said. He was waving a remote-control unit in Mark's face. "There's something wrong with this controller – the one you always give me for the red car."

"Well, you love Ohio State so much, you always want that one – and you claim you're older."

"I am!" Matt said.

"By three minutes," Mark said. "Three stupid minutes – that's it. So, you always get the car you want. You lose because you must stink at driving."

Jimmy pushed Matt off Mark. "What the hell?" he asked.

Mark took on the role of the victim. "I was minding my own business and playing with Luther."

Jimmy looked at the ventriloquist dummy lying next to his brother – Mark had gone nuts when he got it two Christmases ago.

"You stink at that," Jimmy said. "Why do you keep trying?"

"Got to get better," Mark said. "I want to be the next Jeff Dunham."

"Well," Bob said, "why don't you just put Matt on your lap and let him talk? Everyone would think you're a genius. And Matt is sure convincing as a dummy."

Jimmy, Mark, and Bob giggled. Matt fumed.

"Come on, Jimmy," Matt said. "You're supposed to watch out for both of us. Besides, I think Mark is cheating with the race car set. I always lose. He did something to the controller."

Jimmy took the controller from Matt. It was sticky – and it smelled.

Jimmy looked at Mark and laughed. "How long before you think the honey will short out the circuits?" he asked.

Mark rubbed his hands together like an "evil genius."

"Long enough for me to complete my plan for world domination. Besides, I only put a little – a very precise application with one of Mom's sewing needles."

Jimmy looked at Bob who'd collapsed on the floor. Bob wiped tears from his eyes. "Honey in the controller – brilliant. That's Hall of Fame stuff right there."

While Matt fumed, Jimmy helped Mark to his feet. "Okay guys," he said. "I know the racing is fun, but we've got bigger issues."

"You get the board?" Matt asked.

"Yes – did you numb nuts come up with any questions?"

Matt and Mark stared at their feet. "We got distracted," Mark said.

Jimmy looked at the pad he'd left for questions. The twins had gotten as far as a big, bold question mark on the top line.

"You guys are idiots," he said.

"Well," Matt said, "the 'idiots' got you in the attic, right?"

"Good point," Jimmy said. "Did you hear anything from, you know, up there?" He pointed toward the ceiling.

Looking at Mark for confirmation, Matt said, "No, we haven't heard a single peep. Maybe we scared it."

Bob unpacked the board, "Let's find out."

The four boys sat around the board. Bob and Jimmy's hands hovered above the planchette. Mark held the journal, although he had no intention of writing in it. He was leaving that up to Jimmy and Bob.

"Do you need me to get the flashlights?" Matt asked.

Jimmy looked at the window – the sun blazed through the panes. "I think we're fine without them for now."

He and Bob placed their hands on the device, and Bob said in a soft tone, "To the entity living in the attic, who are you?"

Nothing.

Bob looked at Jimmy and repeated his request. Once again, nothing happened. Bob and Jimmy took their hands off the planchette.

"Do you think the cross is interfering with our ability to speak with it?" Bob asked.

"Maybe," Jimmy said, "but I was able to speak with it through the barrier upstairs."

"Maybe you need to ask." The boys put their hands

on the board again. Jimmy asked, "To the entity living in the attic, do you agree to speak with us?"

The planchette began to move across the Board.

The boys were expecting a "yes" or "no." Instead, the planchette moved to the "L," just below the "no."

It slid across the board: E.

Then, to the center: T.

Mark figured he ought to start writing.

"L-E-T," Bob said. "Let."

Jimmy looked at the board. Tendrils of black mist seeped upward – they dissipated one inch from the surface.

"Can you guys see that?" Jimmy asked.

"See what?"

"There's a dark mist rising out of the board."

Matt and Mark backed away. Bob hung in with his hands on the board.

"It's fine," Jimmy said. "It's disappearing as quickly as it's appearing."

Bob's finger touched Jimmy's hand. "Light pressure, buddy," he said. "We're not drilling for oil here."

Jimmy relaxed and the viewfinder began to move.

"M."

"Mom!" Matt said.

"Shut up, Matt," Jimmy said. "It's not Charades."

"E." Bob looked over at Jimmy. "Let me?"

"Stay with it," Jimmy said. "Focus."

The last letters came in a flurry.

"O…U…T."

"Let me out – let me out!" Mark and Matt were screaming and bouncing on the bed. Jimmy looked at Bob. They moved the planchette to the top of the board.

"No!"

"Hell no," Matt said. "Never!"

Jimmy spoke towards the ceiling. "What is your name?"

The planchette scooted away from the fingers and moved with a mind of its own.

"L-E-T-M-E-O-U-T."

"No!' Jimmy said. "What is your damn name?"

They watched in horror as the planchette spelled out:

"B-U-B-E-Z-L-E-E-B."

Bob snatched the journal from Mark and copied down the letters.

"Bu-bez'-leeb, Bub'-ez-leeb, Bube – zleeb'… no… Bube'-zleeb, I think."

Jimmy kept asking questions. "What do you want?"

"L-I-F-E-F-O-R-C-E-U-S-E-D-O-L-L."

"Doesn't make sense," Matt said.

"Yes, it does," Bob said. "It's not one word. Break it down; Lifeforce. It needs nutrition – fuel. That's the message."

"What about the Use Doll part?" Jimmy asked.

"Dunno. Something like Barbie?" Bob looked confused.

"No," Matt said. He pointed to Luther. "Something like that!"

"It wants to eat Luther?" Mark's eyes bulged. "No way, Jose!"

Matt tugged at Luther's arm, "Come on, man. Let's put this little clown in the woodchipper!"

Mark started to cry.

"Cut it out, Matt," Jimmy said. "I don't think that's what it means."

"Hang on," Bob said. He looked up. "You want Luther?"

"Y-E-S."

"I don't think he wants to eat it," Bob said. He reached for the doll. "I think Bubezleeb wants to speak through it."

He pried the doll from Mark's hands and handed it to Jimmy. The dolls eyes were flat – vacant. Jimmy propped Luther in a sitting position on the board. Only Jimmy saw the mist rise from the board – hundreds of vaporish snakes filling every pore and orifice on the doll.

But everyone could see Luther's eyes when they shone with a cold, dark fury – an enraged Rottweiler. The eyes darted back and forth. The mouth hinged up and down without Mark's manipulation. Matt and Mark jumped into the far corner. Jimmy and

Bob scooted back from the board – poised to flee if necessary.

The doll spun its head to Jimmy. The voice sounded like sand mixed with static – course – buzzy – difficult to understand – a malevolent tone in contrast to Luther's sweet and sunny painted face.

"You must let me out; I must feed."

Jimmy opened his mouth. Nothing came out. Bob began to stammer. "F-f-feed on w-w-what?"

The head swiveled to Bob. "Lifeforce."

Mark had moved up behind Jimmy. His voice quavered. "What's lifeforce?"

"Living essence – power."

Luther collapsed onto the board.

Jimmy said, "I'm not sure what the hell Lifeforce is, but I'm not giving *that* any damn thing."

Something moved in the attic. They heard a squawk.

"Bird," Bob and Jimmy said at the same time.

Luther 's head moved. "Bird…lifeforce…need more."

The doll mumbled something and collapsed again.

"What did he say?" Bob asked.

"He said, 'goodbye,'" Jimmy answered.

Mark picked Luther up. He gave the doll a hug and wrapped it in a blanket. "Sorry you had to do that, buddy," he said.

Bob put the board away, while Jimmy scribbled notes in the journal.

It would be a long time before they removed the dead robin from the attic.

CHAPTER 21
BUBEZLEEB

FALL 1983

For the next few weeks, Bubezleeb did not speak to the boys, either through the Ouija board or via Luther. Jimmy could tell Mark was pleased when Luther's body remained lifeless. Mark was fond of the doll and became increasingly resistant each time Jimmy asked to use it.

"I figured something out," Jimmy said.

"Give it," Bob said.

"We don't need to put Luther on the board to figure out if Bubezleeb wants to talk."

"Really?"

"All I have to do it look at the board. If the Shimmer's there, it's showtime."

Despite the demon's absence, Jimmy went to bed every night expecting to awaken at 3:33 AM to the sound of an invasion coming from the attic. But each morning, he opened his eyes to a bright sun and a beautiful day. When he climbed out of bed, he didn't know whether to be grateful or disappointed.

On the first day of the new school year, Bob and Jimmy test drove their tale of summer adventure with a few friends, but no one bit. The saga of the "Attic Dweller" found no traction.

Besides, most of their classmates had graduated from ghouls to girls.

Once things cranked up at school, the boys had less time together and attempted to contact Bubezleeb less often. But they talked about it every day on the route to and from school. They loved going to the high school varsity football games on Friday nights and having sleepovers on Saturdays. Their favorite new activity was "channel changing."

Every house in Bellevue used the same cable system and every remote in the neighborhood emitted the same signal. Bob, Jimmy, Matt, and Mark loved to sneak from house to house, peak in over the window ledge, and change the channels on their neighbors' televisions. Jimmy did not know how many fights they started between husbands and wives, but he was pretty sure their shenanigans caused a divorce or two.

One Friday night, the "Channel Gang" huddled in the hedge next to Mrs. Skyler's house. She was watching *The Love Boat*.

Bob and Jimmy each had a remote. They started slow – a single change. Bob maneuvered the old woman's television to *Airwolf*, a 9:00 PM favorite for the boys. Mrs. Skyler glared at her set, picked up her remote and flipped back to *The Love Boat*. The boys waited another minute and went back to the *Airwolf*.

Jimmy fired up his "cosmic channel ray" and sent Mrs. Skyler off to the world of *Mama's Family*. Bob spun her over the *Airwolf*. The boys soon had the television dancing.

Mrs. Skyler screamed to no one across her empty den, "Mother Mary, send your blessed angels to remove these demons from my TV."

The boys made wild banshee noises as they ran off into the night. "That'll teach her to make her yard off limits to Ghost in the Graveyard," Bob said.

After their evening of mischief, Bob spent the night at Jimmy's whose parents were dining at the Eagles Lodge. Heather was at Clancy's Burgers with some friends.

Once again, Angie had agreed to watch Matt, Mark, Jimmy, and Bob. She had one request. "You can do anything you want within reason," she said. "If you bother me when Alex comes over, all bets are off, you go to bed, and I tell Mom and Dad you did something horrible."

"Why should she believe you?" Jimmy asked.

"Because I am a responsible almost adult – and I don't lurk in the bushes and change peoples' channels."

Bob and Jimmy stared at her in horror.

"You guys think you're all James Bond and shit. The only one who doesn't know it's you is Old Lady Skyler. She thinks it's demons from the underworld."

When Alex knocked on the door, the boys went upstairs.

"MAN, BELLEVUE LOOKED pretty good last night," Jimmy said. He was tossing a plastic football back and forth with Bob. "You think we'll make the playoffs?"

"They have to beat Willa—" Bob stopped. "Were those footsteps…in the attic?"

Jimmy quit lobbing the ball into the air. He cocked his head to determine the direction of the sound. He nodded and pointed up to the ceiling. Bob tiptoed to the closet, took down the Ouija board, opened the box, and placed the game in the center of the room.

"Spirit, are you there?" Jimmy asked.

The dark mist filtered up from the board and swirled around the planchette. Bob's eyes asked a question – Jimmy nodded. Bob mimicked a writing motion in the air. Jimmy pointed to his desk. Bob took a pen, a pencil, and the journal (right where it should have been – right side of the middle drawer) and sat next to the board across from Jimmy.

The planchette moved: "Yes."

"Where have you been?"

"L-O-E-H-S."

Bob repeated the word, "Loehs," doing his best to pronounce it correctly. "Something familiar about this word," he said.

"What is Loehs?" Jimmy asked, his face pointed to the ceiling.

The boys waited impatiently as the planchette moved and paused…moved and paused. "S-O-U-L-S."

Bob shrugged. "What else should we ask? I can't think of anything."

"You don't need to," Jimmy said. He pointed to the board. "Look!"

"L-E-T-M-E-O-U-T-S-E-E-B-R-O-T-H-E-R."

"That doesn't make any sense," Jimmy said.

"That thing has seen Matt and Mark – it's not going to show you anything. What do you think it means?"

Jimmy rapped his knuckles on the floor. "I have an idea," he said. "See brother where?"

Bob nodded. "Good – that's good."

"F-I-N-D."

"That makes a lot of sense," Bob said. He looked up. "Tell us something we can use."

The planchette moved again.

"Y-O-W-I-E."

The veins in Jimmy's neck throbbed and he jumped to his feet. "Tell us something useful, you demonic dirtbag!"

Bob could not remember ever seeing his friend so angry. "Don't let him get to you," he said. "He's just screwing with your head."

Bob was glad Paul and Maggie weren't home because Jimmy was throwing things at the ceiling, screaming, and swearing like an NFL defensive coordinator. "Tell – us – something!"

"Look," Bob said.

More letters.

"F-I-N-D."

Jimmy charged to the attic door and began to kick it. "We know, we know, we know!" Spittle flew from his mouth. He pounded on the door. "What? Find what? Yowie-wowie – what the hell is that? Give us something we can use or get the hell out of my attic!"

Bob's voice was soft but firm. "Jimmy," he said. "Another word."

The planchette moved. The letters leaked onto the board with the pace of cold motor oil.

Jimmy stopped raging and both boys stopped breathing.

"J."

"O."

"S."

"H."

CHAPTER 22
INSIDE THE SHIMMER - JOSH
ENTRY

SHORTLY AFTER JOSH "shimmered" into nothingness and Jimmy disappeared, someone scooped Josh up and carried him into the woods. When they stopped, he saw a short, stocky woman – shorter than Mommy. The woman wore a tunic of fur. Her copper hair swung down her back in a long braid.

She put her finger to her lips. Her eyes reflected terror. Her voice barely registered. "Shh, Stompers."

Josh's started to cry, his face scrunching like he'd eaten a lemon. The woman slapped her hand over the boy's mouth, picked him up, and began to run. The cold creek water stung his body, little icicles of pain as the woman darted across the shallow trickle. They crossed a moss-covered hill and cowered in an outcropping of large rocks. Josh's breath came in short, shallow bursts. They moved from boulder to boulder – her eyes darting right…left…right. They stopped, crouched, listened – and waited.

The sound came from the left – a dense, dark place

where the trees grew without restriction and the under-growth looked impassable. Two creatures – large and wooly unlike anything Josh had ever seen – thundered across the plain below. Josh stared at the "big monkeys." They grunted with each earth-shaking step, not in pain but with an aggressive, savage sound – a noise Josh's young mind could only interpret one way.

Attack.

Only later did he learn he was wrong. The grunts meant: *Dinner if we can catch it.*

And the preferred meal was human flesh.

Thirty minutes or so later, the woman stood and offered her hand. Josh took it and they walked back to the small creek. She knelt, scooped water into her hands, and held out her cupped palms to Josh. He lapped like a dog until he felt better.

The redhead reached over, cradled his jaw, then licked his cheek. Confused – and slightly grossed out (as Heather would say, wherever she was) – he raised his hand to wipe away the saliva. But when he looked at the woman's eyes, he saw something – something primal – something familiar.

He saw a mother.

His hand dropped and he smiled a little.

Several hundred yards downstream, the brush moved. One of the hairy beasts stepped into the clearing, this one large and reddish. It was bigger than the ones they'd seen before – at least 10 feet tall. Long, yellow fangs protruded at the corners of its mouth. It tilted its head and sniffed. It found the wind and followed the scent until…

…it looked straight at Josh.

Josh felt the piercing, baleful howl at the base of his spine. Within 10 seconds, three other creatures – all brown – stepped onto the bank. Without any discernable signal, but in perfect coordination, the quartet erupted into a flurry of movement. Two charged straight at them. The other two split out in flanking movements – one left, one right.

The woman's voice nearly shattered Josh's eardrum.

"Loon!" Even in his terrified state, Josh understood the command: "Run!"

She snatched Josh to the right, just in time. The beast's momentum careened past them. Josh smelled body odor – filth – and something else.

Blood.

The beast bellowed in frustration and skidded to a halt. Josh burst into tears – the dam of his fear breaking into a thousand terrified pieces. It didn't matter, stealth was not important now, only speed and shelter.

They ran along the shallow creek bed. The woman veered left, diving into the underbrush. She dragged Josh towards a large rock then, looking just like Ken Griffey, she slid on her hip – full speed – along a small, almost invisible trench and disappeared. Her hand appeared. Josh grabbed it and she pulled him under the boulder with her.

Josh's eyes adjusted to the darkness. He saw a series of tunnels and small caves. It looked like the rabbit warrens he'd discovered in the fields when he went exploring with Jimmy. This tunnel was tall enough for him to walk upright, although the woman had to hunch over from time to time.

They walked and crawled for a while – Josh had very little concept of time. He just knew he was tired – and scared. They rounded a corner and stepped into a large room – it seemed to Josh that it was as big as his house in Bellevue. A man stood.

"Evie," he said.

"Annu," she said.

And they embraced.

JOSH MUNCHED ON a "strillie," or as he knew it, an apple. He could see Evie talking to Annu. They were quiet but Josh knew what an argument looked like. Evie kept pointing to him – Annu kept looking at Josh and shaking his head.

Annu looked unmoved by Evie's argument until she unleashed the ultimate weapon – she began to cry. Annu shook his head again, but this time in resignation, and embraced her. Annu shuffled over to Josh and touched him on the head. Evie picked Josh off the ground and hugged him.

She did the lick thing again – *ugh.*

The cave was not as big as Josh initially thought, but there was room for straw mats and a fire.

No TV, Josh thought.

He looked at the walls. Simple paintings displayed what he understood were people. He saw other pictures – crude and horrifying – the beasts chasing and catching people – tearing them apart – *eating them.*

Evie pointed to one of the beasts. "Stomper," she said. "Stomper."

Josh was not allowed to go more than about 10 feet from the opening to the cave. A long time passed – at least it seemed long. Day after day of heat and bugs. Whenever Annu left, Evie pulled Josh back under the rock and they waited. Annu always returned with something to eat – berries, grapes, sometimes even a fish or two.

The weather grew cooler. Sometimes Evie let Josh lie on top of the big rock where he would soak up the warmth of the sun. His clothes were gone. They'd gotten weirdly small. Evie replaced his little jeans and pullover shirt with a tunic of animal skin.

"Kalis," she said when she stroked the fur.

Looks like squirrel to me, Josh thought. But he smiled and said, "Kalis."

His shoes began to hurt. They pinched his toes and made them raw. Annu used a stone knife and cut off the ends of the shoes. It worked for a while, but by the time snow covered the ground outside, Evie presented Josh with a pair of woven sandals.

Spring came. Josh could tell he'd grown. He had to duck when he went in and out of the cave. Annu showed Josh how to fashion a spear from a sapling – how to stand in the water of the brook without moving – and how to gaff a fish, which smelled wonderful cooking over the fire – and tasted even better. "Tanta," Evie said when she pointed to the fish.

Josh did not understand everything, but he was dreadfully aware of the ever-present danger. In case he forgot, Evie reminded him every time he prepared to go out. She stood at the opening of the cave, took his face in her hands, looked him in the eye, and – in a voice ripe with terror – said, "Stompers."

Inside the Silver Shimmer:
July – One Year After Entry

Josh stood in the middle of the waist-deep water. He moved less than an oak tree on a windless day, his spear held in a cocked right arm, his eyes unmoving from the brook. A large *tanta* swam lazily between his legs, its fins moving only enough to maintain position, while the fish fed. Without moving his left arm, Josh flipped a handful of ants onto the water about five feet ahead and watched them flow back towards him. He waited. The *tanta* rose to the bait.

Josh tensed slightly, prepared to stab the fish. Something caught his eye, and he looked up. His sudden movement alerted the fish to danger, and it darted away with a swift flip of its tail, but Josh did not notice.

He was too busy focusing on the approaching Shimmer. It was just like the one he'd stepped into when Jimmy disappeared, only bigger.

He heard movement to his left and turned, ready to flee. Annu stood on the bank, disappointment etched on his face. The man gestured, palms up: *What did you do?*

JOSH POINTED TO the west. The Shimmer was expanding, and Josh could see the dome rising high into the air. Annu looked in the direction Josh indicated, then back. Again, the palms went toward the sky, and he shook his head as only a disappointed father can.

Josh looked at the Shimmer, then at Annu.

He cannot see it.

Annu motioned, "Come." He was not pleased. Josh waded out of the brook, and they went home empty-handed.

CHAPTER 23
READING IN A MIRROR
FALL 1983

Jimmy and Bob talked about the encounter the next day. As soon as they'd seen the message, "Josh," Jimmy had thrown the board against the wall and cursed. Bob took the explosion as his clue to leave, He knew how to be a friend, which meant he knew when his buddy needed a little space.

Now, they were sitting in Jimmy's room again. Bob saw the Ouija board box on the top shelf of the closet.

"Weird day yesterday, huh?"

Jimmy's face was stone – his eyes dull. "Yep."

"I figured some things out," Bob said.

"Like what?"

"Well," Bob said, "I know where our friend (he pointed to the attic) was for a while."

"Where?"

"Well, this takes a little set up."

"It's Saturday – got nothing but time – at least until my golf foursome with Jack, Lee, and Tom."

Bob hit Jimmy in the head with a pillow. "Like Nicklaus, Trevino, and Watson are going to play with your chop butt."

"Well," Jimmy said, the gleam returning to his eyes. "It took some convincing because I beat 'em so bad last time. But The Bear wanted a chance to get his money back."

"Shut up," Bob said. He dodged the "return pillow fire."

"Okay – tell me."

"Well," Bob said, "you remember you missed the first few days of Vacation Bible School, right?"

"Had a cold – sure."

"You had herpes and you know it," Bob said. "Anyway, Father Reed got all fired up in one of his 27-hour lectures and started talking about, let me get this right…" Bob stood, clasped his hands behind his back, and began talking through his nose… "the biblical manifestations of the Afterlife."

Jimmy grimaced. "Herpes sounds much better. But so what?"

Bob smiled. "He talked about hell…hades… Gehenna…and, get this, the Hebrew place of the dead called Sheol."

"So?"

"Spell it backwards."

"L…o…e – oh shit!"

"Yep, 'Sheol' spelled backwards is 'Loehs,' the place

our furious friend up there said he visited while he was gone."

"Okay," Jimmy said. "So, what's the big deal about Sheol?"

Bob face had no color. He swallowed – hard.

"Jimmy, that thing said he went to the place of the dead. Which means—"

Jimmy interrupted, "Which means it's something from the Afterlife – and not Heaven."

"Right," Bob said. "And—"

Jimmy started pacing – his eyes alive. "And if we can figure out where it went by spelling the location backwards, we can probably also figure out its name the same way."

"Right again," Bob said. "I already did that. So the demon's name is…"

They spoke at the same time. "Beelzebub."

Jimmy yelled down the hall, "Matt and Mark, get in here."

Bob's voice was intense. "Beelzebub. He's known as Lord of the Flies – often blamed for lust."

Matt, and Mark didn't know what to say, so they listened intently.

"And Beelzebub is associated with the deadly sin of gluttony."

Jimmy clapped his hands. "That explains the lifeforce thing – he can't get enough. Even when he's satisfied, he wants more."

"Right – when he was pressing on your chest, he was trying to push out your lifeforce. When you hit him with the cross, he went after Matt."

Jimmy shuddered. "If Matt had disappeared into that laundry chute…"

"He would be gone," Bob said, looking at Matt.

Matt's face had drained of all color. "You mean we conquered a demon?"

"Not sure he's conquered," Jimmy said. "Right now, he's simply held at bay."

Matt said, "Good enough for me."

High fives all around.

"Bob?" Jimmy voice barely registered.

"Yep."

"You think *you know who* can show me where Josh is?"

Bob put his arm on Jimmy's shoulder. "We're scientists and investigators. What are the facts?" He held up fingers as he ticked off his list. "Despite all reason to the contrary; One – we have a demon in the attic. Two – we know demons are bad. Three – he claims he knows where your brother is. Four – demons don't get to be demons because they are truthful all the time."

Jimmy held up a hand. "Got it – the butthole's lying. Let's go get a soda."

A FEW WEEKS later, Bob, Jimmy, Matt, and Mark filched the skeleton key from Dad's "secret hiding place" and went up to the attic. In the corner, Jimmy could see the faint remnants of the dark Shimmer, now no bigger than a kickball, he relaxed a little.

Under Jimmy's direction, the guys threw things at the spot – a tennis ball, a handful of screws, even a small box. Everything disappeared briefly, then reappeared on the other side after having passed through the dark misty spot. Jimmy did notice that every time something was thrown through the Shimmer, the sphere got a bit smaller. Then, Jimmy threw a larger ball through the mist. It was the same exact size as the Shimmer. The ball went through, the Shimmer shrunk slightly, and the ball did not return.

Jimmy said, "interesting, I wonder why it didn't come back."

Bob was deep in contemplation trying to think through the riddle when he saw Jimmy's outstretched hand approach the Shimmer.

Taking the cross in his hand, Jimmy approached with extreme caution and pressed his finger against the darkness, while the others watched in hushed fascination.

"Anything?' Bob asked.

"No pull or anything like that." Jimmy tried to keep his voice level – scientific – observant and dispassionate, even though he was sure he might wet his pants at any minute.

"Damn!" Jimmy snapped his finger away. "Something bit me."

Bob began to laugh "Don't be a sissy— oh, crap."

Blood dripped from the tip of Jimmy's index finger and pooled in his palm.

"It's just a flesh wound," Matt said.

Bob whirled. "Now is not the time to quote *Monty Python and the Holy Grail,*" he said. "Whatever that is, it chomped your brother something fierce."

Jimmy held up his hand.

Matt gulped. "Sorry. You okay?"

Mark was already headed to the stairs. "I'll get the First Aid kit."

Jimmy and Matt had the same thought. "Don't let Mom see you."

THEY DIDN'T RETURN to the attic for a while. Jimmy's finger healed, but he had to make up a story about getting it caught in his bike spokes. Mom threatened to take him for a tetanus shot but Paul "talked her down."

He'll be fine. Boys have accidents."

Maggie smiled and said, "Okay," but Jimmy saw her hand trembling, which led to a lecture on bicycle safety.

Repeated attempts to contact Beelzebub proved fruitless and a quick perusal of the attic revealed the dark Shimmer had disappeared. They checked the entire house but could not find anything.

Jimmy went over to Grandma Leona's.

"Any more contact with Grandpa Will," he asked through a mouthful of cookies.

"And all this time, I thought you came over for my sparkling wit and conversational skills," she said.

Jimmy started to protest, then saw the twinkle in her eye.

"No, honey," she said. "My Wilfred moved on to his permanent rest, and I am at peace with that. He always took care of me in life – and even for a little while after he was gone. He's earned his tranquility."

Jimmy and his grandmother discussed the attic, what had happened, how the boys had captured the creature, communicated with it, and ultimately watched it retreat to Sheol. Leona expressed concern. She'd seen the dark Shimmer in the attic's recesses on the day the pastors purged the home. She was sorry to hear they had not entirely gotten rid of it, but proud her grandsons and friend had taken care of it once and for all.

"Jimmy be careful. Your gift allows you to interact with all sorts, including those associated with Hell. Those creatures lie and will try to trick you."

"I know, Grandma," he said. "I'll be careful."

"You left the cross up, didn't you?"

"Of course, Grandma," Jimmy said.

He decided not to talk to her about Josh.

Ten years later, when they laid her to rest next to her beloved Wilfred, Jimmy wondered if he'd done the right thing.

PART II
THE OTHER SIDE

CHAPTER 24
R.I.P. GRANDMA
SPRING 1993

JIMMY WALKED INTO Frazer's Funeral Home and hugged his two brothers.

"Jimmy, how are you?" Mark asked. Jimmy, bald and thin attempted a smile.

"Getting there," he said. "Had my last treatment today."

Matt kept his hand on Jimmy's shoulder. "What's the prognosis?"

"Good," Jimmy said. "Chemo and radiation are over. Cure rate is around 90%." He grabbed Matt's hand. "Just make sure I don't fall down, okay?"

"You got it, brother," Matt said.

"Grandma, huh?" Mark said.

"She was a good one."

All three said, "World's best cookies."

Matt pointed behind Jimmy. "Watch your six," he said.

Jimmy turned into Bob's open arms. The old

friends embraced, though Bob obviously didn't squeeze too hard.

"How you feeling, Coop?" Bob asked.

"About the same as I look," Jimmy said, "but still strong enough to kick your scrawny butt."

Jimmy turned back to his brothers, "Bob's been a big help," he said. "He's got a series of charts you would not believe. He tracks the tumor size, my weight, everything. A true Ohio Stater!"

"Go Buckeyes," Bob said.

They walked towards the visitation room. "How's physics?" Matt asked.

"Well, I've got the E=MC² thing down, but gravity still baffles me," Bob said. "I should have picked something easy like your brother."

Mark punched Bob's shoulder. "He only chose psychology so he could understand you," Mark said.

"Fair enough," Bob said.

Matt lowered his voice. "Seriously, thanks for all the help with Jimmy. You know, since Mark and I are stationed overseas – it was nice to know you were there looking out for him."

"That's what friends and roomies do," Bob said.

Matt held the door. "After you Egon."

"Still with the *Ghostbusters* after all these years," Bob said.

"It's a classic," Matt said.

Bob stopped. "Why am I always Egon? No one wants to be Egon."

"Precisely," Matt said.

Bob turned to Jimmy. "Sorry about Grandma Leona. One of a kind. World's greatest cookies."

"We mentioned that," Jimmy said.

JIMMY STAYED A while after everyone left.

"I'll get a ride," he said to Bob.

"Hell you will," Bob said. "I'll wait outside. Take all the time you need."

Grandma lay in the oak casket. The family had selected one of her favorite dresses.

"A little casual, don't you think,?" Maggie had asked.

"It's fine, Mom. She ought to be comfortable every day," Angie said.

Leona wore a double strand pearl bracelet on her left wrist, her Timex on her right. As always, her crucifix encircled her neck.

Jimmy leaned in and kissed her forehead.

"Thanks for everything, Grandma," he said. "You helped me – a lot. I love you. Enjoy the rainbow Shimmer with Grandpa Will."

An all-too-familiar, post-chemo queasiness tightened his throat, so he sat in a chair next to the casket. He picked up a Bible from a nearby table and held it against his temple – the slight pressure helped with the nausea.

Something vibrated.

Jimmy looked to the side and saw a Shimmer glistening in the corner – pearl white with flakes of color. He heard Leona's voice.

"Jimmy, everything will be okay. I have one thing more to tell you. Josh is stuck but you can find him."

Jimmy didn't move. "Where?"

"Look for him in the Shimmers. Be careful. Stay away from the dark ones. They are places of pain and malice. Find Josh. I see Wilfred waiting. Goodbye, dear boy."

The voice faded, and the Shimmer slowly diminished in size until it disappeared.

Jimmy sat a long time, then went outside to meet Bob.

CHAPTER 25
BACK TO THE LIBRARY

SPRING 1993

"Bob, I know how crazy this sounds, but I am telling you, Grandma spoke to me," Jimmy said.

"I get it, buddy," Bob said. "But you've had chemo, radiation – you've had a fever and you're under a lot of stress. Could have been a hallucination."

Matt and Mark stood to the side. "He's got a point," Matt said.

"Hard to argue the logic," Mark said.

"Why don't you Jarheads go shoot something?" Jimmy said with a hint of humor. His brothers smiled.

"I'll give you a hundred-meter head start and take you down in two steps," Mark said.

"Too much trouble," Matt said. "Easier to hit him with a mortar."

"But not nearly as much fun."

Matt grew serious. "Before yesterday at Frazer's, when was the last time you noticed a Shimmer?"

"Over a decade," Jimmy said. "And I don't think this had anything to do with my illness. It seemed real."

"All right," Bob said. "As a scientist, I'm willing to listen. God knows we've experienced some weird shit thanks to you."

"Thanks," Jimmy said. "Let's consider for a moment that my twin brother, (he pointed to Matt and Mark) your brother, may still be alive – somewhere. Why not go with it and see where we end up?"

"I'm still on leave," Matt said. "What do you have in mind?"

Jimmy looked at Bob. "My memory's a little shot right now. When the thing in the attic – Beelzebub – told us to look for Josh, where did he say to go?"

Bob rubbed his chin. "Damn, man, it's been 10 years. Let me think – ah… 'woyie'… something like that."

"No," Mark said. "Right letters – wrong order – it was *Yowie.*"

"That's right," Jimmy said. "Applying the backwards spelling concept, the demon meant someplace called *Eiwoy*. Won't hurt to look for it – at least for a little."

The gang all nodded and headed to the library. They walked into the stacks. Each one grabbed a couple of books off the shelves, flipped to the glossary, and began searching. Thirty minutes later, they closed the last of a stack of book.

"Nothing," Matt said.

"Zippo," Mark said.

"Nada here," Bob said.

Jimmy rest his head in his hands. "We're zero for four," he said. His head jerked up. "Or…"

Bob knew the look. "Or what, buddy."

Jimmy began to grin. "You remember the day we were talking about the demon and you made the list."

"Ah…no," Bob said.

"You said, "Demon in the attic – demons are bad – demon claims to know where your brother is – and—"

Bob slapped the table.

"Shh," came from the Circulation Desk.

"Sorry," Bob said. He turned to his friends. "Then I said, 'Demons don't get to be demons because they are truthful all the time.' I think ole Beelzebub was screwing with us. He knew we'd figured out Sheol. When the board forced him to respond, he decided he'd play a little game. He gave us the right name. He said if we wanted to find Josh, we had to find—"

"Yowie!" Jimmy said.

Everyone grabbed a book. Fifteen seconds later, Matthew slapped the table. "Winner, winner, chicken dinner," he said.

Bob saluted. "Is there anything you can't find?" he asked.

Matt looked up, breathed on the tips of his fingers, polished his nails on his shirt, and said. "Ladies and Gentlemen, back by popular demand, Detective Matthew P. Cooper."

Mark smirked from across the table. "Yeah, the P stands for pin-head."

"Quit horsing around and give me the book," Jimmy said. Despite his weakened condition, he still commanded his brothers' respect. Matt slid the book across the table.

"*Yowie* – here it is." Jimmy scanned, then summarized. "It's not a place – it's a thing – from Australian folklore. Yowie is a creature. It ranges from 7-to-12 feet tall. Huge feet."

Matt and Mark began one of their favorite routines – from *The Young Frankenstein.*

Matt: For the experiment to be a success, all of the body parts must be enlarged.

Mark: His veins, his feet, his hands, his organs *vould* all have to be increased in size.

Matt: Exactly.

Mark: He *vould* have an enormous *schwanzstucker*.

Matt: That goes without saying.

The group dissolved into laughter. Within seconds, they heard, "Shh."

"Sorry, Mrs. Lutz," Jimmy said. Then he whispered. "She's got to be a thousand-years-old."

Matt looked at Jimmy. "Is this Yowie thing a joke – you already know about it?"

"No," Jimmy said. "I swear. And we got so wrapped up with the Sheol stuff and Josh that I never gave Yowie a second thought." He turned to Bob. "You?"

"It's new to me," Bob said.

"Okay, "Matt said. "Where does that leave us?"

Bob had been scribbling in the journal – the same one he'd started a decade before. He put down the pen. "Let's move out of the realm of what we can see, feel, taste, and smell and wander over into the kingdom of the possible. We've seen some weird stuff, right?"

Everyone nodded.

"Certainly not anything normal for Bellevue, Ohio, right?"

More nods.

"So, consider for a moment that we have somehow – I don't know how – but somehow intersected with another dimension – another Universe."

Jimmy tapped his fingers on the table. "The Shimmers."

"Right."

"So," Jimmy said, picking up on Bob's train of thought, "18 years ago, my brother – our brother – Josh, accidentally stepped through the door to another universe—"

Bob interrupted. "One on a different evolutionary arch than ours. We have…ah…giant apes. They have—"

"Bigfoot," Jimmy said. "You know what this means?"

Despite the tension, Bob could not stop smiling. "Yeah, buddy," he said. "We found it – we frickin' found it."

ON THE WALK home, Bob draped his arm across Jimmy's boney shoulders.

"Seems to me, old friend, that your gifts are extant. They just took a little, 10-year vacation."

"Not sure I want to go digging around those things, guys. I still remember the last run in," Mark said.

"Yeah," Matt said. "Some nights, I can still feel the walls of that laundry chute."

Bob laughed. "Check out The Few, The Proud, The Marines," he said.

Matt shot him a withering look. "I just prefer enemies I can see."

Jimmy interceded. "No one's calling you a coward, little brother – he's just bustin' your balls a little."

Bob said, "Hey Matty, if I was bustin' your balls, I'd tell you to go home and get your shine box."

"Gotta love a *Goodfellas* reference," Matt said. He relaxed – the Marine faded as he settled back into his old, familiar role of the annoying little brother.

Bob held court as they walked. "Let's consider what we understand already. We have all experienced what Jimmy can see via temperature change, even though we can't see it. I think we've proven the existence of both demons and hell. And we know we can hold those powers at bay – the crucifix and the Bible. Jimmy said he always saw a black mist whenever the demon was around. Do we think Josh is trapped with the demon?"

"It's been a long time," Jimmy said. "but I am confident Josh stepped into a lighter Shimmer – not a black one."

"What color was your Grandma's Shimmer?"

"Multicolored – a rainbow."

"Makes sense," Bob said. "If black is Hell, a rainbow would be the opposite."

"Heaven, wow," Mark said. "But I don't think we'll find Josh there."

Jimmy stopped walking. "Why not?"

"Easy, brother," Mark said. "Nothing against Josh – we never met him, but you loved him, so we know he was a good guy. But I think Grandma or Grandpa would have mentioned him, right?"

"True."

"Okay – you remember telling us about Eddie?"

Jimmy nodded.

"What color was his Shimmer?"

"The Shimmer in our old basement was white."

Bob picked up the thread. "Okay – Josh is not in a white one either. We know Eddie and his sister, Clara, have been dead a long time. They aren't in Hell, black – you didn't see a rainbow, so we can rule out Heaven. That leaves Purgatory and Limbo."

"Hm," Jimmy said. "Purgatory is a place of continuing penance. Sounds a little painful. Eddie talked about his hideout – never said anything about pain or unpleasantness. Let's go with Limbo."

"So, we're down to the gray mist in your grandmother's backyard and the silver Shimmer that enveloped Josh."

"Grandma Leona mentioned gray ghosts – wanderers. Why would they wander?"

Matt spoke up. "Searching for atonement."

"Purgatory," Mark said.

"I concur," Bob said. "So, we're left with silver. Didn't your grandmother see silver?"

"Yes," Jimmy said. "Twice – I've seen it once."

"So, what is silver?" Mark asked.

Bob, thoroughly enjoying the mental gymnastics, said, "Where, is a better question. Some believe the Afterlife is no more than another dimension. If it is a place and we can travel there, it might be an alternative universe. With that said, Josh did not leave his body behind; it went with him. I think he has traveled to an alternate dimension, one much different from our own – and substantively different from Heaven, Hell, Purgatory, or Limbo because it exists not on a transcendent plane but on a physical one."

"I just remembered something," Jimmy said. "The silver Shimmer was the only one with texture, lattice work – ah, a crisscross pattern – like a non-stick skillet."

Bob's face lit with excitement. "Jimmy, years ago you saw one when we were playing Ghost in the Graveyard. It was in the sky over St. Paul's. Did you know there was also a UFO spotted that night in Clyde?"

"If you told me, I don't remember." He tapped his forehead. "Chemo brain."

"Okay," Bob said, "so, if we go with the parallel universe or alternate reality scenario, the silver Shimmer is a place where – for lack of a better phrase – all weird things dwell."

Matt bounced with excitement. "Like Bigfoot, Nessie, UFOs, all that shit, right? How do we get there?"

"The Shimmer is the portal. Sometimes it's big – you could slide an entire house through it. Sometimes, it's like the one that took Josh, small – opens and closes fast. We find the Shimmer; we can get in – I guarantee it."

Mark coughed. "Ah, this is good stuff, but shouldn't we worry about how we get back? Didn't work out too well for Josh."

"I think we can get out, but I am still not exactly sure why Josh got stuck," Jimmy said.

"Sorry, Jimmy. I am still unsure about how the dimensions work."

They walked into the Cooper house and surrounded the kitchen table. Bob said, "I think I can help explain that." Bob drew a dot in the center of a page in the journal.

"This is a point; it contains zero dimensions. It has no length, no width, and no depth. It is an infinitely small point."

He drew another dot and connected it to the other

with a line. "This is the first dimension. It only contains lines and points."

"Gee," Matt said. "I bet your dad is happy he spent *all that money* on a college degree for you."

"Shut up," Bob said – but he was grinning. He drew a perpendicular line. "This is the second dimension. He completed the drawing: a square. "This is what it looks like when we watch TV. We can see length and width, so it is like a flat projection on a screen."

He drew lines vertical to the square and said, "This is the third dimension, the one we are accustomed to living in."

He picked up a book and held it in front of them. "You can see it has length, width, and depth. These three dimensions are the world we experience when we look at objects. You with me."

Everyone nodded.

"There's a fourth dimension: time."

Bob tossed the book to Matt, who caught it with ease.

"See?" Bob said. "Matt identified the length, width, and depth to track the book and analyzed the movement through time. Because he did so correctly, he caught it. If he'd miscalculated the time, the book would have smacked him in the mouth."

"Got it," Mark said. "Go on – can you draw a fifth dimension?"

"I can," Bob said, "but not in a way that will translate into a reality any of us would understand. We cannot see the fifth, sixth, or seventh dimensions, well, most of us can't, because of human limitation. Seeing multiple dimensions simultaneously would probably be more than the human mind could handle. All of this is, of course, very theoretical."

Jimmy stood and began to pace. "How do you explain what I see?"

"Excellent question, and I hadn't figured it out until right now. You never claimed to see other dimensions – a very important point. You simply see the intersection – the Shimmers – and meet visitors from them, like our not-so-friendly friend, Beelzebub."

"He was a peach," Jimmy said.

"Right," Bob said. "And although you could not see *where* he came from, for some reason, you could see *how he gets here.*"

"The portal – the Shimmer."

"Exactly," Bob said. "You may be able to see the dimensional surfaces where two dimensions overlap. It is the same as a Venn Diagram. At least that is what I believe now."

Matt walked to the refrigerator. "That's some heavy stuff," he said. "And I'm hungry."

Mark could not resist. "No more yanky my wanky – The Donger need food."

Everyone laughed. They almost choked when Jimmy put his finger to his lips and said, "Shh!"

CHAPTER 26
CEDAR POINT
SUMMER 1993

OVER THE NEXT few months, Jimmy continued his studies in Columbus. He was fascinated by multiple aspects of neuropsychology and parapsychology. With his treatments at The Arthur G. James Cancer Institute over, Jimmy attacked his studies with renewed vigor. His doctors were surprised by his quick rebound to normalcy.

He still roomed with Bob who had declined a spot in the Honors Dorm across campus. "I like it fine here," Bob said. "Plus, we are closer to the bars."

Bob elected to continue his academic studies over the summer, but Jimmy felt like he needed a break. In honor of Jimmy's departure, the friends celebrated at the Bier Stube. Bob made his way to the bar, while Jimmy staked out a booth.

Bob came over with a pitcher of beer and two chilled mugs.

"What are we drinking this time?" Jimmy asked. He loved Bob's adventures into all things beer.

"PBR," Bob said.

Jimmy blinked with exaggeration. "Robert Finsmere Bellard, noted physicist and brew snob, deigns to sip the domestic swill known as Pabst Blue Ribbon?"

"A tribute to your father, the one and only Paul J. Cooper!"

"Gotta love it," Jimmy said. He raised his mug.

They clinked glasses.

"Cheers, brother," Jimmy said.

Bob asked, "So when do you leave?"

"COD tomorrow," Jimmy replied. "I start working at Cedar Point in a couple of days, but I have to check in at the office tomorrow. Kind of nice to be working the place I visited with my family."

"What part will you be working?"

"They have me scheduled for Kiddieland."

"Why in God's name would you work those rides where kids spin around and puke?"

Jimmy grinned. "Aren't you supposed to be the smart one of this duo?" he asked. "Think about it. The staff in Kiddieland is mostly feeee-male."

Bob returned his smile. "I may have the GPA, but you've got the strategy, my man!"

The conversation turned to their past adventures and Jimmy's "special vision."

"Jimmy," Bob said, "you might not have a super-power, you know."

"Does that mean I have to get rid of my spandex suit? Crap, I look good in a cape."

Bob just laughed. "Like I said, you might not have Spidey Sense, but you may have the ability to see the intersection of our dimension with another. I've been doing a lot of theoretical stuff in my off time."

"Which explains your social life," Jimmy said. He mimicked a deep, pseudo-sexy voice, "Baby, wanna come to my room and see my hypotheses on intersecting dimensions?"

They both laughed. "Come on, man," Bob said. "You know girls have always been a little bit of a mystery to me. Besides, I'm saving myself for one of your sisters."

"Oh vomit," Jimmy said. "I may never eat again." He shook his head. "You've always had a thing for Heather – or was it Angie?"

They raised their glasses, clinked, and drank.

"Anyway," Bob said. "Since, I'm starting my master's program next semester, part of my curriculum involves an internship at Edison Labs. Thought I'd ask a few questions and see what I could figure out."

"One geek to another?"

"Well," Bob said, "maybe more than one."

"What do you mean?"

"Buddy," Bob's excitement bubbled. "I'm going to try and get permission for a guest. You're starting your master's program in the fall, too. If I can get you in, why not take a little time and come with me? God knows you've earned a little adventure after everything you've been through."

Jimmy did not hesitate. "I'm in. Won't understand anything you guys say, but I'm sure there's got to be a place I can get a beer."

JIMMY CHECKED INTO Cedar Dorms the next day, one of the residences for the Kiddieland staff. He was thankful he didn't have to work.

Might have had a few too many last night, he thought. *Maybe six or seven.*

The two old friends had lost track of time – and quit counting beers – as they discussed the mysterious worlds they hoped to encounter.

Jimmy opened the door to his room. One of the two beds had been slept – and apparently eaten – in. Jimmy counted three empty Coke cans lying in a nest of an empty Cheetos bag and multiple candy wrappers.

My roomie's here, Jimmy thought.

After a good nap, Jimmy headed over to Operations to pick up his badge, name tag, uniform, and to check on his training schedule.

6:00 AM CAME early. Jimmy had walked the entire park after closing the night before, then spent some time getting to know his roommate, Ben.

At least I feel better this morning than I did yesterday, Jimmy thought after he left to begin his shift.

"Good morning, I'm Andie Pruitt. This is my second summer here. One of my jobs is Training Supervisor. Welcome to Kiddieland."

Andie was tall, lithe, dark-haired, and stunning. She had an easy manner, a quick wit, and a polished presentation. Within an hour, Jimmy was doing trial runs on the rides from all angles – as a passenger, a greeter/seater/safety instructor, and an operator.

"You've got to know these things inside-out," Andie said. "You don't have to repair them, but you may have to trouble shoot from time to time. Now that you've gotten your feet wet, let's tackle the big boys: Bumper Cars and the Carrousel."

Andie could not stop smiling. "This is my favorite ride to work on. It gives off a nice breeze, so while everyone else is melting, at least you get to cool off a little. You gotta nail the spiel."

She put on her best Don Pardo voice. "Welcome to the Kiddieland Carousel, please watch your step as you enter and exit the ride. There is no side-saddle, backward, or double riding. Please remain seated at all times. Parents are always welcomed to join our younger guests. If you want to accompany your child, please stand to the inside of the animal your child chooses. Place one hand on your child's back and one on the nearest pole. If anyone gets dizzy, sit down immediately, and one of our helpful staff members will assist you. As always, enjoy you day here at Cedar Point!"

"You ever thought about a career as a television announcer?" Jimmy asked.

"I wish," Andie said. She leaned towards Jimmy and whispered. "Full disclosure – some of our employees don't like to close down this ride at the end of the evening. They say it's haunted."

"You don't believe that do you?" Jimmy asked. He kept his voice skeptical, but his pulse quickened.

"I don't know," Andie said. "Last week, I was the last one here. It was after midnight. Right after I put the cover on the control board, I looked up and – well – I thought I saw something or someone, sitting on the armored horse."

JIMMY GOT INTO the swing of things quickly. While being a good employee required attentiveness – sloppiness could lead to injury – nothing was very complex. In fact, there were days when the responsibilities were mind-numbingly routine. Still, Jimmy knew every ride was someone's first time, so he worked hard to remain enthusiastic and friendly.

Nineteen young adults were working Kiddieland – three guys – 16 girls. Jimmy liked the odds. Long hours on the job led to long evenings on the town. A month in, Jimmy requested a transfer to the late afternoon - evening shift. Given his light complexion (and his continuing recovery) he preferred the cooler time of the day. More importantly, Andie worked the late shift.

Two weeks into his new assignment, Jimmy closed the carrousel for the first time. He'd worked the ride a lot but had never seen anything weird. He opened the small door underneath the mechanical beast – time to power things down. He slid the massive power handle to the "Off" position and listened as the ride groaned its way to sleep.

When he locked the door, he looked around. No moon – a gloomy evening.

And nothing else.

More than a little disappointed, Jimmy trudged towards the office to clock out. He noticed Ben shutting down the Octo-Whip. Jimmy despised the ride. Most of the young riders who got off were a little disoriented because of the centrifugal force they'd endured. Invariably, someone tried to exit the wrong way or cracked a knee on one of the eight cars.

When Jimmy had "Octo-Wipe" duty, his shirt was invariably covered in tears, snot, or dried vomit.

Jimmy waved and kept walking. He saw Andie. "Need some help shutting down Bumps?" he asked.

"Sure," she said. "I see chivalry is not dead."

Jimmy walked over and helped push the cars into storage position. When Andie shut off the lights, they walked along the path leading to the dorms.

"Hey," Andie said, "What gives over at the carousel. Didn't you just shut that down? Management will have your ass if you didn't do it right."

Jimmy stopped mid-stride. A white mist covered everything – the pointed top, the glittering flags, the elephants, lions, and giraffes.

"Eddie," he said.

"What?" Andie looked at him, her head cocked.

"Nothing," Jimmy said. "I did it right." He was afraid to ask, but he had to. "What do you see?"

Andie's voice wavered a little – like someone speaking into a strong wind. "For a second, I thought I saw someone sitting on the armored horse."

"Seriously?"

"Seriously," she said. "A kid – a little kid. Very dark hair – maybe seven or so. And then, he was gone."

Jimmy decided to wait.

Andie continued. "No – I must be tired. There's nothing."

"If anything was ever there," Jimmy said. But he knew…he knew.

"Right," Andie said. "I probably need more fluids during the day."

"Well, I guarantee we need some fluids after we change, right?"

Andie came to a jump stop, then bounced to face Jimmy.

"You move like Bluto outside the sorority in *Animal House*," he said.

"Well," Andie said, a mischievous smile on her face, "last one back buys the first round."

She pushed him and sped away. Jimmy stumbled, recovered, and gave chase. He didn't make much of an effort to catch her, however.

There are worse things than buying a drink for a pretty girl, he thought.

EVERY NIGHT, JIMMY walked past the carousel before he turned in for the night. By the end of the summer, he'd seen the white Shimmer three times – about once a month. The appearance coincided with the new moon – when the sky was darkest.

The second time, Jimmy saw the boy. The child sat on the armored horse, swinging his legs like he didn't have a care in the world. Jimmy stepped onto the carousel with caution, his hands raised in a sign of peaceful intent.

The boy, young and dark like Andie said, wore a floppy hat, a white shirt, and baggy pants held in place with wide, bright red suspenders.

The boy opened his mouth. "Thank you for the ride, sir."

Then he was gone, and the Shimmer absorbed into the ceramic animals. There was no portal.

The last appearance came on Jimmy's last night. Jimmy saw the Shimmer from across the park. Instead of heading towards it, he went over to Bumps.

"Hey, Andie."

She looked up and held up her index finger. Jimmy waited while she shut off the lights and secured the safety gate. She trotted over.

"'Sup?" she asked.

"I want you to come see something," he said.

They walked in the direction of the Shimmer.

"You see anything?" he asked.

"How can I," Andie said. "It's like a tomb – no moon – no stars."

They passed through the safety gate and stepped onto the carousel – Andie a few steps behind Jimmy.

"See anything?" he asked.

"Jimmy." He turned. Andie was standing, hands on her hips. "Seriously, dude," she said. "You need to step up your game. If you wanted to go make out, man up and ask— Oh Wow!"

The last two words were spoken so quietly, they barely registered. Andie pointed over Jimmy's shoulder. Her eyes were the size of Frisbees.

Jimmy turned slowly but he already knew what was behind him.

The little boy, clad as before, waved from the armored horse. Jimmy felt Andie pressing into him. He felt her breath on his ear.

"What the hell?" she said.

Jimmy waved. The boy smiled.

"Ask him something." Andie sounded like someone running out of air.

"What's your name?" Jimmy asked.

"Bishwa."

Sounds like a little lamb.

"Anyone with you?" Jimmy asked.

The ride was off, but the child bobbed up and down. His longish hair streamed behind him as if in a breeze.

"Grandma and grandpa brought me – but I don't see them now."

Andie worked up the courage to join the friendly interrogation. "Where do you live?"

"In a nice place with my parents and grandparents."

"Is it heaven?"

"No. we don't believe in Heaven."

Jimmy spoke over his shoulder. "He's from the subcontinent," he said. "Probably Nepal. I went to OSU with a guy who sounded like this."

Bishwa settled onto the saddle; his hair quit moving and fell to his shoulders.

"Thank you for the ride, sir," he said.

"Where did he go?" Andie said. "And – what – the – hell – was – that?"

Jimmy spent the rest of the night explaining to Andie how he knew the little boy was going to be there. He had to go back a long way – all the way to Bellevue…and the attic. When he finished, she stared at him.

"This isn't bullshit, is it?" she asked. "I can tell. This isn't a joke."

"Absolutely not," he said. "I've lived with this for a long time."

"Where's Bishwa from?"

"Based on my experience – and the theories I worked out with Bob – I'm guessing Limbo. And I bet he'll be back."

"SOUNDS LIKE YOU had a hell of a summer," Bob said.

"Yep," Jimmy said. "Let's hit Papa Joe's, and I'll brief you on everything."

The place was packed, and the beer was cold. "Bob," Jimmy said, "I want to find Josh. I know he's out there. I think we can analyze the patterns and unravel the mystery."

Bob was uncharacteristically serious. "We've been doing this a long time, buddy," he said. "You know I'm in, but I'll question everything – I'll challenge every hypothesis. But I'm in this to the end – just like always."

"I think we need my brothers."

"Yep," Bob said. "Couldn't hurt to have two jarheads on the team."

Jimmy held his mug aloft. "Adventurers and Friends," he said.

Bob tapped his glass against Jimmy's. "Friends and Adventurers," he said.

When they put their glasses down, Bob said, "Oh, by the way, I got permission for you to come to Edison Labs. Dr. Palmer wants to meet you."

CHAPTER 27
EDISON LAB

FALL 1993

"THANK YOU FOR taking time to show us around today, Dr. Palmer," Bob said.

"Mr. Bellard," Dr. Palmer said, "Your professors tell me you are on the fast track at OSU to becoming Dr. Bellard. We are always looking for top talent here, and your paper on *Quantum Fluctuation Theory and Alternate Realities* has piqued our interest. I have a few questions about the Veil Identification Theory you proposed in your paper."

Bob sounded like the farmer who won "Best Cucumber" at the County Fair. "Well, thank you, sir. Whenever you wish, I'd be honored." Bob pointed to Jimmy. "I'd like you to meet someone. Coop – I mean, Jimmy Cooper. He's my roommate from OSU and my lifelong friend."

Palmer's handshake exuded confidence. He tried the time-honored "up and over" move of dominant personalities. Jimmy held the grasp firm at vertical and saw a flash of recognition – and respect in the scientist's eyes.

"Jimmy is it?"

"Yes, sir – Jimmy Cooper."

"Well, Doctor Cooper."

Another test. "Not yet," Jimmy said. "Someday."

"Well, until then, Jimmy, welcome to Edison Laboratories."

Bob jumped in. "Jimmy majored in psychology."

"Anything specific you like?" Palmer asked.

"A bit of neuropsychology, child psychology, and parapsychology," Jimmy said.

"Quite the pair you two are," Palmer said without any sarcasm. He was impressed by the young men. "I think you will both find some interesting things here."

Dr. Palmer guided Jimmy and Bob on an extensive tour. They visited areas associated with chemical, energy, biological, nuclear, and computing science. Each section demonstrated cutting edge technology and innovation.

Jimmy leaned into Bob. "Close your mouth, you're drooling on the floor."

"Ever seen anything like this?" Bob asked.

"It's pretty special, but try not to embarrass me, okay?"

The old buddies smiled and walked into Palmer's office.

Dr. Palmer sat behind an expansive desk, while Jimmy and Bob plopped onto an overstuffed sofa.

"Bob," Dr. Palmer said, "would you be so kind as to expand on your work in Columbus?"

"Certainly," Bob said. "I need a little runway room – it's a little involved."

Jimmy trusted his friend but hoped Bob would not delve too deeply into his paranormal research. The area was often viewed like voodoo in scientific circles.

"Please continue," Palmer said.

"Jimmy and I have a long history of studying what you might call the abnormal. It started with the usual childhood interests, including Bigfoot, UFOs, Loch Ness, ghosts, and the Mothman. Jimmy began to consider these events as stemming from the unconscious mind, hence his research into psychology. In contrast, I began to look at these phenomena as potentially manifesting from alternate realities."

Palmer's shoulder slumped – but only a little. "You are not suggesting these creatures exist, are you?"

"No, not implicitly. Jimmy is studying whether sightings and the like present themselves in the human mind through psychological factors, possibly even through extrasensory perception. I wonder if they are vestiges of the past, present, or future, almost like double exposure on a film. The differences of reality would be due to shared time and space."

The slumping shoulders disappeared. "Interesting – potentially provocative," Palmer said. "But I am not sure how one would prove such a thing through physics."

"I am not exactly sure either - right now," Bob said. "However, if I am correct, we need to investigate time, our fourth dimension, and dimensions five through seven with considerably more diligence."

Bob was rolling now. Jimmy had seen his friend get fired up. "As you know, we can only perceive time in a linear fashion now – a human limitation. However, if time is flexible, we raise the possibility of two distinct times and, by extension, two distinct locations overlapping and occupying the same space simultaneously. Once we establish the possibility of multiple dimensions, a creature such as a large, hairy, bi-pedal animal might exist in an alternate reality, especially given our evolutionary history. I am not claiming anything like that lives on Earth now, but it might exist in a concurrent and wholly different time and space. If our worlds happen to share the same space by some cosmic accident, then the 'other place' (Bob used air quotes) might appear to us in a visible/tangible way during the incidence of overlap."

Dr. Palmer stroked his chin. "I understand a bit better. You hope some of the quantum collision experiments we are doing here might provide the information you need to postulate – or prove – a theory of multiple dimensions or alternate realities. Truly fascinating! If we were able to show this overlap in some way, you could expand upon your work."

"Exactly," Bob replied.

"Dr. Palmer," Bob said, "without your work here, and that of your colleagues at The European Organization for Nuclear Research in Geneva, we might never understand some of our Universe's complexities. If we are able to prove the existence of other dimensions, we will eventually ascertain how to observe them. More importantly – and of greater scientific interest – we might determine how to control our intersection with them."

Jimmy's eyes were beginning to droop. "Well," he said, "it'll all be fun and games until one of you guys opens a black hole and we all disappear."

Palmer looked like he'd smelled something unpleasant. He was about to explain the lunacy of Jimmy's joke when Bob interrupted.

"Jimmy knows that isn't true; he's just fooling around."

"Seriously," Jimmy said, "let's say we can verify other dimensions, realities, or universes, do either of you worry about whether we could accidentally tear the curtain, so to speak – you know, rip the fabric separating the worlds and cause some cataclysmic and irreversible overlap?"

"You have a point, Jimmy," Dr. Palmer responded. The skepticism on his face had been replaced by a look of respect. It wasn't often a non-scientist made so much scientific sense. "As of now, we are simply colliding subatomic particles into one another to determine if some slip out of our Universe into another. If so, we might be able to verify existence. We need more power, however. Our current calculations indicate we are nowhere near the force needed to reach the – what's the best description – the, ah, puncture level. Even if we could locate the wall between realities, we are not equipped to punch through."

Jimmy raised his hand.

Palmer laughed. "The Chair recognizes the distinguished academician from Ohio State University,"

At the same time, Bob and Jimmy said, "*The* Ohio State University."

Putting on a stuffy British accent, Palmer said, "Quite so…please proceed Mr. Cooper."

"I know this is not my field of study," Jimmy said, "but maybe you don't need a bomb blast. Maybe the only thing you require is a pin prick."

"A legitimate and salient point," Palmer said. "That is one of the reasons I wanted to discuss Bob's Theory on Veil Identification. I'd like a better understanding on the thickness or viscosity of the veils."

"Doctor," Bob asked, "do any of your tests account for the level of thickness to the veil?"

"No," Palmer said. "We don't even know if other universes exist. So, I am not sure the thickness would matter."

Bob stood and began to pace. "Imagine if you will, the fabric of our Universe looks like a soap bubble. There's another bubble – a parallel universe – close by. Perhaps the two bubbles share a common wall – one side is the interior of our world—"

Palmer interrupted. "The other side forms an interior wall of World Two."

"Precisely," Bob said. "The worlds, though technically connected in a physical sense, remain completely separate – but, and here's the important part, *not by much.*"

Bob picked a paper clip from Palmer's desk and began to straighten it. He held a metal point in front of him. "What it we figure out how to (he jabbed forward with the point and made a popping noise with his lips) burst through the wall? Would we have conjoined bubbles – a three-dimensional Venn Diagram? Would we create something new?"

"Or," Dr. Palmer's voice was grave, "would we destroy two worlds at the same time?"

"Precisely," Bob said. "Now for the sake of argument, let's imagine our Universe's surface is a bit heartier, such as human skin. When Jimmy and I were young, we both pricked our fingers and then held them up to one another to be blood brothers. It was a simple rite of passage for boys back in the early '80s. We shared surface area but did not merge into a single being. If the surface of our Universe is more like human skin, we may have certainly shared some of our biological information from time to time (albeit in minute amounts), but we have never blended into a single, indistinguishable cosmic blob."

"How do you propose we would recognize the difference?" Dr. Palmer asked, now understanding why Bob was such a highly regarded student.

"Well, it's conjecture at this point," Bob said, "but if another universe leaked into ours – as in the human skin example – I image we might absorb bits and pieces without any drastic changes.

Bob had wandered into Jimmy's field.

"Let's look at the false memory phenomenon," Jimmy said. "Do you remember Mr. Roger's Neighborhood?"

Dr. Palmer nodded. "Won't you be…m'neighor. Of course."

"Okay, in the theme song, most everyone remembers the song lyrics as *It's a beautiful day in the neighborhood,* then it goes on from there."

Dr. Palmer said, "Yes, that is it."

"But it isn't. The lyrics say, 'It's a beautiful day in *this* neighborhood.' Either the verse has changed, or we have a mass false memory. My guess is, as the veil breaks down, we will begin to see an increased number of these false mass memories, the human skin analogy."

"If the universes were significantly different," Bob said, "such as alternate realities, and the surfaces were like bubbles, we just might permanently live in a world with Nessie, Bigfoot, and UFOs."

Dr. Palmer, deep in thought, said, "You have given me a great deal to consider. I have some colleagues, Dr. Kline and Dr. Springer. We were doing a bit of this research in the early '70s when we ran into something highly unusual – 1973 to be precise. We have yet to replicate the experiment, but I will certainly postulate your theory at our next meeting. Interesting stuff."

Jimmy said, "When in 1973?"

"Spring," Palmer said. "We witnessed a small, spherical anomaly in the chamber. It is kind of famous around here – a horror story of sorts. We saw (he paused as if unsure about sharing) – we saw an appendage – hand like – definitely non-human."

An awkward silence smothered the room. Palmer stood.

"Mr. Bellard, when you are ready, please consider joining us here at Edison. We could use a mind like yours. And Mr. Cooper, you have some very interesting observations – for a psychology major. No offense."

"None taken."

They shook hands; Bob and Jimmy headed for the door.

"A pleasant evening to you both," Palmer said. He closed the door.

CHAPTER 28
INSIDE THE SHIMMER: JOSH
AUGUST – TWO YEARS AFTER ENTRY

A NOTHER WINTER PASSED. Annu and Evie now let Josh go outside alone. He knew the ways of the Stompers, and he was faster without Evie. He'd been spotted a few times, but he could outrun the beasts, so he didn't worry too much unless they were in large packs. The only one that scared him was Yellow Fang – the red one – the smart one – the leader.

One afternoon, Josh spotted the Shimmer – a silver arch just over the nearest hill. Without Annu to stop him, he decided to see if he could get close to it. He moved quietly through the brush, sniffing constantly. His nose would tell him if a Stomper got close. They smelled worse than bear scat and three-day-old dead possum, combined.

Josh checked the wind – out of the west. He knew the location of the Stompers' camp.

Just avoid a hunting party.

Josh put his finger in his mouth, then held his wet digit above his head.

Still downwind.

As he got closer to the Shimmer, he spotted Yellow Fang at the head of a column of Stompers. They were moving towards the silver arena. They moved with slow intent, no growling, no chest bashing. They were neither hunting nor attacking.

They're traveling.

Moving as fast as he dared and with the stealth of a prowling panther, Josh followed at a safe distance and stayed on the high ground. Stompers were strong and unbelievably agile, but their lack of footspeed was exacerbated whenever they tried to labor up a hill.

Josh was now close to the Shimmer, an ever-widening wall of Silver mist. He passed through it. Yellow Fang and his pack were walking on a wide, black path – it had a solid white line running down the middle. It looked familiar, like something Josh had seen in his old life.

A road – that's what it's called, he thought. *We used to get in...the car...and...ride*

The Stompers disappeared behind a low hill. Josh remained concealed until he could reacquire the Stompers' location. He then began to hear someone approaching from the west. It was faint but growing louder.

He saw movement. He looked left along the road. A figure came through the Shimmer – a human – a girl – an older girl – someone who looked more like... *Mommy.*

She was running – leisurely pace. A brunette

ponytail bobbed out of her baseball hat. She glanced at her wrist, checking her pace – her heartrate – all the things runners think is important.

She sniffed, wiped her nose, shook her head in disgust, then looked up and stopped dead in her tracks. The road ahead was blocked by a wall of hair, gleaming eyes, and bared teeth. He heard the woman scream, and began to run back towards the way she came. Josh noticed she wasn't that far into the Shimmer.

He stood up and yelled. "Run!"

Without looking to see who shouted the warning, the woman turned and sprinted in the other direction. At the same time, Yellow Fang and the rest began a lumbering towards her. It took time for the Stompers to gain any speed but soon they were moving like a fleet of 18-wheelers rolling down a steep hill out of control. Two of the younger Stompers picked up speed by dropping to all fours and running like bears.

The woman looked over her shoulder. Even from a distance, Josh could see the terror painted on her face. She screamed again, caught her toe in a pothole, and skidded across the blacktop on her palms.

The woman rolled like a paratrooper at the end of a jump, came up on her feet, and continued her flight – although limping hard on the left side. Josh's breath came in short spurts as he watched the younger beasts gaining – now less than 20 feet behind the woman.

Fifteen feet…

…the wall of the Shimmer, only five feet away…

…10 feet…

…Josh saw one of the pursuers gather and leap forward – a vicious dive, claws extended…

…Sheer terror-induced fatigue set in and the woman stumbled into, and through the Shimmer. The Stomper also went through the Shimmer mere seconds after her. Josh heard a bellowing howl as the Stomper returned through the Shimmer empty handed. Josh knew, she had safely returned to her world outside of the Shimmer.

Yellow Fang stopped his pursuit and howled in frustration and rage. He looked in Josh's direction. Perhaps he could still have some success on this hunt.

But the boy was already gone.

September – Two Years After Entry

The leaves were turning again. Josh was on his third pair of sandals, and Evie had made him another "squirrel dress." The world around him was strange. He could communicate with Evie and Annu, but all they cared about was food, water, and the Stompers.

Sunset was not far off when Annu came into the cave. Josh was alone. He signaled to Annu that Evie had gone out to pick berries.

The color drained from Annu's face. He signaled, "Follow," and darted deeper into the cave. Josh followed along the series of tunnels stringing their family's dwelling with other caves. Josh did not spend any time in the other caves. Why would he? In the two season cycles he'd been with Annu and Evie, Josh had seen exactly four children. He was glad they had not become his friends. The Stompers specialized in catching little ones. Now, there were no other children – anywhere.

Annu and Josh crawled out from underneath the boulder concealing the northern entrance to the cave complex. They could hear the Stompers as soon as they surfaced.

At the base of the hill, about a hundred yards away, a cluster of juvenile Stompers had surrounded Evie. She was trapped in a ring of hair, teeth, claws, and stink. One of the Stompers, a dark brown male about six feet tall, jumped towards Evie. When she shrank back, she ran into a tan female who sent her sprawling with a sweeping backhand. The earth shook as the Stompers jumped up and down with glee.

Another one picked Evie up by the hair and hurled the small woman headlong into the base of a tree. Evie screamed in pain.

They want to torture her – play with her – before they kill her, Josh thought.

He stepped forward but felt a firm hand on his shoulder. He turned. Annu shook his head.

Josh watched as the Stompers batted Evie back and forth. *Like the Pong game – like when I played with Jimmy.*

Josh heard a shout – a human shout. He looked to his right. Annu had positioned himself on a rock and was yelling at the Stompers. The young creatures stopped their game and stared as Annu picked up a large rock and hurled it at them. The stone hit the dark brown Stomper between the eyes.

Josh knew it was not luck. Annu could kill a bird in flight with the strength of his arm and a projectile. Annu threw another stone and found his mark again. He began to jeer at the Stompers, mimicking their movements and mocking their grunts.

The dark brown Stomper took three steps towards the base of the hill. Annu hit him with another stone. This time, Annu laughed – a scorn-filled screech of derision. He pelted the young Stomper again, this time in the groin, and kept laughing.

Josh heard an unmistakable roar – Yellow Fang. He saw the red, monstrous leader of the Stompers at the edge of the forest. The creature's eyes brimmed with murderous rage. Yellow Fang bellowed and pointed at Annu.

The young Stompers climbed up the hill, sure their target would run for his life. But Annu stood firm on the rock, hollering his defiance even as the beasts began to tear his limbs from his body.

Josh slid under the boulder and beckoned Evie towards him. Evie arrived, bruised and battered but otherwise unharmed, Josh curled up in her arms and cried himself to sleep.

Annu had made the ultimate sacrifice.

PART III
QUIETLY INTO THE NIGHT

CHAPTER 29
REUNION
LATE SUMMER 2003

D
R. ROBERT BELLARD (PhD, Quantum Physics, Cal Tech) loved working at Edison. Being away from home for six years had been tough, but his perseverance had helped him land his dream job. In the past three years, he had perfected several techniques for studying veil density. He was steadily working to verify the existence of "bubble" universes.

Partnering with Lionel Kline offered Bob the enviable opportunity to work alongside a legend – and a fellow Cal Tech grad. The colleagues were studying the time and space factors impacting the relative strength or weakness of the veil. Bob postulated the closer the given universe, the thinner the veil and, potentially, the bigger the overlap – he just hadn't proved it yet.

Jimmy spent his days at OSU as a member of the faculty in the Psychology Department. He was on tenure track and had already made some waves in the academic community with his papers on parapsychological phenomena.

Bob's voice came through the phone. "How's it going, man?"

The old friends chatted as they did every first Wednesday of the month – 8:00 AM. They'd committed to keeping in touch. As Bob liked to say, neither of them believed in "disposable friendships."

"Everything's good, buddy."

"How are your brothers?" Bob asked.

"Matt's running his construction business; Mark's traveling the globe with his work. He should complete his mechanical engineer degree in May."

"Hard to believe those guys got out of the Marines without getting locked up."

Jimmy laughed. "They've come a long way since the Tornado Twins."

"Clean up on Aisle Five," Bob said.

"More like on the lawn," Jimmy said. "When Mom came home and saw all that furniture outside the window, I thought she was going to blow an embolism."

"We're still on for the lake, right?" Bob asked.

"Starting Memorial Day weekend – The Team will get together again."

"And Stacie, Bridget, and Andie will be as thrilled as they always are, Bob said. "See why I haven't gotten married?"

"You might have a better chance of meeting, you know, *anybody* if you'd get out of that lab coat and hit the town every so often," Jimmy said.

He could hear the resignation in Bob's voice. "I

know, Jimmy – I just want to figure this stuff out so badly."

"Buddy," Jimmy said, "you know I love you – I just don't want you by yourself. I think your dad said the same thing – right?"

"Yeah," Bob said. "About two weeks before his heart attack, he said his biggest regret was not finding someone after Mom because when we all left the house, he was alone."

No one spoke for a while. Jimmy could hear Bob fidgeting with a Rubik's cube.

"What's your best time?" Jimmy asked.

"I can solve a 3-by-3 in less than 10 seconds," Bob said.

"Nerd."

"Dork."

The tension alleviated: they turned the conversation to their plans. They always spent a week at the family lake house where they swam, played tag football on the beach, drank (way too much), and – armed with a battered copy of *Ohio Ghostly Greats* – visited sites with, as Matt liked to say, "potential for weird crap." Most of the places proved worthless (although Jimmy had seen a couple of Shimmers) but this year, Bob was particularly hopeful about Vermillion Orphanage. The old home had burned to the ground in the early part of the Twentieth Century, before killing dozens of adults and children. After midnight, one could hear the cries of the children who had perished – or so the legend went.

A COOL BREEZE blew from the east. The guys sat on what was left of the orphanage's foundation and sipped cans of beer. The full moon cast long shadows across the ruins. Bob looked up and shuddered.

"Ugh," he said. "Bats."

"All the stuff you've seen, and those little things bother you?" Mark asked. "You are one weird dude."

"Takes one to know one," Bob said.

Mark reached into his pocket. "Hey doc," he said. "I brought you something."

He withdrew his hand and lifted his middle finger.

"Somehow, that never gets old," Jimmy said. "Just remember, you may be a combat veteran, but if Mom ever sees you do that…"

Mark flinched. "I'd rather take my chances with that thing we locked in the attic."

Matt straightened. "Hear that?"

They all nodded.

"Kind of freaky," Jimmy said. "Probably just an animal or the wind going through the trees just right, but it sounds a little like a baby crying."

"Or it could be the first time we've actually found something," Mark said. "We've been at it a long time."

"You getting bored?" Jimmy asked.

"With seven days of nothing to do but screw around and drink beer? I don't think so."

Bob tapped Jimmy on the shoulder. "See anything?"

"Nope."

"Any chance you've lost your touch – you know, like aged out of your special power?" Matt asked.

"Possible," Jimmy said. "Last time I saw a Shimmer was two years ago."

"Sorry, buddy," Bob said. "More like five – Ohio State Reformatory – 1997."

The Shimmers had been gray and white, but the guys had not established contact with anyone – or anything.

I wonder, Jimmy thought. *It's been too long – maybe I don't have it anymore.*

Bob held up his hand – the group fell quiet while the physicist made an audio recording. He switched off his portable equipment. "Everyone back in the car."

"You scared, Egon?"

"You know better," Bob said. "I just want to test a theory."

They piled into Jimmy's Yukon and headed to the highway. A hundred yards from the access ramp, Bob said, "Pull over."

Before the car stopped, he was out of the car with this equipment.

"What the hell is he doing now?" Matt asked.

"There's a fine line between genius and insanity," Jimmy said.

Several minutes later, Bob clambered into the front seat.

"Listen to this! First selection is from the orphanage."

They heard the moan-like noises.

"Now, this," Bob said.

The noises were different, most certainly cars zooming by on the highway.

Mark shook his head. "Different noise – but it's the same pattern. The trees and the distance distort everything and make it sound like babies crying."

Bob's face was glum.

"Another lead shot to hell," Matt said.

"Man, let's get back to the cabin," Mark said. "Wait…I can hear something."

"What?" The other three leaned in.

"It's a voice…it says…it says… 'Mark…Mark…I'm cold…I'm so cold…come help me."

"Is it a child?" Jimmy asked.

"No, moron," Mark said. "It's the beer at the lake house."

They all laughed, and Jimmy gunned the engine. On the way back, Bob broke the silence.

"Fellas, I love doing this every summer, but we're not kids anymore. We need a strategy. I've been working on something at Edison. It's a little out there but it's all I've got."

"Hit me," Jimmy said.

Matt and Mark immediately went into their Pat

Benatar routine. Matt played air drums, Mark held a fake microphone and sang at the top of his lungs.

Hit me with your best shot

Why don't you hit me with your best shot

Hit me with your best shot

Fire aw-a-a-a-a-y!

"My God," Jimmy asked. "How is it you have gotten worse?"

Mark looked hurt. "Whatdaya mean, bro," he said. "That's primo rock n' roll."

"Primo, my ass," Jimmy said. "And Matt, you keep dropping beats on the drums."

"Bite me," Matt said.

Bob rapped his knuckles on the car's ceiling. "Hello," he said. "Anybody home."

Jimmy, Mark, and Matt chimed in at the same time, "Buehler…Buehler!"

"Shut up," Bob said. There was a little edge in his voice.

"Sorry man," Jimmy said. "We're just having a good time."

"I know," Bob said. "I'm just a little wound up."

"Continue, Professor," Matt said. "No more concerts."

"Yeah, sorry," Mark said.

"Okay," Bob said. "Dr. Kline and I have been going over all the data from a mysterious event in the lab in 1973."

"That's the same year Josh disappeared," Jimmy said. "If they caused this—"

"Relax," Bob said before Jimmy could get too fired up. "We haven't found anything to indicate a connection, but the timing is interesting. It could indicate a pattern in the chaos."

He looked over his shoulder, "And if anyone of you chuckleheads say, 'There's a disturbance in The Force,' I will stop the car and leave you out here for the bears."

Matt and Mark looked at each other and elected survival over humor.

Bob continued. "Based on the evidence we've seen and adding in the events in Bellevue—"

"You mean the man from hell in the attic?" Jimmy asked.

"Yep," Bob said. "Anyway, everything points to a potential appearance of another Shimmer in late fall of this year – possibly sometime around Thanksgiving."

Matt's voice came from the back without any hint of his customary sarcasm. "So, we go from not knowing crap to a semi-specific date? How's that possible, Egon?"

"Bear with me here – remember it's all theory." Bob eyes bored into the road. "When I was investigating the incident in the lab, I discovered there were a number of other disappearances in '73 – about 10. They all vanished within a month or so. At the same time, there was a spike in Bigfoot sightings."

"Ten years later, Edison labs started keeping tabs on anomalies– Bigfoot reports, UFO sightings, stuff like that. We ascertained there had been a similar explosion of missing persons in Dundee, Michigan, about that time – a decade after all the stuff in Ohio."

"Question," Jimmy said. "Correlation or causation?"

"Very good," Bob said. "I believe the missing persons are a result of Bigfoot encounters." He heard the guys in the back shifting in skepticism. "Hang on, hear me out. There was another event in Potterville, Michigan, in 1993."

"So?" Matt asked. "Do any of you have a map in your car?"

"Reach in the pocket behind my seat," Jimmy said. "There's an atlas."

"Roger that," Matt said.

Jimmy pulled into the drive. "Bring it inside."

Jimmy nudged Bob as they headed for the front door. "Do you remember what I told you about what I told Mom when Josh disappeared?"

"You know I do," Bob said. "'Poor Josh – he's stuck in the ball with the monkey.' You always thought it had something to do with monkey in the middle."

"Yep," Jimmy said. "But I talked to her last week. That's not how she remembers it."

Bob stopped walking. Matt and Mark went into the house. They knew better than to disturb the two old friends in the middle of a heart to heart.

"How does she remember it – exactly?" Bob asked.

"She says I kept saying *big monkey.*"

Bob nodded. "Exactly the way a three-year-old would describe Bigfoot."

"And the same thing our friend in the attic meant when he said *Yowie*."

"Yep," Bob said. He patted Jimmy on the shoulder, and they walked inside.

Once they were settled, Bob turned to Matt.

"Okay, Matty. You're an expert in orienteering, or so you claim.'"

"10-4," Matt said. "Like Daniel Boone said, 'I've been powerfully confused for a few days in a row, but I've never been lost.'"

Bob smiled. Matt always cracked him up. "Draw a line from Potterville to Dundee."

Matt used the back side of his hunting knife as a straightedge and scored a line on the map.

"Extend the line to the edge of the page, then keep your knife at the same angle it is now."

"Done," Matt said.

Bob slid the atlas out from under Matt's blade and flipped a few pages. He put the atlas back under the knife.

"Here is Ohio." He positioned the book. "Start at the western edge and continue drawing."

Matt complied – then stopped and looked up.

"Son of a bitch," he said.

"What town did you hit, Matt?" Bob asked.

"Bellevue."

"So where does that put our next target?"

Matt flipped the page back to Michigan and moved the knife, and pointed – "Newaygo, Michigan."

Jimmy said, "No kidding, Andie's Aunt Marty and Uncle George live up in that area."

CHAPTER 30
THE CABIN

2003 – DAY 1 - SUNDAY, NOVEMBER 23

A FTER A GREAT debate, they decided, Jimmy's wife, Andie, Matt's wife, Stacie, and Mark's wife, Bridget, would join them for the adventure.

The night before the trip, Bob called. "Mind if I bring someone?" he asked.

"Not sure why Dr. Kline would want to join us in the middle of nowhere for Thanksgiving, but I'm fine with it," Jimmy said.

Please God, let me be wrong, he thought.

"Rest easy, my friend," Bob said. "Her name is Rhonda. I took your advice as soon as I got back from our trip. We've been dating since late June."

"The more the merrier," Jimmy said.

The "cabin" turned out to be an expansive deer lodge. Five separate bedrooms spider-webbed their way from a central den and kitchen. With a woodburning stove in the middle, the cabin was toasty warm when everyone gathered on the overstuffed couches and only slightly "coolish" in the bedrooms. Thick comforters offset any evening chill. The rooms were designed for maximum efficiency but not overly private – counting bunkbeds and the couch, total occupancy - 14.

They headed for the isolated location in Newaygo County (about an hour east of Lake Michigan) in Hummers owned by Matt and Mark. Jimmy rode with Matt. They had a 15-minute lead.

Surprised this thing doesn't have a mounted 50-cal," Jimmy said as they lurched along the heavily-rutted dirt road.

"Couldn't get it in a matching color," Matt said, "but at least the exhaust doubles as a rocket launcher."

"Weather could be a problem," Jimmy said. "Dark skies says a cold front might move in."

"If we get snow, it'll help with tracking," Matt said.

They approached from the west, the most elevated point of the property. The cabin sat in the flat at the base of a small hill. A deep ravine ran along the eastern property line. Undulating hills spotted the horizon to the north and south. The only problem presented by the spectacular landscape was the dense forest.

"Visibility could be an issue," Jimmy said.

Andie snorted. "Who cares? This view is spectacular."

Jimmy's bag contained a week's worth of clothing; Andie had brought enough food for all eight people – for about three months. Jimmy's ever-expanding waistline bore witness to her determination that no one would starve on her watch.

One year after they met at Cedar Point, Jimmy and Andie had married. She moved to Columbus and finished her degree – also in psychology. Her interest lay more on the clinical side – assisting people to develop coping skills, guiding troubled souls towards peace.

She knew Jimmy had gifts. Instead of analyzing, she accepted them and tried to assist Jimmy in every endeavor – however improbable.

Jimmy had been to the cabin a few times before. It belonged to Andie's family, including her parents. They lived just outside of Dowagiac, Michigan, a small town lucky enough to survive the decimation of rural America. Their home sat on Dewey Lake, just out of town.

Earlier that summer, Andie, Jimmy, and Andie's parents, Patrick and Nancy, were sitting on the deck overlooking the lake. It was about an hour and a half after twilight. Jimmy saw fog rolling in from the north. He was ready to point it out when he realized it was an expansive silver Shimmer – the first he'd seen since childhood. He had first thought that maybe Bob's calculations were incorrect, and this was the predicted anomaly, but he soon discovered it was something quite different.

He tried to look casual as he went to the railing. The Shimmer bore a unique checkerboard pattern. Andie, ever attentive, slid up next to him.

"What is it?" she asked.

"See anything to the north?" he asked.

"You didn't marry me because I'm Sacagawea – you married me because I'm irresistible. I get lost when I go to Walmart, remember?" she said. "Do you think I know north?"

"Left," he said. His heart filled with anticipation as it moved closer.

She faked a yawn, stretched, and stole a glance. "Nope."

"Probably nothing," he said.

The silver glow undulated across the sky like a massive bubble floating on an ocean. The Shimmer swept close to the water – and to the house. When the Shimmer passed directly over him, the air turned cold.

Josh.

Nancy said, "Patrick, is there supposed to be a cold front coming through?" but Patrick did not answer the question.

Instead, he said, "Never seen anything like that."

"Neither have I," Andie said.

Oh my God, they can see it.

"What is it?" Patrick asked, his eyes transfixed into the sky above him. Andie, too mesmerized by the incredible sight.

"It came out of nowhere," Andie said.

When Jimmy squeezed her hand, she looked at him.

He put his lips to her ear. "No, it didn't," he said. "Not out of nowhere." She squeezed his hand in understanding, but she knew better than to start the discussion in front of her parents.

Then, she gasped.

"Jesus Christ on a cracker," she said.

A large, pill-shaped craft hovered about 200 yards above the lake's surface. Multicolored beams shone from the ship, reflected off the water, and bounced back up. The craft rotated 90° and moved with purpose until it floated directly over the house.

With the customary calm of a mother in time of crisis, Nancy walked into the house. "Getting the video," she said.

Jimmy could now see the back edge of the Shimmer approaching. Without warning, Andie and Patrick screamed as their feet lifted off the deck. Jimmy flailed with his arms and caught an unmatched pair of ankles: Patrick's left and Andie's right, then wedged his foot under the railing.

His father-in-law and his wife continued to move upwards – slowly – steadily. Jimmy could feel his grip slipping. Warm air brushed his face as the back edge of the Shimmer passed overhead. Then, they fell – Andie on top of Jimmy and Patrick into the hedge on the other side of the rail. Patrick, a physical fitness fanatic, scrambled to his feet. Blood trickled from a scrape on his forehead, but he was fine.

"What in the holy hell was that?" he asked. He sounded more fascinated than frightened.

Andie pushed herself off Jimmy and came up angry. She shrieked into the sky, "Come back here, jerk!"

Despite his pounding heart, Jimmy chuckled. "You are fearless, aren't you, baby?"

Andie locked him with a piercing gaze. "Gone?"

"Mostly," Jimmy said. He could see the retreating silver edge.

"Had to be a UFO," Patrick said.

The screen door banged against the wall. Nancy panned the sky with her camcorder like a machine gunner spraying a battlefield. "Dammit, I missed it."

They gathered themselves, sat, and reviewed the events until late in the evening. Throughout the discussion, Jimmy kept thinking how lucky they had been that Nancy went inside.

If she'd stayed, being three of them, and Jimmy only having two hands, one of them would be on the evening news in a week talking about guys with huge heads, tentacles, and invasive anatomical investigations.

Multiple reports dominated the news for the next few days. The U.S. Army claimed it had "helicopter reconnaissance" training in the area, but no one bought what Patrick labeled as, "Typical government bullshit."

DESPITE ITS BEAUTY and comfort, the cabin did not have electricity; all the food had to be kept on ice. Jimmy had just carried the last of four coolers into the house when the other Hummer roared into the drive. Bob stepped out, beat his chest, and released a Tarzan yell.

"Now, this is what I call a vacation," he said. "Blue skies, cool breezes, soon to be a warm fire, and a little something for the soul to share with my friends." Bob reached in the Cleveland Browns duffle bag on his shoulder and extracted a bottle of Balvenie 25.

Jimmy embraced his friend. "Dr. Cooper," Bob said.

"Dr. Bellard," Jimmy replied.

Rhonda looked at Andie, "What dorks."

Andie hugged Bridget, then exchanged pleasantries with Rhonda.

"Jimmy, help them with their things," Andie said.

Mark and Bridget were already headed inside with their luggage.

"No need," Bob said. He held aloft two middle-sized backpacks. "Got everything we need in here. We travel light."

"My dad was in the Army," Rhonda said. She put on a huffy male voice. "Take only what you need for how long you will be gone. Everything else is unessential."

"Well, if that's all you've got, let's get at that Scotch."

"Not so fast, Kemosabe," Bob said. "These are our clothes, but the sciency stuff is in the back."

He opened the tailgate. Multiple large storage bins filled the back space, each emblazoned with EL.

"Do your colleagues know you stole the entire lab?"

Bob smiled. "Well…some of this stuff is here on, let's say, an unofficial basis. We just need to be damn careful."

Jimmy tugged on the first bin. It didn't move. "What do you have in here, a pipe organ?"

"Some new technical gear for testing in a live field situation. I got a nice grant a few months ago. Nothing dangerous in there, but it's extremely sensitive."

They each grabbed an end and lugged the container into the cabin.

Bob admired the interior. "This place is a fortress. Look at the size of the logs – they could withstand canon fire."

"Hope it doesn't come to that," Matt said. "I've seen enough action to last three lifetimes. But if the situation escalates, we'll need to pay attention to those." He pointed to two large windows, one on either side of the cabin. "Those are areas for potential breach."

Andie laughed. "Think again, General Patton. My family don't play. Those are one-way, military-grade, bulletproof glass. My uncle was always worried about some drunk hunter firing a reckless round."

"Outstanding," Matt said. "Hell yes."

Mark said, "Hell yes indeed."

Bob's girlfriend stepped back. "Don't worry, honey," Bob said. "They're all harmless. But (he pointed to Matt and Mark), keep your finger away from their mouths at dinner time."

Rhonda smiled – a little weakly.

Andie put her arm around Rhonda." Andie said. "The asylum takes some getting used to – it'll be fine."

CHAPTER 31
THE FIRE

SUNDAY NIGHT, NOVEMBER 23

VERYONE ELSE LOUNGED around the fireplace. A single battery-operated camp lantern provided the only illumination.

Matt's voice boomed from the door. "Hey brother, where's the head? I'm about to blow out the back of my pants."

Jimmy laughed. "Damn, you are one classy dude," he said. "Outhouse down the path. Take a light. You don't want to walk up on a wolf or a cougar."

Matt stomped past the group, exaggerating his arm movement. "No need," he said. "Super Gy-rene warrior here."

He flipped his night vision goggles down from the brim of his hat and walked towards the woods.

"Hey, Sergeant Basilone," Jimmy said. "Might want to take this."

He spiraled a roll of towel paper at Matt. "Nice catch," Jimmy said.

"You'd expect nothing less from anyone who wore the same uniform as Gunny Basilone," Matt said. "Medal of Honor winners don't grow on trees, you know."

"Be back in a sec," Matt said – and he disappeared into the dark.

Matt thrashed through the undergrowth for about a hundred yards. He made plenty of noise. Most forest creatures, regardless of ferocity, preferred to avoid human contact. Having relieved himself on the battle-field, Matt saw no need to bother with the outhouse. After ensuring he was downwind, he "dropped trou" and completed his mission.

The second he finished buckling his belt he heard rustling in the bushes behind him. With instinct birthed in combat, he reached for his Beretta M9.

"Damn," he said in a low voice. "I knew I shouldn't have left it. Civilian life is making you soft, Matty."

He flipped his goggles down again and saw a hairy, clawed arm stretch through the branches of a pine tree. He circled to his right.

Create position and distance, he thought. *Give yourself time to react.*

He reached into the lowest pocket of his tactical pants and withdrew his MTech rescue knife. He pressed the lever. The spring-assisted 5-inch blade locked into place.

Better than nothing. When it charges, stick it twice and run like hell.

269

He cocked his arm, preparing to strike when two bear cubs ran past him from the left. The paw extended from the tree and cuffed one of the cubs sideways. Ever the disciplinarian and protector, Mama Bear lumbered into view and put herself between Matt and the cub that was still standing.

She let out a low growl. *She hasn't lowered her head,* Matt thought. *She's warning me – but she's not going to charge unless I piss her off.*

Matt held up his palms – a meaningless gesture in the wild but he wanted to avoid any movement the fidgety mother could interpret as aggressive. She growled again and Matt could smell her fetid breath.

He backed away with great care – never taking his eyes from the mother.

Twelve feet…15 feet…20 feet.

The mother gathered both babies and shooed them into the brush. As she walked away, she glanced over her shoulder at Matt.

"Oh, no ma'am," he said. "I would not dream of messing with your young'uns."

Matt returned for the end of Jimmy's UFO story. He'd heard it before – but it still fascinated him. A crooked grin creased Matt's face when he surveyed the assembled crowd.

Here it comes, he thought. *This should be good.*

"The craft slid overhead," Jimmy said. "Then—"

He broke off and stared into the trees.

"What do you see, honey," Andie asked.

Everyone looked up. A bright light shone from 15 feet off the ground.

"Oh my God, what is that?" Rhonda asked.

Matt stifled a giggle as he watched Bob moving towards his equipment bag with as little noise as possible. He was bending to open the duffle when a high-pitched whistle pierced the night.

Everyone around the fire jumped.

"Hey, Mark," Jimmy said. "Cut it out, asshole. You ruined a great story."

Maniacal laughter filled the night. The light pivoted and revealed Mark, grinning like a lunatic from the branches of a pine tree about 20 feet off the ground.

"Scared the shit out of you, didn't I?" he said.

"Yes, you did," Bridget said. "And your reward is a night on the couch – alone."

The group released a collective, "Ooooooooooooo."

Mark shinnied down, plopped into a rocker, and opened a beer.

"Come on, babe," he said. "That was funny."

"It was," she said. "But you're still on the couch.

Rhonda shook her head. "Bob said you guys were a little different, but I thought he was just kidding."

After Jimmy finished his tale, Mark jumped in.

"I've been waiting for the right time to tell this," he said. "Bridget is the only one who knows it. You mind if I tell 'em?"

Bridget gave the go ahead.

"When I was in Afghanistan, we heard a lot about giants – you know, sort of like Goliath and such."

"We've heard about the Giant of Kandahar, the 10-foot guy shot by the Marines," Bob said.

"Yeah," Jimmy said. "Smelled worse than a skunk."

"Yep," Mark said. "What I'm about to tell you happened before all that. No one knows this story – classified now, but what are they going to do to me?"

Andie frowned. "This already sounds like bullcrap."

Mark's face turned to stone. "It's not," he said. "Cost one of my buddies his life. I was there. It's real as a heart attack."

"Sorry," Andie said.

"No problem," Mark said, "Only reason I believe it is because I saw it – everything."

"Go on, brother," Matt said.

"We were on patrol investigating some caves about a click south of our base in Kowgak. The caves sat above a sheer cliff with only a small shelf, maybe five feet from the entrance. We had to scale a 75-foot sheer face – 10 of us moving up on two different lines. I was fourth on the second cable. Culbertson had already reached the top of the shelf – I was about 40 feet down when we heard this unholy howl followed by quick burst of auto-fire. Culbertson screamed and then came flying over my head. He died on a rocky outcrop at the base of the cliff."

"That's terrible," Bridget said. "My daddy saw men die in combat. Rough, huh?"

"Thanks," Mark said. "It was bad, but it was strange, too."

"How so?" Bob asked.

Mark drew in a deep breath. "Culbertson was a moose – 6'5" – 270 pounds. I was directly below the summit. If he'd taken a running start and dived off, he might have missed me by four feet. Remember, he was in full combat gear and carrying a full load – somewhere between 90 and 120 pounds."

"Okay, so?" Bob said.

"He cleared me by 15 feet – easy," Mark said. "Do the math, Egon. Something propelled him off that cliff with a lot of force."

"Damn," Jimmy said.

"That's not the end of it," Mark said. "Wallace was ahead of me – second place on the first line. As soon as Culbertson took a header, someone yanked on Wallace's rope. He traveled the last 20 vertical feet in under two seconds. Like I said, someone – or something..."

"What happened?" Matt asked. He'd never heard his twin's story either.

"Wallace is a smart cookie. He swung to the side, hit the quick release on his binding about a foot before he reached the top, and grabbed onto the guy below him on the other line. I started humping it down the rope, but I swear, when I looked up, I saw a massive head. I fired a couple of quick bursts and whatever the hell it was got out of dodge."

"Anyone else see it?" Jimmy asked.

"Not in my unit. They were too busy trying to get their asses off that cliff. But we called in air support. I talked to the gunner on one of the Apaches. He said they fired a shitload of ordnance into that cave. When they veered off, something came out. My buddy said it was a 12-foot tall man."

"Twelve?" Bob said. "Sounds like a fishing story to me."

"Maybe," Mark said. "But even if my friend exaggerated by a yard, the dude was still almost two feet taller than anyone in the NBA!"

"Good point," Jimmy said. "And, you have to admit, we've seen some pretty weird things in our lives."

Silence settled over the group – and the temperature started to drop.

After 30 minutes, Andie stood. "I don't know about you guys, but I'm cold. Heading in."

Everyone stood.

"But before we go, let's get something straight," Andie said, "You guys aren't going to sit around for the next six nights and tell ghost stories."

"Of course not, honey," Jimmy said.

Matt started laughing.

"What's so funny?" Jimmy asked.

"Dude, you are so dense," Matt said. "She wasn't asking you a question."

CHAPTER 32
BEEFALO BONES
DAY 2 - MONDAY, NOVEMBER 24, 2003

T HE NEXT MORNING, everyone woke up to find breakfast hot and ready. Matt and Mark, both early risers, had sausage, bacon, hash browns, and pancakes on a portable grill. Mark presented freshly sliced melon and an assortment of pastries. There was even a pitcher of Bloody Mary on the table to help fend off the worst of the hangovers. The group gathered around the picnic table.

"Well, George and Marty won't be here until later today. I think around 4:00 PM. What's the plan?" Jimmy asked.

Stacie liked to take charge. "Well, we could drive over to Lake Michigan to check out the sights, stop back at the Newaygo Tavern on the way back, and come back here and play a few board games before they get here for dinner."

"Scenery, beverages, games, and food – all sounds good to me," Bob said.

They cleaned up from breakfast, loaded into the

Hummers, and took off on their morning adventure. They came home in time for a late lunch and had just finished a cutthroat game of Monopoly when George and Marty wheeled up the drive. Just before their truck stopped, Andie looked around. "Remember guys," she said, "my uncle has lived up here for decades. He's not quite as polished as the rest of my family."

George unloaded two cases of wine. Marty handed Andie and Bridget a pumpkin pie.

"We'll save these for the feast on Thanksgiving, but the wine is for now," Marty said.

Jimmy was the first to greet his aunt and uncle. Even though they were related only by marriage, Andie's entire family treated Jimmy like one of their own.

"George, Marty, thank you so much for allowing us to use your cabin," Jimmy said.

"Hey, Jimmy," Marty said.

Marty hugged everybody in the cabin with the ferocity of a Sumo wrestler. George, a bit more reserved, greeted everyone graciously but left the hand-to-hand combat to his wife.

Andie and Rhonda served heaping bowls of piping hot chili.

"Watch out," Jimmy said. "Burns both ways."

"Going in and coming out," Matt said.

Marty roared with laughter. George offered a thin smile. The sun was slipping into bed for the night when they settled around the firepit outside and George began – and the transformation commenced. He looked at each person around the fire, then launched into an animated recitation.

Born actor, Jimmy thought. *Introverted until the curtain goes up.*

"Alright, kids," George said, "I have one hell of a story to share. Try not to wet your pants." He paused as he looked from one face to the next. When he was sure everyone was settled, he began.

"About a month ago, up at my home," he turned and pointed towards west, "I was sitting by the lake enjoying the sunset, just like every evening. There were birds, raccoons, rabbits, deer – even saw a moose, I think – a little slice of heaven. The animals all creep out of the tree line for a little water, you know. Well, that night was different. Nuttin' was movin' – I mean nuttin'. Very unusual – sorta spooky. Dint hear much - dint overthink it. Just sat next to m'fire and watched things unfold. Ya' know, it's a peaceful existence—"

Marty's voice issued a sift prod, "Get to it, George. You don't need to tell the story in real time."

"All right, dear, don't rush a master in the middle of a tale. Anywho – nuttin' moved. All of a sudden-like, Rousse, that's m'dog – world's best birder he is. He can find a pheasant—"

Marty cleared her throat. The second warning.

"Sorry – get a little carried off sometimes. So, Rousse takes to sniffin' – nose goin' 90-to nuttin'. He's part wolf – alpha predator type. His hackles stand up like porcupine quills – dog looked like he'd signed up for the Marines with that prickly hair. But his tail's all tucked between his legs, and he's whimpering. I've seen that hound run a full-growed bear out of our yard. He's not 'fraid of nuttin,' but he wanted no part of whatever the hell was out there."

"Language." A soft reprimand from Marty.

George glared a little but kept plowing. "I couldn't see nuttin' – too dark – but I heard something all right – loud and clear – and whatever it was, was big."

George took a long pull on his beer – the master storyteller reeling in his audience.

"So, what was it," Jimmy asked.

"Hold your equine there, buddy. I'm getting to it. You gotta let me finish the yarn. Anywho – for the next few weeks, I decided to come up to the house before twilight, just to be safe, you know, especially when I could hear the creatures vocalizing."

Bridget sat up. "More than one?"

George nodded. "A regular choir it was. Not like a pack of coyotes either – you know, just caterwauling and the like. Nope, this was sequential – tree knocking and whistles – whatever was out there was communicating. Sometimes, it got real spooky quiet – I mean everything shut down all at once, like there'd been a signal or such. Some nights, it sounded like marching band practice."

An owl hooted. Everyone flinched a little. Rhonda let out a nervous giggle. "City girl, you know," she said.

Bob patted her arm.

"Couple of friends went with me to scout the place. Couldn't find nuttin' 'cept a few broke trees, but even that was strange."

"Uprooted?" Jimmy asked.

"No," George said. "Snapped off like a toothpick about eight foot off the ground. I'm not talking saplings here – these wuz full-growed birches and cottonwoods."

Mark moved to the edge of his seat. "Did you try to trap it?"

"Well, devil dog, hell yeah, we did. Set a big ass (Marty coughed) – sorry, set a big ole' bear trap. Used a deer we'd shot for bait. Don't kill many of them – they never done me no harm, and they taste like sh… I mean, I don't care for the meat. But this one had a broke leg, and I didn't see any reason for it to suffer."

The fire was nothing but embers – the night crept in at the edges of the group like a plastic bag.

"That trap was bigger than hell. Took three of us to pry it open and set it. Would have taken an arm clean off. We were pretty sure we'd find a severed leg in it the next morning."

"What'd you catch?" Mark asked.

"Jack shit," George said.

Marty rolled her eyes and muttered. "I give up."

George rolled on – undeterred. "We found the trap in the shallows of the lake the next day. It had sprung, and the deer was gone. But whatever we caught got out of the trap, ripped the chain out of the post we'd driven into the ground, and tossed the whole thing into the water."

"Blood – hair?" Bob asked.

"Blue gill cleaned the trap before we got to it."

Andie put a hand on George's knee. "Uncle George, maybe you caught something, and it dragged itself to the lake before it died. Then, the fish ate it."

George let out a belly laugh. "Blue gill, honey," he said. "Not piranha. No – that thing got caught, opened the trap, and tossed it in the lake. Had to be strong as a full-growed bull."

"That's some story," Jimmy said. He started to rise.

"Not finished, Dr. Egghead," George said. "Here's the really weird part. I raise Beefalos."

Jimmy, stinging a little from the rebuff, said, "Three-eighths bison – five-eighths bovine."

"Very good, Poindexter," George said.

Everyone laughed except Jimmy.

"Well," George said after grinning at Jimmy – "Nothing personal, just having some fun – these animals are no joke. Fifty-five inches tall, 1,500-2,000 pounds. I go down to feed 'em and Ole Billy's missing – my prize stud. The gates closed. The lock is secure. And the fence is six-foot tall. These ain't jumpers. I search the area and find Ole Billy – well what's left of him – about half a mile in the trees. His head is bashed in – not shot – caved in with a rock or a club. There's nothing left on his skeleton – stripped clean. And his leg bones is shattered, and the marrow gone."

"Did you report it?" Bob asked.

"Hell no, son. You think I want people to think I'm

losing it? No one would believe that story. But Marty can tell you it's true. She saw the whole thing. Helped me bury poor Billy – he was her favorite."

Marty nodded and daubed at eyes with a handkerchief.

Jimmy looked around the circle and saw reminders of Angie and Heather watching *Jaws*. All the girls had pulled a blanket up to their chins – eyes like saucers.

"Last part," George said. "Marty and I came up here to spring clean the cabin this week. Massive prints everywhere – not like anything I'd ever seen. I took my thirty-aught-six and followed 'em all the way to down the ravine."

George's voice lost momentum, like he was running out of air.

He's terrified, Jimmy thought.

George was determined to finish. "I found some bones – beefalo bones – had to be Ole Billy's. They weren't scattered – no sir – they was tied together with vines – made into a tool-like thing. Whatever killed Ole Billy ain't no dumb beast – it's a smart, strong, and stealthy killing machine."

He locked eyes with the men, one by one. "I know you boys are smart, and Andie tells me you are fearless. If you go looking, you better pack some heavy firepower."

"Copy that," Matt said.

"And if you find 'em – God help you."

CHAPTER 33
THE VISIT

DAY 3 – TUESDAY, NOVEMBER 25, 2003

THE NEXT MORNING, Bob and Jimmy set up breakfast.

Andie looked at "the spread" and shook her head. "Are you guys 12?"

"What?" Jimmy said. "It's a buffet – fruit, grains, dairy—"

"Cut the crap," she said. "There is not an ounce of fruit in a Pop Tart. Everything else is sugar cereal."

Bob nodded. "Yeah, but we've got the classics: Count Chocula, Boo Berry, Fruit Loops."

Stacie, Bridget, and Rhonda joined the chorus of complaint. Bridget threw up her hands. "Can someone at least find me an effin' bagel?"

Matt and Mark came downstairs, their hoots of delight drowned out all opposition.

"You girls are so easy," Jimmy said. "We've got bacon and sausage on the grill outside, and Bob's headed out with an omelet pan – geez, you guys are gullible."

After breakfast, the women headed into town with George and Marty. Matt, Mark, Jimmy, and Bob set up for their hunt.

"Hey Jimmy, catch."

"Jimmy caught the Silly Putty Egg and laughed.

"Tell me you're not serious," he said.

"Just thought I'd give a little nod to our days at Greenwood," Bob said. "I've got casting solution and everything else we need in these cases."

The quartet laid everything out on the floor of the great room: recording equipment, tripwires, detection flares, a pair of Stealth Angel folding shovels, laser pointers, canteens, night vision goggles, binoculars, two AR-15 assault rifles, four packs of ammunition, a half dozen side arms of various sizes and calibers, and an odd-looking camera.

"Hey, Bob, what's this?" Matt asked. He bounced the camera in his hands, acting like he might drop it.

"It's a Hasselblad H6D-400cc Medium Format DSLR Camera, High resolution – great color – exceptional for low-light situations."

"Looks expensive," Matt said. He was still juggling the camera.

"It's only about 48 grand," Bob said. "Belongs to the lab, but I'm sure they'd sell it to you *if you broke it.*"

Matt lay the camera on the sofa and backed away. "Notice, it was in *perfect* condition the last time I touched it," he said.

"Okay," Bob said. "Let's leave the artillery. We don't want to look like some militia group."

"Right," Mark said. "Besides, X-ray Vision Boy over there can see if we are going to run into any trouble. You *can* still see Shimmers, right, brother?"

Jimmy nodded.

Matt holstered a Colt Python and shoved two boxes of .357 shells into his backpack. "I'm ready," he said.

"Enjoy your pop-gun," Mark said. He slipped a heavy lanyard around his neck. From it hung an odd-looking, long-barreled revolver."

"What the hell is that?" Jimmy asked.

Matt answered in a reverential tone. "Shit, that's a Pfeifer-Zeliska .600 Nitro Express. I've never seen one."

"Yep," Mark said. "Bought it special just for this."

"With that barrel, it could double as a pool cue." Jimmy said.

"Thirteen inches." Mark started to grin, "Just about the same size—"

"Don't even try," Matt said. "First, you know I will ask Bridget."

"Go ahead. It ain't braggin' if it's the truth."

"And second, I'll tell her you bought that bad boy – she doesn't know, does she?"

Mark hung his head and got very busy polishing the grip of his hand canon.

"Well, it's scary looking as hell," Jimmy said.

"That's not the point," Mark said, looking up.

"Costs about 17 grand – and each 900-grain round costs about $40, which explains why I have fired it exactly twice. It's not for target practice, but this sucker will knock about anything down – like a charging bull elephant."

The only noise in the room was Bob snapping the closures on his backpack,

Jimmy broke the awkward silence. "Let's hope we don't need it," he said. "Maybe you can get a refund and send your kids to college."

THEY HEADED AWAY from the ravine. Jimmy felt foolish only with his walking stick, flashlight, and water bottle. "Just remember, guys," he said, "when all your fancy equipment fails, get behind me."

He swished the spiked end of his walking stick like a sword.

"We'll leave all the small woodland rodents to you, big brother," Matt said.

They'd walked about a mile when Jimmy stopped and pointed.

"Over there," he said. "Two hundred meters – silver Shimmer."

"Okay," Bob said. "Like we discussed. Set up some flares and then move out." He turned to Jimmy. "Last time you saw a silver one, what was it?"

"The UFO at Patrick and Nancy's. This one is lower though."

Mark asked, "Do you think that's what it is?"

Matt said, "God, I hope not, or they might use that pointy walking stick for a little probing." He clinched his butt and said, "Oooooch."

"Okay, guys," Jimmy said. "Let's quit screwing around. Show time."

THEY FANNED OUT in a search grid. Before long, each one found tracks, the largest of which lay south of the cabin.

"I don't like it," Mark said. "Looks like these are moving to higher ground. Puts us at a serious strategic disadvantage."

Matt and Mark set flares and trip lines, while Bob and Jimmy took castings.

"I got some hair samples," Jimmy said, "but they all came from low to the ground – probably fox or wolverine."

After they took the imprints, Bob brushed away the tracks.

"Why did you do that?" Jimmy asked.

"Good thinking," Matt said. "If something sets off the flare, we'll have a fresh set of tracks – we'll know exactly what's out here."

Jimmy glanced at his watch. "We've got 30 minutes of daylight," he said. "Let's check out the Shimmer, then book it home."

"Can you still see it?" Mark asked.

"It dipped out of sight when we came over the ridge, but I'm sure it's still over there." Jimmy pointed.

They crested the hill. Jimmy saw a massive translucent plate – a wall of silver with a crisscross pattern. Jimmy's throat tightened.

"Looks different in the daytime," he said.

"How so," Bob asked.

"It's more of a feeling. In the twilight, it looks serene. Now, it's…hell, I don't know… it's ominous."

Jimmy quit walking. "Stop! It's right there."

"Where?" Matt reached for his pistol. Mark's hand fingered the canon looped across his chest.

"It's just closer – like it moved towards us," Jimmy said.

Jimmy placed his hand against the Shimmer – it quivered and gave way. He turned his hand, fingers forward, and eased into the viscous structure.

He heard a faint buzz.

"You hear that?"

Matt and Mark nodded.

Bob shook his head. "You know I don't. Describe it."

"Not as loud as the one in our old basement – louder than a cicada."

Bob was making notes. "How wide is it?"

"I thought it was a wall – it's a dome – curved, like a giant half-bubble."

Mark tapped the face of his watch. "The plan says we start back in 15, guys – we can't get caught out here after dark."

"Agreed," Jimmy said. He looked at each of the guys in turn. "I'm not the scientist and I'm not a combat vet, but when it comes to these things, I am in charge. Copy?"

"Copy that," they all said.

"What do you guys see?" Jimmy asked.

"Forest, leaves, sky, clouds," Bob said. "Regular stuff."

Matt and Mark nodded.

"Okay," Jimmy said. "Follow directly behind me. Be ready to boogie on my command."

Following Jimmy, each man walked into the Shimmer – now a mile wide. The terrain did not change – the view was the same.

"My God, that stinks," Bob said.

They all pulled camouflaged face masks over their noses. Mark and Matt moved with the assurance of combat vets. Bob dug in his bag looking for a piece of equipment. Jimmy tried to look everywhere at once. They were in the Shimmer no more than five minutes when Jimmy stopped in his tracks and saw something large and hairy behind a tree. He began to yell instructions. "Guys! Out – now! Run straight at those ash trees." He pointed. "Get the hell out. Move it."

Jimmy saw the thing running toward them. Matt and Mark made it out with ease. Bob was not far behind. Jimmy, larger than his friend and brothers, struggled to keep up.

Matt, Mark, and Bob were already on the other side of the Shimmer. Jimmy could hear the creature closing in on him. Jimmy left his feet and dove through the Shimmer. He felt a tug on his shirt as he flew through the air. He face-planted at Bob's feet appearing out of thin air to them. He stood up and spun around. Nothing was behind him.

"Way to stick the landing," Bob said. He grew serious. "You disappeared for a second."

"Yeah, I was on the other side of the Shimmer," Jimmy said.

They pulled down their face masks. Matt took a deep breath. "Mother of God, what was that smell?"

Jimmy said, "A big monkey," then he waited. Everyone stood silent for a moment.

Matt said, "Are you serious?"

Jimmy just returned his look. Matt knew he was serious.

"Oh shit," Bob said. He took some restorative breaths, then said, "Tomorrow, we bring the measuring equipment and figure this thing out."

"Okay," Matt said. "And Mark and I will bring more firepower."

They turned for the cabin.

AFTER BURGERS COOKED over the firepit, Jimmy and Bob debriefed the girls, while Matt and Mark went inside for a weapons check. They came out with more trip wire flares and established a perimeter 75 yards around the cabin in all directions.

"I should have brought some Claymores," Mark said. "We'd have a better fire plan."

"True," Matt said, "but you'd have to tell Mom we killed Bob when he dragged his weak-ass bladder out here in the middle of the night to take a leak."

"Point taken," Mark said. "But I'd blame it on you."

"Jimmy, we went in and out of the Shimmer," Mark said. "What's to keep something in there from dropping by for tea?"

Bob interjected, "The same reason Jimmy disappeared on the other side of the Shimmer. I can't believe I didn't figure this out before. We only converge in that shared space. Once we leave it, we no longer share that world."

Matt gnawed on a cold brat. "Makes sense," he said.

"How's that?" Mark asked.

Bob used a pencil and drew a circle on a piece of

paper. "Big bubble. I know it is a circle, not a sphere, but bear with me," he said. "You get it?"

"Yes."

Bob picked up a Sharpie and drew another circle. "Okay, when the spheres overlap, it creates a shared space. He pointed to the overlapping part of the Venn diagram. That represents the Shimmer. He then pointed to the first circle in pencil. This is our world. We can only walk around in this circle."

They nodded.

He then grabbed the sharpie and said, "This is their world, maybe where Josh is, and they can only walk around here," pointing to the sharpie circle. "Still make sense?"

Jimmy said, "Yeah, that makes a lot of sense. But what about Josh?"

"I also have a theory regarding why Josh got stuck based on some of the work I have done on bubble dynamics and the ball that disappeared in the attic." Bob drew two spheres. The first, he drew quite large and then he drew one much smaller with a thicker outline. "The smaller the sphere, the thicker the membrane.

"So, the Shimmer decreased in size increasing its containment capacity – so Josh got stuck," Jimmy said.

"Very good for a shrink," Bob said.

Jimmy said seriously, "So we have to hope Josh finds his way into the Shimmer, then we have to find him, then we have to make sure he is in the center of the Shimmer when it closes. That is a lot of things that have to happen."

Matt undeterred said, "Well hell, let's do this!"

Andie's voice broke into the conversation. "We have a long day tomorrow – we should get some sleep."

"Aw, Mom, do we have to?" Matt was laughing, as were the others, but the guys all stood and shuffled off to the bedrooms

---

THE FLARES WENT off like skyrockets.

Jimmy glanced at his watch. "4:23," he said.

The guys took up assigned positions, one at each corner of the cabin. Jimmy heard Mark click his AR-15 into "fire" mode. He flared into shooting position when three shadows skittered through the clearing about 30 yards from the cabin.

"Deer," he said.

Andie was on the night vision scope about 10 feet from Jimmy. "I see a lot of movement – animals – running like hell – south to north. You think there's a fire?"

"No," Jimmy said. "Don't smell anything."

"Predator?"

"Could be a cougar or a bear, but it seems weird that one animal would spark a stampede."

A black bear lumbered across the clearing.

"He's got to weigh 600 pounds," Jimmy said.

The beast skidded to a stop, turned and sniffed the air. Then, just as suddenly, it took off.

"That's not what they're running from, is it?" Andie asked.

"Don't think so," Jimmy said. "That was prey behavior."

"Shit – I thought so."

Bridget came out of the back door with a Glock .9 mm in her hand. "Where's Mark?"

"Other side," Jimmy said. He glanced at the pistol. "Yours?"

"Since I was 17," Bridget said. "Don't worry, I know what I'm doing."

"Not a lot of knock down power," Jimmy said. "Don't think it'll stop that bear." He nodded in the direction of the bear's route.

"It'll stun him long enough for me to run," Bridget said.

Jimmy raised an eyebrow. "You faster than a black bear?"

"Don't have to be," Bridget said. "I just have to be faster than you, Professor."

Bridget returned to her post. Jimmy left Andie and moved along the side of the house to where Bob and Matt were positioned – at the tip of the spear.

A silver dome crept over the tops of the trees.

"You don't see that, do you?" Jimmy asked.

"Shimmer?" Bob asked.

"Yep – it's moving this way – same as this afternoon."

Bob's jaw tightened. He clumsily worked the bolt action on his deer rifle. "If you say it's there, that's good enough for me. Is it coming this way?"

Jimmy watched for a moment. "No," he said. "The movement is lateral."

They heard a warning whistle, the signal, they'd adopted to ensure no one was mistaken for an intruder. Bob returned the signal, and Mark appeared from the darkness.

"Who's on your post?" Matt asked.

"Stacie," Mark said.

"Good, she's a better shot."

Mark ignored the insult. "Wanted to make sure you guys heard that," he said.

Bob and Jimmy cocked their heads. "I hear it," Bob said.

"Me too," Jimmy said. "Thunk, crack, thunk, crack." He knelt and placed his cheek on the ground. "And there's vibration. Those are trees falling."

"Why are they knocking over trees?"

"Not sure," Mark said.

The three stood still and heard a rhythmic thumping.

"Drum corps?" Bob said.

"Don't think so," Matt said. "Sounds more like this." He balled his fist and slammed it into his chest.

"That's it – but it's something a whole lot bigger than your scrawny ass."

"Yeah," Jimmy said. "And a whole lot more of them than the eight of us."

CHAPTER 34
BELLOWING BEAST

DAY 4 – WEDNESDAY, NOVEMBER 26, 2003

THE REST OF the night passed without event. The group awakened to find Mark on watch and Matt cooking sausage. Bridget wiped Mark's mouth.

"Finished the Boo Berry, didn't you?" she asked.

"How could you tell?"

Bridget shook her head. "Telltale blue moustache. Gives you away every time."

They sat around a large picnic-style table inside the cabin.

Bob waved a fork. "Andie, been meaning to ask. Why is there a brick embedded in the middle of this, otherwise, lovely table?"

Andie smiled. "The legendary Murphy and Peterson brick exchange."

"Do tell," Bob said.

Andie began. "Many years ago, my grandfather Vern Murphy, and his stepbrother, Roy Peterson and a few more buddies, went hunting. When they got back from the trip, they split all the meat up into four, neat piles, each bit wrapped in white butcher paper. They were one roast short. Well, Roy had been out of the room at the time, so my grandfather Vern wrapped up a brick and placed it in Roy's pile. About two months later, Roy's wife wanted venison roast. Try as she might, she could not get the – ah – 'roast' to thaw. When she finally undid the paper, the battle commenced."

Jimmy had heard the story many times. He slipped outside.

"Over the next 40-odd years, the two brothers took turns gifting the brick back and forth on birthdays. It showed up in boxes, bags, flower arrangements – you name it. One year, Vern opened his birthday gift – no brick. Roy had paid to have it baked into Vern's cake."

Everyone smiled and chuckled. They all needed a break from the tension.

"On the day of Roy's funeral," Andie said, "Vern placed the brick into the casket. The end – or so he thought. But Roy, who'd been sick and knew his time was up soon, had commissioned a custom-built picnic table with a hole in it…(she rapped the brick)…and it's been here ever since.".

JIMMY STEPPED THROUGH the door.

"Guys, time to go – *now!*"

Matt looked at his older brother. "What is it?"

Jimmy's scowl brooked no argument. "Lock and load – double time, grab the walkie talkies."

They loaded the Hummers and spun out down the gravel drive. Matt and Mark guided their oversized vehicles with careful precision along the rutted dirt road.

"Damn roads in Iraq were better than this," Mark said.

Jimmy's voice came over his headset. "Less talk, more focus."

"True dat," Mark said. He spoke over his shoulder. "Bob, Rhonda, you guys ready?"

Bob was digging through an equipment bag. Rhonda worked the slide on her .9 mm and said, "Ready."

A mile down the road, Matt slowed. "Road's blocked," he said. "Mark, lay back a little in case we have to bug out."

"Copy," Mark said through the crackle of static.

"What is it?" Jimmy asked.

Matt eased the Hummer forward. "Big ass tree blocking the road," he said. He turned halfway towards Jimmy. "And some ugly mo-fo standing behind it."

Jimmy's voice pulsed with urgency. "Matt, look out!"

The front windshield exploded, showering Matt and Stacie with pebbles of tempered glass. Matt shook his head. "Stace, you get any in your eyes?"

"All good," she said. "What was it?"

"Incoming!" Jimmy yelled.

A boulder the size of a beach ball smashed into the Hummer's grill. Before Jimmy could shout instructions, Matt slammed the vehicle in reverse and gunned the engine. The 6.5-liter, V-8 roared, and the truck lurched back just as another massive rock whizzed past on the right.

Andie screamed. "Jimmy, look!"

A half dozen creatures were charging – all well over eight feet, covered in hair, and carrying clubs the size of lampposts.

Jimmy's voice was a hoarse croak. "Mother of God."

Matt floored the Hummer, let off the gas momentarily, and cranked the wheel left as fast as he could. He straightened the wheel and stomped on the accelerator – a perfectly executed J turn.

"Shit!"

A monstrous body flew over the top of the low-slung vehicle right after they heard the thump.

"I hit that sumbitch," Matt said. Instinctively, he slowed.

"Keep driving, dammit," Jimmy yelled.

An enormous hairy hand crashed through Jimmy's window and grabbed his shirt. The interior filled with a vomitous smell. The smell overwhelmed Jimmy. Coupled with the pressure of the creature's hand on his throat, the odor threatened to knock him out.

A series of shots exploded inside the car – firecrackers in a tin can. The creature howled, threw its hands up to its face, and staggered. Andie was already reloading her Glock.

"I put at least two in his left eye," she said. She looked at Matt. "Don't stare – drive us the hell out of here."

The Hummer fishtailed around a curve, barely missing Mark's vehicle. Mark's voice echoed over the headset. "Bugging out?"

"Like a bat out of hell, brother. Hit it. If you run up my ass, it's fine."

The two vehicles flew along the narrow road as fast as the drivers could push them. Jimmy could smell blood, the creature's stench, and something else.

Fear.

THE ATMOSPHERE AROUND the picnic table was considerably less jovial than it had been during the "brick saga."

"What – What the hell was that?" Matt asked.

"You know what it was," Jimmy said. "You just don't want to admit what you saw."

"Looked like a goddamn Bigfoot," Matt said.

"Wrong," Jimmy said. "Looked like a flock of them."

"You get any pictures?" Bob asked calmly.

Matt bolted from his seat. "Are you crazy, man?

This isn't Junior Adventurers Club. Those suckers tried to kill us."

Jimmy put his arm on Matt's shoulder. "Easy, brother," he said.

Matt lowered into his seat, still glaring at Bob. He ran his tongue around the inside of his lips. "I know, I know," he said.

"We need to get the holy hell out of here," Rhonda said.

Stacie sat in the middle of the room crying. "We are going to die."

Mark was pacing back and forth with his finger on the trigger of the AR.

Matt said, "This shit is pretty damn hairy."

Jimmy started laughing – "hairy." Everyone looked at him. "Matt, you're pissed about Bob's wanting pictures, and you're making bad puns?" A spontaneous release of tension and fear filled the room, and everyone instinctively exhaled.

Matt grinned.

Mark took his hand off the gun and raised it like a kid in school. "Professor Bellard? What is the plural of Bigfoot? Bigfoots? Bigfeets?"

"Scary mo-fos, I think," Bob said.

Everyone laughed aloud.

Andie spoke up. "I thought those things were supposed to be shy and introverted. At least, that's what the beast was like in *Harry and the Hendersons.*"

"Well, they weren't this time," Matt said. "What we saw was pure, predatory instinct."

"No, it wasn't," Jimmy said. "It was worse."

"What do you mean?" Mark asked.

Jimmy was quiet for a while. Then…

"They weren't on a hunting party – or roaming around like a wolfpack looking for food. That was a trap – an ambush. They had a plan, and they executed it almost to perfection. Annie Oakley over here messed up their scheme."

Andie had turned white. "I just reacted," she said.

"Good thing," Jimmy said. "Otherwise, I'd be someone's captive right now."

"Or dinner," Bob said.

There was no humor in his voice – and no one smiled.

***

ANDIE STARTED THE conversation after an uncomfortably quiet dinner of Vienna sausages and biscuits.

"Alright, but would someone mind telling me what the hell we really ran into out there?"

Everyone looked at Jimmy, who deferred to Bob.

"No one really knows exactly," he said. "There have been sightings of this creature all over the world. The names change depending on the region: Bigfoot,

Sasquatch, Yeti, Yowie, and a host of others. Each legend is a little different."

He looked around – he had everyone's attention.

"Perhaps clusters of these beasts differ in personality and tendencies, depending on where they live. Some may, indeed, be as gentle as Harry was in the movie. Some may be curious, others more aloof. Apparently, we've run into a strain of pretty aggressive dudes."

"Easy with the technical science jargon, Professor," Matt said.

The mood around the table relaxed a bit.

Bob poured a finger of Scotch in his glass and passed the bottle. "I think we learned something today. They aren't fleet of foot – but they are definitely not stupid. The ambush today was well planned and almost flawlessly executed. I don't think they see us as a serious threat – I would hazard that they view us as prey."

"No shit, Sherlock," Jimmy said. He was rubbing ointment over the gashes on his chest where the beast had grabbed him.

Bob looked at Jimmy. "Is there any correlation between the beasts and the Shimmer?"

Jimmy buttoned his shirt. "I don't believe in coincidence. The Shimmer shows up – a silver one – and we're dealing with these guys. I think it's best to hunker down until the Shimmer dissipates."

Rhonda asked, "Well, how long is that?"

"No clue."

"How come Jimmy's the only one who can see the

Shimmers?" Rhonda asked. "Any chance he's making it all up just to scare us? I mean, he's been doing it for years, right?"

Anger began a low crackle around the table, but Bob jumped in. "Rhonda, I know you're scared – we all are. But you're also sort of new to the group. All the guys here have known Jimmy could do this since we were kids – and I, for one, do not doubt his ability or his motives."

"I'm in on that," Matt said.

Mark added, "Hell yes."

"My work at Edison is trying to replicate what is obviously Jimmy's natural ability. I don't understand it at all – but I know it's the real deal."

Matt jumped in. "Listen, when I was younger, I thought Jimmy was full of crap too, but what we experienced cannot be dismissed. Whatever we call those things, they almost totaled my Hummer, nearly ripped Jimmy out of the back seat, took several shots to the face, and ran off into the woods. We can't write any of this off as the idle ramblings of a demented kid."

The group fell into an uneasy silence. Howls and barks sounded from outside. One of the flares sparked and flew into the late afternoon sky.

The guys formed up and walked to the back of the clearing – Andie acted as rear guard, her pistol drawn and ready. At the bottom of the ravine, they saw two hairy shapes carrying a third.

"Must be the one Andie nailed," Jimmy said.

"You think it's dead?" Bob asked.

Mark lowered his binoculars. "Not moving and those guys are dragging ass. I think it's like a funeral procession."

"That would mean the howls are some sign of mourning," Jimmy said. "That makes everything worse."

"How's that?" Mark asked.

Bob understood. "Because," he said, "now, it's personal."

JIMMY GAZED OUT of the window at the silver Shimmer. "It's growing," he said.

"Fifth time you've mentioned that in the last 30 minutes," Matt said. "Tell us when you've got something new."

Matt went outside to relieve Mark. Jimmy watched Bob, who was at the edge of the ravine, hunched over his data and sound recording equipment.

They'd checked the perimeter. Mark came inside rubbing his arms.

"Getting cold," he said.

"We're probably in for snow tonight," Jimmy said.

When nightfall came, everyone took up their assigned defensive positions in the great room. Matt and Mark stood post at the windows along with

Bridget. Rhonda volunteered to guard the back door. Jimmy had the front. Stacie and Andie were in the center of the room with a pile of ammunition on a table between them.

"You guys got the reload procedure down?" Matt asked.

"Roger that," Stacie said. "We won't let you guys get caught with your pants down."

Mark blew out a long breath. "Right now, that sounds like a great alternative."

When no one laughed, Mark mumbled, "Sorry," and stared out the window.

Bob had his equipment on the picnic table, including enhanced audio and video equipment. Laser guided cameras, direction finders, parabolic microphones, spectrometers, a seismograph, and several things only Bob understood dotted the roof. The scientist positioned a rotating, night vision camera in a large tree – field of vision 270°. A series of 72-volt, 100-amp hours (AH) batteries had been sequenced and arranged along the floor to power the lights and equipment.

"How much juice we got, Bob?" Jimmy asked.

"We'll run out of ammo before we need more power," Bob said. "Don't worry. I got this."

They waited.

One hundred and eighty seconds later, a softball-sized rock spiderwebbed the back window.

"Shit," Bob said. "That glass can withstand bullets

at 1250 feet per second. Someone out there has a major league arm."

They could hear projectiles peppering the side of the cabin. The house shook.

"Someone else is trying out for the Browns," Matt said.

"No one on the Browns has hit that hard in 10 years," Mark said. "Bob, give me a 20 on the bandits. Time to rain on their parade. Bridge – little help."

He stood next to the door. Bridget held the knob in one hand, a Sig Sauer p220 in the other, racked and ready to fire.

"Picture quality's not what I hoped – night vision, you know," Bob said.

"You're not shooting for Spielberg – I just need to know where those creeps are."

Another rock hit the window.

"That thing going to shatter?" Stacie asked.

"Don't think so," Bob said, "but we can't let them stand out there and keeping chunking stuff at us."

Bob scrolled through the monitors, "Mark, the guys who tried to tackle the house have climbed up in the tree next to the door – two of them. You go out, they'll be on you like ugly on an alligator."

Matt said, "Sneaky bastards."

"Well," Mark said, "they can run, but they can't hide." He gave Bridget a nod. She yanked open the door and emptied her clip into the tree. They heard a snarl followed by an earth-shaking thud. Mark stepped over the threshold, AR on full-auto and sprayed the darkness. He'd fired for about two seconds when a hairy hand descended from above him, grabbed the hot barrel, and snatched the weapon from his hands.

As soon as the beast grabbed Mark's rifle, a single howl shattered the night. A half dozen creatures rushed at the house, a stampede of hair, grunts, and terror.

Mark dove back in the house. Bridget slammed the door. "Gas," he yelled. "Hit the damn gas!"

Bob reached for a toggle switch, flipped open the cover, and keyed it. A gasoline-filled trench ringing the property exploded with an acrid whoosh. Four beasts began running away – all were ablaze. But three continued their rush towards the cabin.

"Yank it," Mark said. Once again, Bridget pulled the door. This time, Mark came out in a crouch, stopped six feet outside the door, and checked above him before firing. He hit the first beast five times in rapid succession – the creature barely slowed. Mark switched to single fire. He smoked the other beast in the left eye. The Bigfoot's scream halted his companion's charge. The two hirsute warriors locked arms and helped one another leave the field of battle.

Mark turned to go inside. Between him and the door stood the beast who had stolen the AR. The creature, well over eight feet tall and 40 inches across the shoulders, snarled and raised the assault rifle like a club. His move was lightning fast and his intent clear. His blow would crush Mark's skull.

Mark jumped back and to the left. The creature

hesitated – just a second too long – clearly confused. Twin massive concussions sounded in rapid succession at close range. The beast let out an unholy shriek, a cross between a roaring tiger and a trumpeting elephant, dropped the rifle, clutched his arm, and lumbered into the trees.

Bridget appeared in the doorframe. Smoke curled from the barrel of the Colt Python.

"Good work," Mark said. "That guy was going to take my head off. Glad he left my AR."

"That's not the only thing he left," Bridget said as she rubbed her sore right wrist – the Python kicked like a mule. "He dropped this."

In the dim light, Mark originally thought it was a glove. He got closer and saw blood and tissue.

"Holy Christ," he said. "You shot off his hand."

MARK AND MATT came over. "They won't stop next time," Matt said.

"I have a feeling one way or the other, it ends tomorrow," Mark said.

Bob looked up from his screens. "How can you be sure?"

Mark demurred to his brother. Matt's face sagged with strain. "We've seen probing missions before," he said. "Those guys sent a scouting party to test our defenses – to check us out. They'll bring the thunder tomorrow."

"Let 'em come," Rhonda said. "I, for one, am tired of screwing around. I think we can finish 'em. So does Bob."

All heads turned to the scientist. Bob looked up from his monitor.

"They have a weakness," he said.

"Sure, they do," Jimmy said. "It takes two of them to lift a bus. What the hell are you talking about, buddy? They are huge, and strong, and fearless."

"True," Bob said. "But you've got something they don't."

Matt grabbed himself. "A hot wife?"

Stacie slapped his shoulder with the back of her hand. "Not now, idiot!"

Bob managed a weak grin. "No, I'm sure they don't. But it's something else – something more important, believe it or not."

Jimmy knew when his longtime friend was onto something. "What?"

"We've got good vision – those things can't see for shit."

AFTER THEY CHECKED the perimeter again, everyone gathered around Bob.

"Look," he said. He rolled the tape. "Four of those things are about 200 feet away and firing rocks at the window. They're lined up in a straight line. Watch – they throw, then listen. If they don't hear anything, they shift and try again. They only hit the window a couple of times. Watch the guys who tackled the house. They ran full speed and smashed into the corner."

Matt winced. "Ouch," he said. "That monster must have bounced back five feet."

"Yep," Bob said. "And look at the other one. He's feeling the cabin like he's reading braille. He's trying to find the door because he can't see it until he's right on top of it."

Bridget was unconvinced. "That dude was going to kill Mark," she said. "He would have splattered my man's brains all over the yard."

"Except he didn't," Bob said. "Look." He pushed the play button and narrated. "The creature raises the rifle with intent to strike. Mark jumps back and to the side and freezes. The beast hesitates but he does something else, too."

"Son of a bitch," Mark said. "He shakes his head. I thought he was angry – but he was confused because—"

Matt jumped in. "Because he couldn't find you."

Jimmy nodded. "They are nearly blind, but can see movement."

"The Mr. Magoos of the Wild Kingdom," Bob said. "I think we found something we can use."

Two HOURS LATER, an exhausted Bob slumped on the couch next to Jimmy.

"I got bad news, buddy," Bob said.

"Let's see – we're in a remote cabin with no phone – we have limited supplies, water, and ammo – and, oh yes, we have some primitive or alien ape-guys who seem intent on killing us. And you say you have bad news?"

"I'm not screwing around here, Jimmy," Bob said. "I'm not sure we can kill those guys."

Mark and Matt had been dozing in chairs by the window. They came over.

"What gives," Mark said.

"I've spent the last two hours dissecting the hand," Bob said. "More accurately, the forearm. Human beings have two forearm bones."

"Radius and ulna, we know, Bob," Jimmy said. "Get to the point."

"Well, Fredrick Sykes only has one bone – right in the middle of the arm."

Matt, Mark, and Jimmy all giggled.

Stacie glared. "We're in deep shit here, and you guys sound like eighth-grade homeroom. What gives?"

"Nothing," Jimmy said trying to regain his composure. It was hard because he was exhausted, so sputtering laughter kept erupting at inopportune times. "It's just, we're in the middle of all this stuff and Bob thinks to name one of the creatures."

"So?" The glare had morphed into a scowl.

"He named the thing (snort)– you know, the one Bridget shot (giggle) – he named him after the One-Armed man in *The Fugitive.*"

The guys lost it. Mark and Matt collapsed into their chairs. Jimmy doubled over. All three laughed until tears streamed from their faces. Stacie, Bridget, Andie, and Rhonda formed a disapproving line, hands on hips, not the hint of a smile.

"You guys are morons," Andie said.

"I know," Jimmy said. He was clutching his side and gasping for air. "It's just (snort) – just – I'm so damn tired. And it feels (titter) so very damn good to laugh."

Andie hugged him. "I know, honey," she said. "But could you work a little harder on your maturity – and maybe on a plan that doesn't end with us on a spit someplace with an apple in our mouths?"

The boys sobered and returned their attention to Bob who'd stared at their outburst in confusion. Hs shook his head and continued. "Okay," he said. "One bone in the arm but look at the size of this thing."

Matt opened his mouth to say, "That's what she said," but saw Stacie's flaring nostrils and looked back at Bob.

"My forearm is about 10 inches in circumference

– Matt's is closer to 15. This thing is 23 inches around. The bone is large but not excessively so."

"What makes the arm so massive?" Rhonda asked.

"Thick muscle and this – here." He pointed to a gelatinous layer of gray tissue about four inches thick. When he pried a few sections apart, everyone stepped back. Rhonda gagged slightly.

Bob pointed. "That's it." He was coughing and trying not to throw up. "That's the smell from the Hummer when I got grabbed. What the hell is it?"

"Best I can tell, it's very similar to whale blubber – much denser than fat. I suspect the odor represents some form of natural defense system – like a skunk. But that's not the worst news."

Everyone had pulled a neckerchief around their face.

Andie looked at the guys. "First one who says, 'Stick 'em up,' gets kicked in the jewels."

Matt and Mark's shoulders dropped in disappointment. Andie continued to be the adult in the room. "What's worse, Bob?"

"This stuff is dense – denser than any tissue I've ever examined. It was intended to guard against cuts and scrapes and getting whacked with a club, and unfortunately for us, I think it'll act like natural body armor. Shooting these guys is going to be tough."

The Cooper men walked to their wives. Rhonda came over and sat on Bob's lap.

"What are we going to do?" Jimmy asked.

"I'm not sure," Bob said, "But I think the Cleveland Browns can help us." He paused. "Hey, Matt? You didn't happen to bring a reciprocating saw, did you?"

Matt Smiled.

CHAPTER 35
INSIDE THE SILVER
SHIMMER – THE BOX

DAY 4 – WEDNESDAY, NOVEMBER 26, 2003

JOSH SAW THE dome flicker from his hiding place in the trunk of an old tree.

Evie was gone now. While Josh and Evie were fishing, the Stompers came, ate the cache of *tanta*, then ate Evie.

Josh understood Stompers and how to avoid them. He heard noises from over the hill – cracks and echoes. He did not know what the sounds were, but he knew they were not good. He slid out of his shelter and made his way to the top of a hill. Crawling on his belly, he stopped and peered down at a huge hut. He'd never seen one made from entire trees. I looked like something from his old world – something called, *What?*

Lincoln Logs.

He saw something else – another of the few things he remembered from his old life – his time before Evie and Annu – before the Stompers. He saw cars. He used to play with cars – but the ones he saw were much larger.

Big, he thought. *Not race cars. Not like – Jimmy's.*

He remembered Jimmy…reaching out. *I should not have touched the silver ball – bad silver ball – it made me lose Jimmy.*

Yesterday, Josh had seen the Stompers carrying Igwa. Josh could tell Igwa wasn't breathing. He knew the Stompers were taking Igwa to the sacred rock where they would beat on their chests and yell.

Igwa was young, Josh thought. *Why didn't he breathe anymore? Nothing can hurt the Stompers – they are not afraid of little things like bees and skunks; they are not afraid of big things like bears and panthers. Stompers are not afraid of anything.*

He saw humans outside the hut and gasped. They looked a little like Evie and Annu but had on clothes more like the ones he wore when he stepped into the ball. When he wore…

…Jeans?

…Shirts?

Maybe I can hide with them. Are they friendly?

He made the "all clear" noise with his tongue: "Click-clack…click-clack." One of them, a girl – turned but she did not respond.

Not safe.

Night was here. *Cannot be out at night – Stompers.*

He crept through the forest for a little, then saw a

small structure made of wood. Narrow – tall. He pulled on a handle and heard a creak. He went inside.

Stinks worse than a Stomper.

But he could live with the stench. He could probably not live if he stayed outside. The Stompers would smell him.

He tucked himself into a ball and fell asleep.

CHAPTER 36
TURKEY DAY
DAY 5 – THURSDAY, NOVEMBER 27, 2003 – EARLY

JIMMY BOLTED UPRIGHT. The shriek continued. Jumped off the couch to find Stacie staring a creature pecking against the window.

"You okay, Stace?"

"Just startled me is all," she said. "I don't think I've ever seen a turkey that wasn't wearing a plastic bag that said 'Butterball.'"

Jimmy smiled. "Well, Happy Thanksgiving."

And I hope we live to see Christmas, he thought.

The turkey stabbed away at his own reflection in the glass. Jimmy watched in amusement. The bird jerked upright. Its head twitched left – right. Then, after an ungainly running start, it flapped its wings, rose from the ground, and soared up into the trees.

Jimmy saw what had disrupted the turkey's assault on the window – two armed men had emerged from the woods and were approaching the back door.

"We got company," he said.

Matt racked the slide on his AR. "Let's rock 'n roll."

Jimmy held out his palm. "Relax, Rambo – looks like a couple of local cops." He panned the room. "How we going to play this?" he asked.

Bob walked to the window. "Don't tell them anything you're not sure they already know. If we start talking about Bigfoot and sieges, they'll call in the rubber trucks."

"It's our chance to get out of here," Andie said. "Two more guns to cover our retreat."

Jimmy put his hand on his wife's shoulder. "Babe, anyone can leave any time, and no one will ever say anything about it. But I've got to stay. This may be my only chance to find—"

A knock cut him short. As he moved to answer, Andie said, "I'm in, babe. You know that."

Jimmy heard everyone else's voice give the same assurance.

"Good morning, Officer," he said. "How can I help you?"

"Morning, sir. I'm Deputy Abbott; this is Deputy Snyder. Glad we finally found you."

"Didn't realize we were missing," Jimmy said in what he hoped was a casual voice. "Any particular reason you're looking for us."

"Oh, I'm sorry," Abbott said. "Should have been more precise. George and Marty asked us to look in on you guys, you know, since you're visiting and all. Zeke and I patrol this end of the county. Should have been routine but it was tough going today. Eight downed trees between here and Route 37."

"Gee," Jimmy said. "I guess it's a good thing we weren't trying to leave."

"You wouldn't have got nowhere," Snyder said. "It'll be a day, tomorrow at the earliest before we can get anyone out here to chop those bad boys up – you know, the holiday and all. Those suckers are big." He paused. "Sorta odd though."

"How's that?"

"There was one about every hundred yards and in places where you couldn't drive around 'em. If I didn't know better, I'd swear someone cut 'em down to block the road on purpose."

"Weird," Jimmy said. He felt a tightness in his bowel. *They've got us where they want us. They are not going to let us leave.*

Officer Abbott peered over Jimmy's shoulder. "Full house, huh?"

"Yeah – my brothers and their wives plus and old buddy and his."

Jimmy saw Rhonda elbow Bob in the ribs. Bob rolled his eyes but said nothing.

"Problem with the bedrooms?" Snyder asked.

"Pardon?"

"I just know this cabin is all," Snyder said. George and Marty let some of us use it when we deer hunt – their way of saying thanks. There are…uh…four bedrooms, right?"

"Five," Jimmy said. "What's your point?"

"I just notice all the blankets and pillows there."

Snyder said. "Looks like all of you stayed in the great room overnight."

Jimmy forced a grin. "You know how it is, Deputy," he said. "Holiday – games – a little too much tequila…" He let his voice trail away.

Snyder nodded. "Yeah, I get it – we're just too old for the sleeping on the floor routine, aren't we, Mack?"

"You got that right," Abbott said. "Anyway – we walked through the woods – about two miles back to the car and we've got families waiting at home to dig into the feast – and the Lions are playin." So, if everything's okay, we'll be on the way."

"All good, Deputy Abbott…Deputy Snyder," Jimmy said. "Thank you for stopping by. And Happy Thanksgiving."

"Same to you, sir," Abbott said. The two officers touched the brims of their hats and started to leave.

"Oh, say." Abbott turned around. "You guys might want to be careful with the firearms if you're throwing back a few. You know alcohol and guns – safety first."

"Pardon?" Jimmy asked.

Abbott cocked his head towards the splintered window. "George always brags about the bulletproof glass. Only thing that can vein it up like that is a couple of high-velocity slugs."

Jimmy bobbed his head. "Got it," he said. "Safety first."

He closed the door and breathed a sigh of relief.

CHAPTER 37
FIGHT FOR SURVIVAL
DAY 5 – THURSDAY, NOVEMBER 27, 2003

THE BODY CRASHED into the window an hour later. Even before he grabbed the Glock and went outside to check, Jimmy knew the man was dead. The corpse was so mangled, the only way Jimmy could identify it was the blood-streaked nameplate on the shirt: Snyder.

Jimmy scanned the forest. He could hear grunts and growls but did not see anything other than the Shimmer, which grew even more ominous. He considered lugging the body into the cabin but decided to push it closer to the house.

No use for everyone to keep staring at it, he thought. *If we get out of this, we'll give the man a proper burial.*

He closed the door. Seven faces turned to him. He shook his head. "Snyder," he said. "They got him."

"Where's Abbott?" Mark asked.

Bridget's voice "Oh, my God."

They looked towards the ravine almost 1,000 feet away. Two creatures held a struggling Abbott between them. They had their arms under his; the deputy's legs had given way.

"The big red one – the one to the left with the yellow fangs – he's in charge," Matt said.

"Caesar," Bob said. "You know the other one."

"Sykes," Mark said. He yelled at the window. "Want your arm back, Stumpy?"

"He can't hear you through the glass," Bob said.

Mark looked at the scene. "Poor bastard," he said. "They're gonna hurt Abbott bad."

"And slowly, I'm afraid."

As if on cue, Sykes, raised his free arm (he was propping Abbot up with his stump), and pounded it against the shoulder of his missing limb. He roared, turned to Abbott, and ripped the deputy's arm off. Abbott's mouth opened in an inaudible scream of pain. Sykes held his trophy aloft, then ate it in three enormous bites.

Everyone involuntarily turned from the window. Jimmy vomited. Mark caught Rhonda as her knees buckled. Matt lunged at Bridget as she raced for the door, the AR-15 in her hands.

"You cannot go out there," he said.

She yelled over her shoulder. "I'm not going to let them do that."

Bridget yanked open the door, aimed with the scope, and put a round squarely between Abbott's terrified eyes.

With the door open, everyone could hear Caesar's

howl of rage. He tore Abbott's head from the deputy's shoulders and hurled it toward the cabin – a deranged soldier lobbing a bloody hand grenade – before turning and stalking into the forest. Sykes followed. Bridget fired again.

"You won't kill him – not at this distance," Matt said.

"I know," she said. "But the son-of-a-bitch won't ever sit again without thinking of me. I put one dead in his ass."

TWENTY MINUTES PASSED. 25. 30.

"Oh shit!"

The group followed Matt's finger to the edge of the ravine. A band of beasts, all armed with clubs, crawled over the crest. They formed up and began to march towards the cabin. They marched – coordinated – deliberate. Every five steps, they stopped as a group, pounded in their chests, and roared.

The air echoed with grunts and growls – snarls and guttural shouts – a thousand Bengal tigers at feeding time – so loud the cacophony penetrated the walls of the cabin.

"They're taking their time," Jimmy said. "Intimidation technique?"

"It is," Bob said. "They want to paralyze their

opponent with fear. The want to scare the crap out of us. Make us scatter and run so we are easier to track."

"It's working," Jimmy said.

"Screw 'em," Mark said, but Jimmy noticed his brother's heel wouldn't stop bouncing. Bob pointed. "Notice anything?"

"Yep," Mark said. "They're effin' enormous, but they move like big cats," Mark said. "Smooth – quick. After our first encounter, I figured they'd lumber in like cattle, and we could just pump bullets into them at will."

"Well," Bob said, his voice tense, "even if we can, my calculations say it will take at least five shots placed within a four-to-five-inch circle to penetrate the fat layer. If one of us can do that, there's still no guarantee we'll hit anything vital on the sixth shot.

Andie asked, "Who is directing them?"

"I'm guessing they've already reviewed a plan. There's no doubt it's coordinated – otherwise, they'd just roll in here as fast as they could. No, that big mother has already told them what to do. And since he can obviously whip any of them, they all obey until someone can beat him in a challenge."

"For leadership – like a wolfpack or something?" Jimmy asked.

"Exactly," Bob said.

Bridget rubbed her shoulders. Stacie shivered. "Did it just get colder?"

"At least 10 degrees, maybe more," Bob said. "The

temperature will make their fat layer denser – they'll be harder to kill."

Mark put down his Fujinon Techno Image Stabilization binoculars, checked his weapons for the fifth time, and headed for the door. "That's a load of crap," he said. "If it breathes, it can die. Time to rain on their parade."

"I SEE 15," Jimmy said.

"Sixteen," Bob said. "There's a smaller one behind Caesar."

"Obviously female," Rhonda said. "Elphaba." Her announcement met with blank stares. "Come on, guys. You know, the Witch of the West from *Wicked*. I've seen it a dozen times."

"For real?" Jimmy said.

"Oh yes," Bob said. "Knows *all* the words to *every* song."

Rhonda, obviously giddy with tension, began to sing. *Popular, you're gonna be popular.*

"That's not what I meant," Jimmy said. "I meant are we for real going to talk about this now?"

"Damn, Jimmy," Rhonda said. "Might as well – we're probably going to die."

"Not if I can help it," Bob said. He looked at the creatures. "Here they go. Show time."

The beasts changed their steps. They no longer backed up. They began making slow, deliberate progress towards the group stretched along the back of the cabin.

"Stand clear," Bob said. He signaled through the window three seconds before Bridget smashed it from the inside with a hand sledge. The weakened framing mount moaned, then the glass collapsed back into the cabin.

"What the hell?" Mark asked.

"This makes it easier to reload," Bob said.

"Makes sense."

Matt opened up with the AR. He'd long ago modified it to full auto. He emptied his 30-shots in a little over five seconds. He ejected the jungle-styled clip, flipped it, slammed the fresh clip into the rifle, and re-commenced. Bob, Rhonda, and Mark (whose AR had been ruined when Sykes' Superman grip bent the barrel) fired away with a Glock, a Beretta, a Sig Sauer, and the Colt. Jimmy, who couldn't hit water from a boat, collected spent clips and funneled them through the window to Stacie, Andie, and Bridget, who reloaded until their hands were raw. They also handed out a box of .357 shells for the Colt.

The beasts took their time. They had their prey trapped. The gap between them and the cloud of gunpowder smoke shrank with slow but steady precision.

"Hit it," Bob yelled over the rattle of gunfire.

Stacie and Bridget flipped four switches inside the

house. Sixteen flares, angled to hit the beasts at chest height, fired in sequence.

"They're running," Andie said.

The beasts had backed up – a little – but soon returned to the methodical advance approach.

"No," Bob said. "The flash startled 'em, but they're not going to run."

"Out," Mark yelled. "Ammo!"

"Nothing left for the Colt – you burned through too fast." Bridget's voice reflected panic.

Mark unsheathed his Gerber Prodigy survival knife and rushed the beasts.

"Mark, what the hell?" Even if Jimmy's voice hadn't been overwhelmed by the barrage; Mark's attention was locked on his target. The distance between him and the beasts shrank steadily.

"Damn, he always could run, even for a stocky sucker," Matt said.

"They really can't see him, can they?" Stacie asked.

"They see something – a blur – a blob," Bob said. "They obviously don't think it's a threat. None of them have taken a defensive position. Think about it. How often do you think anything runs *at* them?"

Mark raced past the first line of beasts before his presence registered. Two of the creatures lashed out with their clubs but they were woefully late. Mark had the big one in his sights. Caesar jumped sideways when Mark raced past him. The giant could not react fast enough to the charging ex-Special Forces warrior's blurred form. Mark rushed Elphaba, got within four feet, and launched himself – knife extended. He buried the blade to its hilt in her left eye.

The female creature hesitated, then released a high-pitched, piercing screech. Mark withdrew the knife and stabbed toward what he assumed would be her jugular. Elphaba recovered and lashed out with a vicious backhand. Mark flew into the forest some 30 feet away.

"I'm going after him," Jimmy said.

"Hell no," Matt said. "He's a grown man. Stick to the plan."

By now, the horde was within 50 feet. The unrelenting fusillade had only reduced the pack by four. As far as Jimmy could tell, none of the creatures had been killed, but he'd seen several limped back to the woods, and Elphaba was clutching her eye and whimpering in the grass. Caesar stood behind the group, his eyes blazing with fury – a savage commander watching his troops moving inexorably toward a bloody victory.

"Getting low in here." The call from inside made the gunners' blood run cold.

Matt shouted above the clatter of gunfire and the bellowing beasts. "How much left?"

"Enough for two clips each – maybe."

Bob's voice was clear and loud. "Execute, execute."

He led Matt, Rhonda, Jimmy, and Bob inside. Matt and Rhonda fired from the doorway. Bob and Jimmy went straight to the window. They grabbed one edge of a large piece of plywood. Stacie and Andie hoisted the other end, and they covered the gaping window. Bridget set the first nail with two taps, then swung the four-pound hand sledge with the expertise of a blacksmith and drove the nail deep into the window frame in two quick strokes.

"Gotta love a woman who can swing a hammer," Jimmy said.

Bridget looked through her tears. "When your Dad builds houses, you learn stuff."

Matt was at the door firing three-shot bursts with the remaining AR. "Hurry the hell up," he said. "I just switched to my last clip."

Bridget finished in the upper left corner, the popped five nails along the left side. She wrapped her knuckles on the board. "Good thing this was under the house. But those guys will punch right through it."

"Not if they can't tell what it is. I'm counting on their bad vision," Bob said. "With any luck, they won't see the difference unless they are right up on the house."

"We'll find out soon enough," Matt said. "They've picked up the pace since Mark went all Charles Bronson on them."

The beasts were moving much faster – not gracefully, but with frightening purpose. The cabin echoed with the thunder of a brontosaurus stampede.

Bob yelled to be heard. "Matt, try to get them to rush you – fire away. We want them to charge at the light and the noise – get them away from that window."

"Great plan. Wanna take my place?" Matt responded. He was grinning, but there was not humor in his eyes. He fired short bursts from the AR, then checked the chamber. "One fricking round! Moving to the Glock."

With the assurance of an expert, Matt fired shot after shot – almost no lag when he changed magazines. The creatures were 20 feet from the door when the Glock dry fired.

Matt slammed the door and wedged a 2x4 underneath the knob. "Not sure how long that will hold 'em."

The house shook twice. Stacie said. "They're ramming, right?"

"Yes," Bob said. "And my guess is they are boosting some of the smaller guys onto the roof." He pointed up.

They heard the unmistakable sound of heavy footsteps above them.

"Will they fall through?"

"Not sure," Andie said. "George always said this place was a fortress, but I don't think he counted on an aerial attack."

Smoke began to billow in the great room. Eyes burned and lungs clogged.

"Are we on fire?" Jimmy asked.

"Those guys are smart," Matt said. "It's the stove. They blocked the chimney. They must like their meat smoked."

Jimmy and Andie picked up a large Yeti cooler and ran lugged it towards the stove.

"No!" Bob waved them off, his voice frantic. "Not that one! Use the water jugs.

They got the fire out, but the level of smoke only increased as the flames smoldered. In less than a minute, smoke inhalation loomed as a higher risk than the enemy outside.

"It's time," Bob said. "Let's go. Matt, you're on the door."

"Copy," Matt said.

Bridget struggled to put on her backpack.

"Leave it," Bob said.

She ignored him and wriggled into the straps. "Just move your ass," she said. "I'll be right behind you."

Jimmy, Stacie, and Rhonda pushed a couch away from the wall farthest from the back door to reveal a 24" square hole in the floor courtesy of Matt's reciprocating saw.

"Get!" Bob said. "Hit the ground underneath and move east – it's downwind, just in case." He yelled across the room. "Matt, count to three, unblock the door, and run like hell." Bob dropped into the hole after Stacie. He popped his head back out. "And do not forget about the coolers."

"Roger," Matt said.

An enormous set of hairy knuckles came crashing through the door. Matt kicked the 2x4 out of place and took a step toward the escape route.

"Why the hell not?" he said. With the AR on his shoulder, he ran back, opened the door, and jumped aside just as Sykes came charging through the doorway. The beast traversed the width of the cabin and slammed into the wall. The cabin shook violently.

Two more creatures followed closely. Matt froze, hoping they would not see him. They didn't.

But Sykes sniffed the air, snarled, and turned in his direction. As soon as the one-armed Bigfoot lunged, Matt broke for the corner. Three feet from the hole, he dove and slid through on his stomach. He landed face first in packed dirt of the crawlspace underneath the cabin. Five seconds later he was sprinting for the trees.

He did not see the others, but he had a job to do. The minute he crossed into the trees, he turned to the south and ran until he was in the woods directly behind the house. He watched as the last of the creatures shoved his way into the cabin. It sounded like a demolition crew at work. Matt swung the AR off his back and checked the chamber again – one round.

"This better be good, old man," he said. "You haven't done any real target work in a long time."

He drew a bead on the mass of Tannerite Rhonda and Stacie had secured to the outside of the plywood. His finger tensed on the trigger.

Oh God, he thought, *did I open the Yeti coolers?*

He lowered the weapon and tried to remember.

"Only one way to find out."

He took aim again – long exhale – and squeezed.

The Tannerite exploded in a burst of red flame followed closely by a concussive blast as the four Yeti coolers full of gasoline from the Hummers ignited. The shock wave knocked Matt onto his back. When he recovered his equilibrium, he looked at the cabin.

There was nothing left but a burning hulk and the smell of roasting Bigfoot.

MATT STAGGERED INTO the fading sunlight. He sensed movement to his right and turned, assuming a fighting stance.

"If you hit me, Mister, it'll be the last time you ever see me," Stacie said.

They embraced as Bob, Rhonda, Jimmy, Andie, and Bridget joined them in a group hug.

"Hell of a plan, Bob," Matt said.

"Thank the Browns," Bob said. "Nothing works better than a screen pass – sucker the defense in – let 'em think they're in control – then, whammo."

Matt rubbed his scalp. "Well, when I was sliding into that hole, with those things on my heels, I didn't think you were such a genius."

A voice came from behind. "He was a genius because he wasn't the one in there getting chased."

"Mark!" Bridget dropped the backpack, raced to her husband, wrapped him in a bear hug, smothered him with kisses, then stepped back and shoved him

- hard. "Where the hell have you been? You scared the hell out of me."

"Old Eliza—"

"Elphaba," Rhonda said.

"Whatever," Mark said. "She didn't take too kindly to my putting my knife in her eye socket. She knocked me out. I have one hell of a headache – but it's damn nice to be alive."

The group stared at the smoldering ruins of the cabin.

"Bet we don't get invited back next year," Jimmy said.

Andie put her arms around her husband's waist. "Who the hell thinks any of us ever want to come back?"

They peeled off in pairs, walking toward the cabin – Andie and Jimmy, Stacie and Matt, Rhonda and Bob, then Bridget and…

Bridget was still looking at the destruction. She held out her hand behind her. "Come on, babe, let's go home."

Mark's voice sounded like a man with an elephant standing on his chest. "Houston, we have a problem."

Bridget turned – and gasped.

Caesar's hand, the size of a catcher's mitt, was wrapped around Mark's throat. The leader's yellow fangs glistened in the westering sun. He pointed to Elphaba's lifeless body and growled like distant thunder.

Mark's face was turning blue. Unconsciousness was

not far away. Behind her Bridget heard feet pounding the ground. Bob, Jimmy, and the rest stood next to her, panting.

"Oh God," Jimmy said. "Okay, everyone. Fan out. We'll figure this out." Jimmy noticed Bridget's backpack on the ground and picked it up.

They formed a semi-circle around Caesar – about 10 feet away – Bridget in the middle – three on one side – three on the other. Jimmy slid into the beasts periphery.

Caesar stared at Bridget. His red eyes burned with the fury of hatred. His hand constricted and loosened around Mark's throat.

Bob spoke to Jimmy in a voice he hoped Bridget could not hear. "He's making Mark suffer. He could crush Mark's throat any time he wanted. This is revenge."

Caesar looked at Bridget, then pointed from her to Mark – from Mark to her. His yellow fangs glistened in a grotesque grin.

The great beast turned sideways to afford Bridget the optimal view as he held Mark just off the ground. Caesar's jaw unhinged – a snake swallowing a large rat – and lowered his mouth over Mark's head. Everyone was transfixed on Mark except—

When Caesar's head exploded, everyone screamed – everyone but Jimmy who sat on his knees, clutching his right arm, with the smoking Pfeifer-Zeliska .600 Nitro Express lying next to him.

Mark fell to the ground, gasping for breath.

Matt and Bridget picked Mark up and began helping him to his feet. Bob walked over to Jimmy.

"I thought you couldn't shoot," he said.

Jimmy flashed a tired smile. "Lucky shot," he said. "There's something else in the bag for you."

"Let me see," Bob said.

"You'll have to do it, Bob," he said. "I think that damn canon dislocated my shoulder."

ABOUT AN HOUR later, the Shimmer passed over the group and disappeared to the west. Jimmy watched as the Shimmer dissipated, hoping his brother might be miraculously inside. Nothing was left but an unusual looking fern, which Bob scooped up and put in a bag.

They'd left just enough gas in the Hummers to get to the nearest pump. Bob shook his head when he looked in the back of Mark's vehicle – it was empty.

"I think we destroyed about $700,000 worth of equipment," he said. "I'll be working for free until I am 90."

Mark tapped on the metal box Bridget had rescued from the cabin. "Maybe not. They may forgive you when they see what's in there."

He tapped the box Bob was holding.

"You may be right," Bob said. "It's not every day someone shows up with a hairy arm from an alleged mythical creature."

"How come that didn't disappear with the Shimmer?" Rhonda asked.

"I think it's because it was encased in something from this world. It was protected somehow. It is the only explanation."

Bob looked at the box again, "This is an enormous find."

Jimmy frowned. "Still, we didn't find the one thing we came here for."

Andie kissed him on the forehead. "It's okay, babe," she said.

Bob shut the door. Jimmy headed over to Matt's vehicle, started to get in, then said, "Matt, give me a second. I have to use the head."

"Better now than halfway home," Matt said. "Just wander behind that tree over there."

Jimmy shook his head. "I'll just be a second."

Andie said. "Honey, just go to the outhouse. After all, it's the only thing still standing."

Jimmy limped around the corner of the ruined cabin and made his way down the small path leading to the privy. He looked back at the smoldering timbers of the cabin.

"Damn," he said to no one.

He made the final turn, rounded a small bend in the path, and reached for the outhouse door. The hinged creaked – and something hit him in the chest. He fell, then covered his face to protect himself as small fists pounded his face.

A thin, reedy voice shouted, "Stomper…Stomper… Stomper."

Jimmy reached out to subdue the whirling dervish who was beating on him – a boy about six. The child struggled, hissed, and kicked but Jimmy was too big, even with one arm, and the wrestling match ended quickly.

Jimmy peered into the smudged and snarling face – a face from long ago – a face he'd never forgotten.

"Josh?"

CHAPTER 38
HOME

"WHAT'S WITH ALL the mystery?" Maggie had said when Jimmy called her. "And you don't need to get either of us anything at all. It's just another birthday for your father. And it's not even a biggie – like 80 or anything."

"Oh, it's plenty big," Jimmy had said before he hung up.

A week after what the participants dubbed "The Battle at the Cabin," Jimmy, Andie, Matt, Stacie, Mark, and Bridget held hands with Maggie and Paul as they all said grace.

"Bless us, Oh Lord,

and these thy gifts which

we are about to receive from thy bounty,

through Christ, Our Lord.

Amen."

"I thought Bob and his little friend were going to join us," Maggie said.

"You mean Rhonda, his fiancée?" Jimmy asked.

"Honestly, Mom," Matt said. "They've been living together since September. She is *way* more than his little friend."

Maggie scowled in mock fury. "Matthew, you will not make lurid comments at our family table."

The laughter was genuine and loving.

The doorbell rang.

"I'll get it," Paul said.

"No, Dad," Jimmy said. "It's Bob – he'll let himself in. I think he knows the way."

Five seconds later, they heard Bob's familiar, pitch-challenged singing voice, "Happy Birthday, dear Paul. Happy Birthday to you!"

"Oh Bob," Maggie said. "So lovely to see you. Where's your...where's Rhonda."

His grin was as wide as the doorway. "She's bringing in your gift," he said.

"You didn't need to get me anything," Paul said. "A million dollars wouldn't hurt, but I'll settle for having all of you here."

"Well," Bob said. "Might be worth a good deal more, Paul. And it's for – well – it's for everybody."

Rhonda appeared from around the door. Next to her stood a well-scrubbed little boy who was obviously uncomfortable both with his surroundings and with the new clothes he was wearing. But the second he saw Paul and Maggie, his discomfort evaporated.

"Mommy – Daddy!"

AFTER THE TEARFUL reunion, a fabulous, joy-filled dinner, and several helpings of Maggie's apple pie, Jimmy and Bob sat on the porch. The Balvenie was smooth. Bob exhaled a puff of smoke from his cigar.

He held up the stogie with a questioning look. "You sure you don't mind, buddy?" he asked.

"All good," Jimmy said. "But after my treatments, I'm not taking any chances."

"Smart man," Bob said. "This is my one true vice. Rhonda said if I started playing golf, she would call off the wedding."

"Smart woman," Jimmy said. After a moment of gazing at the stars, he leaned forward with his elbows on his knees. "I need you to explain something to me – something I still don't get."

Bob took an exaggerated drag on the cigar and blew a smoke ring. "I am Oz, the great and powerful. Go."

"Okay," Jimmy said. "Josh disappears at three years old and comes back thirty years later at six, as best we can tell from analysis of his growth plates and the like."

"Yep."

"So, I keep thinking about the Roger Byrd guy. He disappears at 16 and comes back in his 80s. Doesn't seem right. I mean, he aged faster than his parents."

Bob sat up with a twinkle in his eye. "Some mysteries are too great to understand, my friend."

Jimmy looked around for something to throw.

"You're lucky I don't have a bucket of water, buddy. Don't give me the same baloney the priest did when I asked about how the Virgin Birth worked."

Bob's face stretched into a broad smile. "I thought Father Robert was going to croak," he said.

"Seriously," Jimmy said. "I can't make it work."

"I'd be lying if I said I had all the calculations in here," Bob said as he tapped his skull. "But the explanation is pretty simple."

"Do tell – is it like time zones?"

"Not exactly," Bob said. "It's 10:10 PM here – 7:10 PM in San Diego, but we are on the same time continuum as the people in California. They may be three hours behind, but we experience time in the same way. Christmas Day in Bellevue will be the same out there."

"Okay."

"When Josh…uh…disappeared…he went to a place where time moves differently: a 1 to 10 ratio. One year in Stomper Land equals 10 here."

"Right. So, why wasn't Roger Byrd young when he came back?"

"Reversed ratios from a different place. Roger obviously did not go to the same place as Josh. Roger reported normal people, normal activity. No Stompers…no smell…none of that. Wherever he went, time moved at a 10 to 1 ratio. He aged 10 times faster than we do. If his parents were both 30 when he was born, it took him only three years in Otherworld to catch them. Three years after that, he was old enough to be *their* parents."

Jimmy sat back. "How many places are there?

"Infinite," Bob said. "And we will probably never know. Who knows, even with your special ability, we may never encounter another one."

Jimmy reached for the Scotch. "From your mouth to God's ear, my friend."

CHAPTER 39
"ABANDON HOPE ALL YE WHO ENTER…"

DECEMBER 2005

"Certainly, Dr. Bellard. We will take care of it," Dr. Springer said.

David Springer hated Bob.

I can't believe they demoted me for this twit.

Bob had no illusions about Springer's feelings. "David," he said, "I'm sorry that you have to work this week – I mean, Christmas and all."

"Don't give it another thought, Doctor," Springer said. "Someone has to watch the newbies. With Kline retired and Palmer at CERN now, I'm the only one who can supervise. You go enjoy your family."

Benjumea had returned to the Fermi Lab. He despised Springer.

"I appreciate that, David," Bob said. "I just feel bad about—"

Springer interrupted. "Forget it," he said. "I had my chance as lead, and I blew it. Rubbed too many people the wrong way. I was too much of a hard charger and not enough of a politician."

Bob chose to ignore the passive-aggressive comment. "Well," he said, "I'll be back on the 28th." I checked the schedule to make sure you can be gone for the week of New Year's."

Springer waved a dismissive hand. "No big deal. The wife and kids left a long time ago. Christmas is just another day for me – I'll be fine."

"Thank you," Bob said.

Might as well try one more time, Springer thought. *All he can say is no.*

"Ah, Dr. Bellard – Bob – can we revisit the decision to shut down the experiments through March?"

Bob had elected to phase down for maintenance of the newly installed Veil Compression Matrix (VCM). Since he theorized the "Stomper Universe" was relatively close to our Universe, Bob wanted to avoid anything that might weaken the veil between the two worlds.

The VCM, a massive apparatus, was intended to reinforce the veil between Earth and all other worlds, but it had not yet been tested to his satisfaction. As a precaution, Bob unilaterally determined to hold off on any experiments until he could oversee the tests.

"If you need me, I'll be at the cabin in Newaygo, Michigan, with my old friends," Bob said.

"Ah yes," Springer said with discernable sarcasm. "The legendary Fortress of Solitude."

Bob waved over his shoulder. *You don't know the half of it, you pompous ass.*

Three hours later, after he was sure the coast was clear, Springer assembled the troops.

"Alright," he said with a condescending tone his young colleagues knew all too well, "we have work to do. Dr. Bellard expects us to get this matrix prepared for his return in February. We have a lot of tests to run and very little time. I have set forth an aggressive schedule not only for matrix assessments but also for running a few preliminary low-level collision tests. Focus – do your jobs – and with any luck, you'll be out of here tomorrow night for Christmas Eve with your kiddies."

THE NEXT NIGHT, Christmas Eve, Dr. Springer looked around the conference table.

"Good work, gentlemen – and lady (he nodded to Dr. Amanda Meiser, who gritted her teeth at his customary misogynism), you've done well. Let's verify everything before you head out for the holiday."

He pointed to his left. "Dr. Steadman, can you confirm that the matrix is set for maximum compression?"

"Set to maximum, sir," Dr. Steadman said.

"Dr. Williams, confirm alignment of the quadrille pole magnets."

"Aligned, sir, plus I triple checked the dipole magnets."

Dr. Meiser did not wait. "Power levels set to minimum, sir."

"Very good," Springer said. "Thank you. Have a Merry Christmas. Now, get out of here."

———

EARLY CHRISTMAS MORNING, Springer walked into the lab. He chuckled to himself. *Those kids think I picked them on merit. Hell, if something screws up, they'll catch the heat.*

He was still furious about Palmer's move to CERN in Geneva. "Should have been me," Springer said. "Then I'd be getting heralded for identifying the Higgs Boson Particle."

Springer still had the ear of a few Board members, and he knew they were unhappy that Edison appeared to be losing status on the global stage. They were unhappy about Bob Bellard's "overly conservative approach to research." Springer had been promised a return to the position of Lead Scientist if he could replicate the "God Particle" at Edison.

Dr. Springer walked to the power control board and moved the setting to "Max." On the next panel – the Compression Matrix – he moved the dial to zero.

"Five…four…three… two…one o'clock!" Springer pushed the execute button on the control board. The accelerator sped up the collection of hydrogen protons to maximum velocity. The Edison Supercomputer began calculating the resulting extraordinary number of multiple proton collisions.

"There it is!" Springer jumped to his feet – his arms extended over his head like a victorious prize fighter. The screen displayed one likely Higgs Boson Particle after another.

"Take that, Bellard, you self-satisfied clown! Who's the scientist now?"

Dr. Springer shut the machine down, but not before the tipping point cascade had been reached. He saw a dark Shimmer forming in Edison's Curve, the point where the collision matrix exists.

No one else heard David Springer's last words. "Dear Jesus, help us all."

CHAPTER 40
"BEWARE THE IDES OF MARCH"

DECEMBER 25, 2005 1:30 PM – NEWAYGO, MICHIGAN

THE CONVERSATION HAD been painful but brief. The child's best interests took precedence over every other consideration, though age played a part in the decision, as had Jimmy's inability to father children – a sad byproduct of his chemotherapy. Jimmy and Andie took on prime responsibility for rearing Josh. Now back in his home universe, the young man was aging at a normal rate – he was a healthy and well-adjusted eight-year-old.

Any time anyone asked about his parents, Josh always asked, "Which ones?"

Despite his harrowing adventures, a loving environment and meticulous counselling had enabled Josh to develop into a happy, well-adjusted adolescent.

Snow fell on "The Ides of March" – they'd all agreed on that name for the rebuilt cabin. Complete with solar panels, a natural gas generator, full plumbing (which included three indoor bathrooms), and a not-so-publicized, fully automated infrared firing system (nicknamed "Twin Tornados" after Matt and Mark who designed it), the woodland getaway was a showcase of technology and comfort.

It had cost a small fortune, but with a little help from an insurance adjuster, who didn't ask too many questions, and some creative, though completely legal, grant "maneuvering," Bob – the best paid of the bunch – had covered most of it. From the outside, it looked like a regular cabin. The construction workers, however, continually commented on the 18-inch, steel-reinforced logs. "You guys expecting an invasion or something?"

Matt and Mark had installed the military hardware themselves, "off the books."

Everyone sat around the fire pit and sang Christmas carols. Rhonda looked around. "Where's Bob?" she asked. She stuck her head in the door. "Bob?"

"Give me a second, hon," Bob said. He was sitting in the great room, elbows on knees, locked onto the television screen. "Something's happening in Ohio."

"Well, get out here and have a drink with us," Rhonda said. "The world is not going to end tonight."

Fred Waring and the Pennsylvanians, a throwback to the recordings Paul and Maggie listened to every Christmas, played through the stereo speakers at the corners of the cabin.

Deck the halls with boughs of holly…

Jimmy stood.

… 'tis the season to be jolly…

"What is it, brother?" Matt asked.

...don we now our gay apparel...

"Shimmers," Jimmy said. "Multiple...more than I can count."

...troll the ancient Yuletide carol...

Bob came out of the house, his face ashen. "I think someone at Edison went too far."

"Talk to me," Jimmy said.

"Weird stuff is happening back home. Sightings... disappearances...unexplained destruction. Looks like Springer screwed the pooch."

"Which means?"

...See the blazing yule before us

"If he cranked things up, he might have degraded our universal barrier to the point of collapse. Everything close – every parallel universe and dimension will open simultaneously."

... strike the harp and join the chorus ...

"If my theory is correct, there's nothing to stop any *'thing'* from coming for a visit."

... follow me in merry measure ...

Jimmy looked at Mark and Matt, who were already out of their seats.

"Firing up the system," Matt said.

Mark turned, raised his fist to the surrounding trees, and shouted, "Come get some!"

...while I tell of Yuletide treasure...

As if someone had dropped a needle onto a spinning

turntable, the valley suddenly erupted in howls and screams. Sporadic gunfire echoed through the trees.

"Sounds like all hell is breaking loose," Bob said.

...Fa la la la la la la la la.

Jimmy picked up an AR and slammed in a clip. "Old buddy, hell's the least of our problems."

THE END
(or is it?)

Dear Reader,

Thank you for your interest in my debut novel.
If you have enjoyed the story of Jimmy and Josh,
a brief review would be greatly appreciated.

Warm regards,
Jon

ABOUT THE AUTHOR
DR. JONATHAN PAUL STRECKER

SHIMMERS IS DR. Jonathan Strecker's debut novel. Born in 1970, Jon grew up in the small town of Bellevue, OH, which continues to be a source of inspiration and appreciation. Jon was influenced by his large family of seven and his strong friendships, which have heavily influenced his style of writing, with copious amounts of dialogue. Living in Pennsylvania with his intelligent and beautiful wife, Stacey, his remarkable son, Josh, and two rambunctious dogs, Bucky and Lucy, he continues to gladly work full-time in the field of education. Even though his life is complete in every way, writing is a way for him to express his artistic side.

In the summer of 2020, Jon, along with his son, Josh, embarked on a family project to write a book and make a short movie. The original short story turned into something more significant, hence the Book, *Shimmers*.

Even though this book is mostly fiction, Jon's unique background gives him experience with matters of life and death. Jon has survived both Stage-4 Cancer (Hodgkin's Disease in 1990) and a significant cardiac event in 2017. Elements of *Shimmers* correlate directly to his past experiences and education.

Made in the USA
Middletown, DE
20 October 2020

22406404R00215